TOYI-TOYI,
CAPE TOWN'S WAR DANCE

By:
SHADLEY FATAAR

Book Two of the trilogy: *In the Shadow of Table Mountain, Cape Town*

Published by SHADLEY FATAAR, 2023.

WHO IS SHADLEY FATAAR?

SHADLEY FATAAR IS A semi-retired radiologist who grew up under the yoke of apartheid rule in Cape Town, South Africa, whose policy of extremist racial segregation was widely regarded as social engineering gone wrong.

His politically formative teens started in 1960 when police shot and killed more than sixty peaceful anti-pass protesters in Sharpeville.

His alma mater, Livingstone High School, in Claremont, was a hive of anti-apartheid resistance. It was a school with the highest number of teachers that were imprisoned, banned and exiled, including his father, Alie Fataar.

After qualifying as a doctor in 1970, Shadley worked as a medical officer in Zululand's Ceza Mission Hospital, then as a GP in a Black township in Cape Town, followed by his time as a radiologist at Groote Schuur Hospital. These professional years coincided with escalating nationwide student insurrection, and police brutality, including the 1976 massacre of more than a hundred demonstrating students in Soweto, in the north of the country.

His personal and professional experiences are a rich source of material for his socio-political and historical thriller trilogy, *In the*

Shadow of Table Mountain, Cape Town. The opus covers the epochal years from Sharpeville in 1960 to the collapse of apartheid in 1994.

Find out more about Shadley at his author/blogsite, *Living with apartheid in the Shadow of Table Mountain, Cape Town* at ◎ https://www.shadleyfataar.com/

WHAT OTHERS SAY ABOUT BOOK 2

LEONIE HENSCHKE, writer, and former Managing Editor at Angus & Robertson Publishers.

Book Two of the trilogy, *In the Shadow of Table Mountain, Cape Town,* continues Shadley Fataar's arresting novels set in the racially segregated, brutal, *apartheid* era in South Africa. In this gripping story, real life issues, true historical events and settings are given voice through fictional protagonists from different worlds. Fataar brings realism to the brutal images, and amidst these graphic depictions are lyrical passages that describe the hauntingly beautiful countryside around Cape Town. The skillful storytelling has woven a plot that reveals the passions and motivations of activists, and of cruel oppression that bred violence against a backdrop of beauty.

ROSALIE SKINNER, author of the eight-book series, *The Chronicles of Caleath.*

In *Toyi-Toyi, Cape Town's War Dance,* Shadley Fataar writes with heartfelt realism to convey the frustration, fear, determination, and courage of people living in oppressive apartheid in Cape Town during the 1980s. The reader can identify with his characters and their predicament. We follow four main characters as their frustration, anger and determination force them to react to oppressive circumstances. The story intrigues us through lives that intertwine, to the extent that we do not fail to empathise with every challenge his characters face. Shadley takes our emotions on a journey of hope and resilience. Some of the content is dark and oppressive, an indication of what apartheid was like but this gripping, gritty story reflects real life, drama, courage, and the reactions of people in historically accurate circumstances.

COPYRIGHT © S FATAAR 2022

For permission requests, contact the author.

Address: PO Box 6145, Coffs Harbour Plaza, NSW 2450, Australia.

Email: zonshad@gmail.com

Website: shadleyfataar.com[1] Living with Apartheid in the Shadow of Table Mountain, Cape Town.

Cover design by Penny Clemens of Rustum Fataar's Minuteman Press, Ontario, Canada, and Sohrab Fataar.

The cover and logo show Devil's Peak, Table Mountain and Lion's Head as viewed from Lagoon Beach, Cape Town

ISBN 978-0-6458246-3-6

ACKNOWLEDGEMENTS

ZONJIA FATAAR (NEE Arnold), my wife, my soulmate, and my closest friend will always top the list in all aspects of my life. After 58 wonderful years together, I am deeply thankful we met.

For her early guidance and editing, I again thank author Margaret Penhall-Jones.

Critical information came from Louis Grammer Jnr regarding the Okapi knife.

Dr Mark Blecher, formerly of the SACLA clinic, provided some details regarding the Fires of 1986 in Crossroads, as did Dr Andre Daniels regarding the Gugulethu Seven funeral.

My appreciation is again extended to Leonie Henschke, Rosemary Skinner with other members of the Coffs Harbour Writer's Group for their regular encouragement.

Exceptional finishing touches to this book came from my editor, Laurel Cohn, and my proofreader, Nasreen Varyawa.

My son, IT specialist Sohrab Fataar from Pi Squard, deserves special mention for setting up my stunning website assisted by Scott Willhite.

For the cover design my thanks go to Penny Clemens, graphics designer at Rustum Fataar's Minuteman Press (Kitchener, Ontario, Canada), and the multi-talented Sohrab Fataar.

Book 2 is, again, the product of many people. I hope I will be forgiven for any omissions.

DEDICATION

1960 marked the beginning of the end of apartheid South Africa after many violent, police-inflicted deaths, especially those in Sharpeville in the north and Langa in Cape Town.

In the student led insurrection of 1976, the first children killed were from the African township of Langa and the Coloured township of Bonteheuwel. These deaths of 17-year-old Xolile Mosie and 15-year old Christopher Truter symbolised the Black unity needed in the struggle to liberate South Africa.

Between 1985-1986, more than 30 marchers paid the ultimate price during the Pollsmoor march to demand Mandela's release; three youths died at the Trojan Horse Massacre as did another seven, in the Gugulethu Seven Massacre. Dozens perished in the Fires of 1986 in Crossroads and KTC[1] while there were many more police-related deaths on the Cape Flats, one of apartheid's refuse tips in the Mother City.

This book is dedicated to the thousands who lost their lives at the hands of the police or their proxies during the tumultuous years of struggle to establish a democratic rule in South Africa.

"THE MEANING OF CAMPAIGN: I need not list the arguments against the Pass laws. Their effects are well known. All the evidence of broken homes, *tsotsism* (gangsterism), the regimentation, oppression, and degradation of the African, together with the straitjacketing of industry leads to one conclusion, that the pass laws must go. We cannot remain foreigners in our own land."

Robert Sobukwe, Pan African Congress leader: Before the Sharpeville anti-pass campaign, 21 March 1960.

PROCEEDS FROM BOOK sales will go towards student scholarships in Cape Town.

FROM THE AUTHOR: THE SEMANTICS OF COLOUR IN SOUTH AFRICA

(From Book1: *Fury and Revenge in Cape Town.*)

THE ISSUES OF HUMAN segregation are a distorted reality of colour, race, religion, wealth, and other diverse means. Apartheid South Africa flaunted a racist disconnect in the face of near-universal condemnation.

The original lines were clear. European or Non-European were simple distinctions between the conquerors and the conquered. In South Africa, as in other parts of the colonised world, colour differentiation became the prime qualifier.

Later, *Whites* or *Non-Whites Only* signs replaced the *Europeans* or *Non-Europeans Only* separatist graffiti in the country's public spaces.

The State's divide and rule strategy promoted Non-White subdivisions into Bantu, Coloured and Indians with a small Chinese population; the latter became *'honorary Whites'* following the establishment of political ties with Taiwan.

The oppressed majority embraced the 1960s Black Consciousness. Black was a sociopolitical banner used by Africans, and many of those classified Coloured or Indian.

A few liberal Whites referred to people as Black or Non-Black. The quaint, pendular swing in terminology was not popular; likewise, the term 'Colourdians', sometimes used in Cape Town. 'So-called Coloured', more commonly used, was more acceptable.

Divide and rule was the State's aim. In contrast, Black unity provided a solution, a concept promoted by Steve Biko, the Black

Conscious Movement leader killed in 1977 during his police detention.

Apartheid's vilified ideology distorted our perceptions of each other in a fragmented nation. In the process, it blighted our lives with an excess proliferation of segregationist and oppressive laws.

Like the author, the more politically inclined rejected *all* classifications; *Homo sapiens* is the only acceptable term for *all* people.

However, in writing this trilogy, one could not avoid the colour issue; it forms the basis of centuries of segregation *and* decades of striving towards liberation.

The author uses capitals to describe Blacks or Whites and other nationalities, e.g., British, Chinese, etc.

WHEN A JUDGE ASKED Steve Biko, "Why do you call yourself Black when you are brown?"

Biko replied, "Why do you call yourself White when you are pink?"

In a nutshell, Biko's brilliant riposte highlighted the absurdity of the South African colour issue.

Timeline of events of the trilogy, *In the Shadow of Table Mountain, Cape Town.*

1960-1976

MARCH 1960: The Sharpeville and Langa massacres of 60 or more people who protested the Pass Laws restricting domicile and work opportunities for the indigenous Africans.

June 1976: Soweto massacre of dozens of protesting students; followed by hundreds more in the ensuing months of student protests around the country. The nation's cemeteries become police killing fields.

Book 1, *Fury and revenge in Cape Town*, covers the months of August and September 1976.

1985-1986

WHEN THE TOYI-TOYI establishes itself as a protest dance during this period, there is another peak in police-related violent deaths in South Africa.

August 1985: The Release Mandela Pollsmoor march cost over 30 lives in Cape Town, with more deaths countrywide.

October 1985: The Trojan Horse massacre took three protesting student's lives during an ambush in which police with shotguns hid in wooden crates on the back of a truck. (The event, filmed by the American CBS TV network, attracted international condemnation.)

March 1986: The Gugulethu 7 massacre involved a planned police ambush using disloyal ANC (African National Congress) turned fighters to set up seven youngsters.

May and June 1986: The Crossroads and KTC Fires of 1986 in which at least 30 people died, with 60,000 rendered homeless. Government-supported Witdoek (White cloth) forces laid waste to informal shanty housing in the two townships.

Book 2, *Toyi-toyi, Cape Town's War Dance,* includes the worst civil violent episodes in Cape Town's latter-day history.

1990-1994

FEB 1990: Nelson Mandela was released after 27 years of imprisonment.

The north of the country experienced its most violent years, with most of the fatalities attributed to heightened police activity before South Africa's first democratic elections.

There was also an increase in extremist right-wing, security police death squad activities in which hundreds around the country died from assassinations, random shootings, and targeted attacks on ANC and UDF (United Democratic Front) activists.

Cape Town went through its own trauma, including the actions of the secretive police Balaclava Gang which created havoc in the African townships. It contributed to the existing mayhem between the ANC and Witdoeke, including the Taxi Wars, and the abhorrent practice of *necklacing* which involved the use of fuel-driven, burning tyres placed around opposition members' necks.

26.4.1994: The day of South Africa's first ever democratic elections.

Book 3, *Cape Town's Necklaces of Fire,* incorporates these calamitous developments from Namibia, all the way to the Mother City.

CONTENTS

CHAPTER 1: THE OKAPI THREE STAR

May 1985

CURTIS FOUCHE WAS PROUD of the striking looks that he inherited from both parents. At six foot tall, his chiselled physique was the result of a rigorous regime of karate practice, combined with weightlifting. His black, widely curled hair nearly reached to his broad shoulders.

He attributed his dark skin colour and Herculean build to his Mozambican slave heritage. A paternal forebear was one of 200 slaves who survived a Portuguese slave shipwreck off Cape Town in 1794. Two-hundred and fifty others died, most still in shackles; all the crew survived. The origin of Curtis's French Huguenot family name was shrouded in mystery. His mixed-race roots meant his rubber-stamped South African designation was Coloured.

It was always with an inner hollowness that Curtis recalled how, along with 60,000 other people, his evicted family had had to leave the central District Six area to live in a municipal housing estate on the windswept Cape Flats. Since the age of seven, the 1968 experience still resonated with him. On the back of an open truck with their belongings, the authorities took them away to Bishop Lavis township. Along with many others, they moved into council housing built in the 1960s during a push by authorities to clear over 250,000 Blacks from the best city areas. Their new estate was a municipal slum where jerry-built houses lined the narrow streets like barracks.

Curtis' father, a labourer on the original township buildings, had told him, "My White foreman says that town-planning provides clear shooting lines along streets during periods of unrest. They anticipated trouble all those years ago."

Poverty, crime, and disease flourished amongst the dislocated masses in many townships. 'You will finish school' or 'Only losers join gangs' were the parental mantras of Curtis' youth. Township gangsters looked the part in their distinctive colours. Their swagger, baseball caps worn backwards, and the visible bum cracks expressed a rejection of society's norms. They magnified their antisocial personas with crude tattoos to add to their ominousness. Tears etched on their cheeks indicated those who had done prison time.

Curtis could not stand the way gang members dressed; he preferred blue denim jeans with a shirt with the collar pulled up, the sleeves double rolled to forearm level. A cheap leather belt and Bata suede sneakers were the only other clothes he wore, besides a sweatshirt when cold.

His most treasured possession was his Three Star, held in his right-hand rear pocket ever since his father gave him the knife on his fifteenth birthday in 1976. He recalled his tremulousness the first time he held his gift with three steel stars attached alongside two lunar crescents on the brown, plastic handle. His love for his father overwhelmed him like never before. Right then, 1976 felt like the best year of his life.

"Your Three Star is a beauty, son, though it's not for stabbing people." The German-made product had probably killed more people in South Africa than any other knife.

It took Curtis weeks to ease the stiff opening mechanism by repeatedly opening and closing the blade with Brasso abrasive cleaner on the ratchet device. Finally, a drop of oil ensured the knife's smooth opening. After honing the weapon on a fine-tooth file, he always shaved a patch of hair on his leg using minimal pressure.

A steel ring attached to the mid-section on the Okapi's spine formed part of a locking mechanism to prevent the open blade from closing onto his fingers. By holding the knife with the index finger through the ring, he could open the blade with a snapping action of the wrist. He recalled the lightness in his chest when he first achieved the feat after weeks of failed attempts.

When he showed the family his new skill, Curtis' father gave him a firm bear hug. He was such a tall, strong man. He recalled the smell of Boxer pipe tobacco on his father's shirt. He could still feel how his rough stubble prickled his cheek when his father had kissed him. Two months later, in August, he was gone, gunned down by the police at Lavistown station on his way to work. Curtis shuddered at the vivid image of his father's bloodied body in the police morgue, where he had had to identify the corpse. It was when 1976 became the worst year of his life.

Two months before his father died, over 60 schoolchildren's deaths in Soweto had set in motion the nationwide revolt led by students. Curtis had had close brushes with death during violent police raids at his school or during township demonstrations. His jaw clenched with the memories of his time at senior school at the way police drove their military Casspir transporters through the school fence; the way they threw tear gas at the students even when they were not demonstrating; the way they beat the girls or tortured everyone they detained. Now, nine years later, rebellion still sporadically erupted throughout the country. Over those years of conflict in the Cape Flats townships, he had managed to avoid arrest, injury or death, the lot of several students.

Curtis had to abandon his formal senior schooling after three years. Gone were his plans to be his family's first university graduate. Not a day went by when he didn't mull over his need to do more than participate in stone-throwing demonstrations. Eventually, the social stew of township disruptions created a revolutionary malcontent ready to increase the stakes. His black belt in karate was not enough for him. By 1984, he prepared himself to use his knife as a lethal assault device.

Curtis extended his karate practice routine to include target practice to perfect his knife blows. The objective was to strike a chosen target area within a second or two of drawing his weapon. To help him, he used Mary, a discarded, headless mannequin wearing a castoff raincoat, with breeze blocks on her base plate to provide stability. A 25-centimetre length of sawn-off broom handle with the rounded end directed forward, simulated his knife.

From all sides of Mary, Curtis targeted the armpits, groin, and neck. He practised on his own under all light conditions, behind the shack where he lived at the family's two-bedroom council house, crowded with three other siblings. Their high, rusted, corrugated iron fence ensured privacy.

To Curtis, Mary represented a policeman. One hot day after a workout on Mary, he saw his reflection in the bathroom mirror after washing his face. His dark eyes stared at him with surprising severity. Through the bathroom window, he could see the barely visible, cloudless Table Mountain with Devil's Peak and Lions Head to the right. He flexed the fingers of both hands; he finally felt ready to start his anti-State mission. It was payback time.

CHAPTER 2: LANGA TOWNSHIP MARCH

27 August 1985

THEMBANI DLAMINI WAS proud of his name. In Xhosa, his name meant hope. He was born on the 21st of March 1960, the day of the Sharpeville and Langa massacres. His father, Nkhosi Dlamini, chose the name despite those stressful days when the State banned the African National Congress (ANC) and the Pan African Congress (PAC). Both organisations launched their military campaigns a year later. These events set in motion the South African revolution, which became Thembani's world.

The United Democratic Front[2] had organised a non-violent, peaceful march to Pollsmoor's high-security prison for the next day. The UDF intended to hand over a letter demanding the release of Nelson Mandela. After 18 years on Robben Island, the ANC leader had been brought to Pollsmoor three years earlier. Days before the banned march, the police arrested the UDF leader, Reverend Alan Boesak and sealed off major access roads to the Mother City to stop busloads of regional people from entering Cape Town.

On the eve of the march, Thembani was at his parents' house, eager to hear the full story of his father's experience in the original Langa march. The story went that in 1960, the jobless 30-year-old Nkhosi Dlamini left a destitute Transkei to seek work over a thousand kilometers away in Cape Town. He left behind his near-term pregnant wife, Thandiwe, for the uncertainty of shanty dwelling in Langa. Nkhosi was aware of the protest against the country's restrictive pass laws. Indigenous Africans had to carry the *Dompas* (the stupid pass) at all times when living in any urban area in South Africa.

Robert Sobukwe, the PAC leader, organised a campaign of absolute non-violence in March 1960. When people without their passes presented themselves at police stations, police gunfire killed over 100 of them in the northern town of Sharpeville, with four more outside the Langa police station in Cape Town. Nkhosi arrived in Cape Town amidst a city in turmoil after the event.

"I remember how hot the day was when the train stopped in Langa," his father told Thembani. "On my head, I carried a few essentials in a folded blanket held in place by crisscrossed ropes. It was my suitcase in those days," he chuckled. "My village friend, Zolani, was there to meet me. My first view of Table Mountain took my breath away, but I soon found myself in a township that was empty of smiles because we passed mourners returning from the nearby cemetery, where residents had buried the four martyrs." Nkhosi paused, staring blankly at nothing towards the end of the lounge of their tiny council home.

"But what was the march like, Father?" Thembani enquired, as he brushed the tip of his nose with his index finger. He knew that his father loved an audience.

"Well son, the march came later. I moved into Zolani's single-roomed *pondok* (shanty) with two other men. We discussed the march due to take place the next day. I shared their hope that the nationwide protests would halt the new law aimed to force our women to carry the *Dompas,* the way the men do." His father rocked his stiff body where he sat on the sofa.

"I was nervous on the day when the local PAC leader, 23-year-old Phillip Kgosana, lead us through 20 kilometers into Cape Town. The University of Cape Town student looked so youthful in his grey shorts, white shirt, dark tie, with an unbuttoned jacket. In those days *we* could still go to UCT. I hope you will have that chance too one day."

His father nodded his head. "The line of De Waal Drive marchers into the city, looked like a cobra wrapped around the base of Table Mountain on our way into the city. It was the first time in my life I saw the beautiful blue sea in the distance. I was amazed to see the huge houses along the way. I could not believe it when Zolani told me how less than five people lived in those houses owned by White people.

"There were so many armed troops, with several on top of their army tanks. My heart was going like this." Nkhosi beat on his chest with a wry smile on his face. "But my spirits lifted when thousands started to sing *Ilizwe Lethu* (Our Land). Then we chanted, *Phantsi ngamapasi* (Down with the Passes). The singing empowered us. I hope you have the same experience tomorrow my boy." He patted Thembani's leg, where they sat on the couch.

"It was heartening to see how so many Coloured people applauded us by returning our Black Power salutes. Many of them joined the march, while the Whites sat there in their locked cars with fear in their eyes." A wide-eyed Nkhosi looked from side to side, while chuckling, as if he was in the past staring at the scared people.

"In the crowded, narrow road near the police headquarters in the city, I became separated from my friends. We heard that Kgosana wanted the marchers to disperse. We were confused, but soon the packed crowd pushed me towards Cape Town's central railway station to the 'Non-Whites only' platforms. The third-class coaches with wooden benches on the train to Langa were packed like sardines.

"Despite our disappointment, we sang our freedom songs with our feet stomping to the rhythm of the train's wheels." His father patted a four-beat tempo on his knees. "We believed change was in the air although we were returning to an uncertain future." Nkhosi sighed, his unsmiling face lined with intensity.

"Outside Langa station, armed police officers beat us with batons or *sjamboks* (short rhinoceros hide or firm plastic whips), while police dogs bit anyone close to them. One of the police officers whipped me with his sjambok. Each stroke felt like a knife blade cutting into my flesh. I bled from every lash while he called me by the hated name *Kaffir* (racist term for an African person)." Nkhosi rubbed a scar on his cheek.

"I was surprised that I could find my way to Zolani's home because there were so many *pondoks*. I thought I would never find the place, but I used the mountains as a guiding landmark." The look on his face reflected how those relived memories were still fresh even after all these years.

"At least there was no shooting," said Thembani. "But why did Kgosana call off the march?"

His father pulled himself upright. "We heard later that the Justice Minister had agreed to meet Kgosana. In the interest of our safety, Kgosana asked the crowd to go home. Once the people had dispersed the swines arrested him. He finally went into exile." Nkhosi clenched his fists, sweat beaded his upper lip.

"None of the other three men had been injured. While they tended to my wounds, Zolani gave me some welcome news." A broad smile highlighted his father's features. "Even now, I feel the joy when he told me about your birth on the 21st of March. I cried at the news as I would've loved to have been there with your mother to hold both of you in my arms. Despite our failed march, I remained optimistic about our future, so I named you Thembani."

"What a beautiful story, father!"

His mother placed a plate of Lemon Cream biscuits and tea on the four-seater dining table. Thembani dunked his biscuit into his cup while his mother raised her eyebrows, before she smiled, shaking her head. The black patch over her right eye always made Thembani quiver even when he was not in trouble.

"So, you'll march tomorrow?" she asked.

"Yes Mamma. Tomorrow will be big as the UDF expects a massive show of unity with all the Black townships participating like never before."

"I wish you a peaceful day, son, unlike the recent Soweto experience. I suppose it's a waste of time asking you not to march." There was no smile to go with her raised brows.

"There may not even be a march tomorrow," said his father. "I heard on the radio that they've banned any gathering within five kilometers of all designated starting points. I would've joined you if my leg was not so painful." He rubbed the hip where the police had shot him in 1976.

"I'll be fine Mamma. My guardian angel will protect me."

"I'm not sure it'll help," she said. "Your father was not even protesting when they shot him at the station in '76." In the same week, she had lost an eye to a rubber bullet while standing at their front door during a police raid in the street.

"I'm fearful too, Thembani, so look after yourself tomorrow, my boy," said his father.

"Try not to worry. I'll be here for breakfast with you in two days." Thembani hugged his parents before going home several blocks away. In the quiet of the streets, he silently hoped their fears would not be confirmed tomorrow. *Would the Pollsmoor march be another Soweto day of bloodshed?*

CHAPTER 3: SCHEMERS AND DREAMERS

27 August 1985

PAT DE BRUIN PUFFED at his Lexington cigarette while lying on his bed. He looked forward to the next day when he and Ebrahim Khan would join the Mandela Freedom March to Pollsmoor prison from Athlone, where the two grew up. Ebrahim was his closest friend who lived nearby in the new Indians-only, Rylands Estate. The pair's resistance politics had started during the mid-1970s while attending Alexander Sinton High School. Their alma mater remained a hotbed of student activism along with most township senior schools.

Pat's neighbourhood had a mix of council-built brick properties with more recently built brick-and-tile houses. Asbestos or corrugated iron roofs were standard in the more established homes, alongside a few all-metal houses. Several residences needed painting while rusted roofs cried out for replacement. Shanties were rare in this more established part of Athlone. An assortment of add-ons reflected the different financial statuses of the owners.

The road where Pat lived ran east-west with Table Mountain as well as Devil's Peak, visible across a winter-green field at the street's tee-junction end. Wind-bent pine trees dotted the area where the pair had often whiled away their childhood hours with cricket, soccer, or rugby. Their cement cricket pitch was the result of a neighbourhood project where the children brought spades to mix the cement. Rocks marked the wickets or goal posts during their games.

Most house windows had simple crisscrossed burglar bars. There was street lighting, storm water drainage, electricity as well as sewerage. Narrow pavements bordered tired-looking front garden patches with low walls, three breeze blocks high. Over the years Pat would have sat on every one of the mostly unpainted walls with his street pals. The memories of his time on each wall included his first kiss with Ebrahim late one night in the shadow of an ancient loquat tree blocking the streetlight. The kiss at number 27 marked the start of their intimate relationship soon after Pat had been released from detention by the security police in 1976.

Pat's incarceration at the age of fourteen marked the darkest period of his life. Detective Warrant Officer Hammer van Zyl had ensured that haunting memories remained seared into Pat's mind in much the same way Hammer had ground cigarette stubs into the backs of his hands and the tops of his feet. 'Hammer's dimple' is what the animal called the burn to Pat's cheek. His invisible mental scars were worse than the visible physical injuries.

Pat attributed much of his healing to the gum chewing Ebrahim, who knew about Pat's ruptured eardrum, while a fractured eye socket, nose, and rib were from Hammer's knee. Ebrahim knew that Pat kept to himself the worst of Hammer's 'treatment' as van Zyl called it. Those experiences were the ghosts that Pat lived with, while his protective shell was the love he shared with Ebrahim. During their intimate moments together, they could closet themselves from the issues around them.

Pat's separate room behind the family home was a well-constructed structure built by an uncle, a builder. There was no backyard on the cramped property. In his spartan room the only wall hanging was a calendar obtained free from the local garage. A threadbare, wall-to-wall carpet provided minimal floor cover. Books lay on a desk with others stacked haphazardly to the ceiling on the top of his narrow clothes cupboard. A secret hideaway below the floorboards held his banned political books, including Isaac Deutscher's biographies of Stalin and Trotsky with the much-thumbed Robert Service's work on Lenin.

He possessed two pairs of shoes: black leather slippers and his daily grey sneakers. Two grey pants with white shirts in need of ironing hung in his cupboard with other clothing essentials in three overfilled drawers. In cold weather, a grey sweatshirt, grey beanie, and anorak were his essential accessories.

A triple knock at the door signalled the arrival of Ebrahim, who let himself in with his key. He was fuming. "I'm sorry I'm late, Pat." Ebrahim, always a neat dresser, was in his standard black outfit with well-polished lace-up shoes and his black and white Palestinian scarf wrapped around his neck.

"Suraya had another epileptic fit before I left home."

Two or three times a week Ebrahim had to cradle his young sister's head in his lap on the floor where she ground her teeth, groaned, and frothed at the mouth. "I hate the way her limbs twitch, jerk, twitch, jerk, jerk ... Every spasm goes through me too while I sing to her until she stops. Her fits lasted much longer today; they're getting worse." Ebrahim blinked his teary eyes, looking briefly at the ceiling, his gum-chewing was excessive.

"Every episode of fits tears me apart. I swear there must be payback one day." Ebrahim's body quivered while his fists clenched tight where he sat on the bed next to Pat.

Pat held him around the shoulders, kissing him softly on his forehead. He knew the story well. "Steady on, love. If our plans come together then we'll have our revenge." Pat was at his most tender whenever Ebrahim was upset about his sister who had been shot in the head by the Riot Squad in the tumultuous 1976 winter months after Soweto. The thirteen-year-old had been on her way to a shop close to home to buy a loaf of bread. The police claimed she had thrown stones at them.

Ebrahim blew his nose. "When are you going to tidy your cupboard, Pat?" He closed the cupboard doors. "I hope you see my cupboard one day with everything neatly stacked in rows." Pat was not allowed at Ebrahim's parents' house.

"I'm not obsessive-compulsive like you," Pat laughed. "Accept me like I am, almost perfect, except I don't iron my shirts, and I smoke while you chew. In different ways we're both hooked," he smirked.

Ebrahim smiled, "But I smell better! On a more serious note, though, what are our plans with Mandela's march tomorrow?" He added a fresh strip of Wrigley's chewing gum to the one already in his mouth as blowing bubbles was easier with two pieces.

"Well, apart from bringing our leader home with us at the end of the day, not much really. I'll have a bottle of water with enough cigarettes to last me the twenty-kilometer walk." A cough interrupted his laugh.

"Twenty kilometers? I can already feel the pain in my legs, but I'm bubbling with excitement at the prospect. Despite them banning the march there should be thousands."

"I'm already a bundle of nerves," said Pat. "I hope the police behave themselves."

"Too true. We can only pray there'll be no deaths."

Ebrahim stroked Pat's hand with his thumb. Ebrahim's body warmth seemed to permeate through Pat's whole body while he wished these moments would last forever.

Will we survive tomorrow? Nagging thoughts like this always preceded any activity since his days at school.

CHAPTER 4: MANDELA'S POLLSMOOR MARCH DAY, ATHLONE

28 August 1985

PAT HAD A PLEASANT lightness in his chest. He rose early to join the Mandela protest march from Athlone Stadium, their nearest gathering point. Pat, in his favourite grey and white gear, drummed his fingers on the table. He was pleased when Ebrahim arrived.

"I see you didn't iron your shirt," Ebrahim raised his eyebrows, a sour expression on his face.

"Relax darling, Mandela won't be able to see me, you know." Pat smiled. "My anorak will cover the shirt so that only the uncreased collar is visible. Look," he teased, pointing to the collar.

The pair set off on the two kilometer walk through the side streets towards Athlone Stadium. Many Muslim men from the neighbourhood wore a variety of skull caps or, like Ebrahim, wore Palestinian scarves as a shared symbol of protest against oppression. Many women were tightly scarfed.

"Large protests are what we have worked towards since the start of our 1976 student rebellion." Pat punched one hand into the other. "Just look at the number of parents here today. There was a time when we only had students protesting, especially in '76."

"It's a sign of hope like never before." Ebrahim's eyes glowed, chewing his gum.

Pat lit another cigarette, before he exhaled with half-closed eyes. "On the downside, the country's new draconian State of Emergency has cost over 500 Black lives around the country." Pat kicked at an empty Mountain Dew can whose clatter equalled his anger. His exhaled smoke appeared voluminous in the wintry air.

It did not take them long to reach the normally busy corner of Thornton and Klipfontein Roads where there were hardly any cars. Police roadblocks kept hundreds of angry noisy people at bay. They were barely a kilometer from the Athlone Stadium, the starting point for the march. Pat felt an emptiness in his stomach. There was a heightening of the collective tension of the protesters in the presence of so many armed, helmeted riot squad officers with their body-length plastic shields ready for action. A brittle tension hung over the area. *What will set things off today?*

Pat felt the customary dryness of the mouth, with the increase in his heart's rhythm as they joined the rowdy crowd close to the police barricades. His inner tension persisted despite deep draws on his Lexington.

"Ours is a peaceful demonstration," shouted a well-shaven Imam with a Koran in hand. "We are here to march peacefully for Mandela's release."

Political banners waved from side to side. "Release Mandela, our leader!" came the loud calls from passionate marchers.

"Let us through," shouted a balding priest with one hand holding onto the fifteen-centimeter-long wooden crucifix around his neck. "You have no right to stop our peaceful march."

"*Amandla, ngawethu!*" (Power is ours!) Defiant calls accompanied dozens of raised fists.

The suspense at the roadblock was palpable. Barely restrained German Shepherd police dogs snarled, barking with menace. Packs of policemen arrested, baton-charged, or whipped people who came too close to the barrier. The noise from the crowd rose as tension escalated. Deep lines etched into the faces of the organising clerics of all persuasions who clustered in a hurried meeting close to the head of the increasingly vociferous crowd. The intimidating police wall edged closer while their sjamboks beat an ominous, rhythmic message on the street surface. The huddled clergymen opted to head a kilometer south towards Hewat teachers' training college.

"From Hewat we'll probably head along Kromboom Road towards the M5 Highway to link with groups from the other townships." Ebrahim informed Pat.

"That's if we ever reach the M5. I don't like the look of our company. I've never seen so many of these police bastards before. They don't want us to march today." Pat had a sharp sense of déjá vu.

"I smell trouble, Pat." Ebrahim's face was a mask of worry.

Along Kromboom Road, they came to a halt at Grasmere Avenue, where military vehicles blocked the way. Far behind the massed troops was the southerly end of Table Mountain and Devil's Peak to the right and the Constantiaberg range to the left, forming a tee in the distance. The setting was surreal.

The tall bespectacled Reverend Russell, impressive with his black cassock over his bright orange altar skirt, addressed the people on a hand-held megaphone. "Following the tenets of a non-violent protest, we'll sit when we're confronted by police. Let them do the violence, let it be a symbol of the country's regime." His voice boomed over the heads of the restive gathering.

Almost by way of reply, a White police officer declared on his megaphone. "Your gathering is illegal. You have two minutes to disperse." He glanced at his watch in a deliberate, exaggerated fashion. His colleagues' bodies stiffened, no longer fidgeting while they fingered their guns' triggers with others beating out a sinister warning with their sjamboks on the street surface.

A passing police helicopter drowned the repeated message in Afrikaans as people started to leave. The high concrete walls of the fringing houses limited the crowds' exit pathways.

Pat's balled fists were tighter than ever before. "There's a side road over there if the crap starts to fly." Pat pointed. He watched a couple of the priests and imams go to the officer who, by his gesticulations, showed he was not interested in any negotiation. A row of clerics with arms linked, separated the police from kneeling protesters in prayer behind them. Pat looked on, fearful about any action against the thin line of brave religious leaders. *Surely they won't attack our spiritual leaders?*

No sooner had they started singing a hymn, than the police charged the thin line of priests and imams, lashing at them with their *sjamboks*, batons and meter-long *rooikrantz* (wattle) staves[3].

"We had better move!" Pat called to Ebrahim. The shooting had begun.

"Rubber bullets and teargas! You know I can't stand the gas," said an experienced Ebrahim as they turned to run.

Shouts of "*Amandla, Ngawethu!*" interspersed with "*Allah hu Akhbar!*" (God is the greatest!) rang out. Women screamed. Men swore. Many rubbed their stinging eyes while children cried, their faces soon awash with tears and snot. The barking, snarling police dogs bared their teeth, and added to the theatre of unprovoked violence.

Pat's limbs shook while his insides felt ready to explode. They had not been so close to the action in ages. The frenzied police charge did not spare anyone - neither the clerics, nor the men, women, and children. A woman with a headscarf dropped to the ground unconscious, felled by a heavy rubber truncheon. The responsible policeman lashed at others in his path. His perspiring, distorted face bristled with the intensity of his clubbing while spittle flew from his mouth as he swore his way along the line of scattering protesters.

Pat signalled to Ebrahim to help him lift the injured woman. Her forehead lump was already the size and colour of a plum as blood from the split skin stained her face, as well as the front of her dress.

"She's pregnant," Pat shouted. "The bloody police bastard must've seen she is close to delivering." His knotted insides felt ready to explode.

Teargas started to sting Pat's skin. He closed his tearing eyes to reduce the burning as he held his breath to suppress his coughing. Screams tore through the air as desperate people scrambled away from the unprovoked charge. The nearly corralled crowd was frantic in their efforts to escape.

When they were about to turn the street corner, Ebrahim suddenly let go of the woman. Pat stumbled, nearly dropping their load.

"What the damned hell are you doing Ebrahim? You can't release her without any warning man!"

Ebrahim's face was frozen. His hands flapped as he pointed to the ground. "Look, look! There's an eye on the ground? Sis man, I'm going to vomit."

With a sense of horror Pat saw the sand-covered bloodied orb while Ebrahim threw up on the grass close by. "Hurry man I need you. I think she may be coming around." With his foot, Pat scraped at the sand to cover the eye on the ground.

Ebrahim, with his mouth still wet, recovered enough to take his place alongside the woman whose eyes had opened. The pair lumbered along the side road with their load between them.

"Quick, in here!" An urgent voice beckoned. A white-haired man directed them into his driveway towards an open side door to his kitchen. "I was so afraid we would have a bit of drama here today," he said. "Let's have a look at your head. What happened?"

The woman stirred; her eyes fluttered open.

"A policeman struck her with his truncheon even though she's visibly pregnant," said Pat.

"Oh good. I felt my baby kicking," mumbled the woman. "I was so worried as I have just another month to go." She patted her belly.

A distressed Ebrahim had located the toilet. Pat heard him retch a few more times.

After dressing the woman's wound, the man brought ice in a plastic bag to place on her forehead.

"The wound is superficial. I don't think you'll need stitches," he said. "What brought you here to march today?"

"It's about solidarity," she said. "I intended to return once we reached the M5 highway, one kilometer away." She patted her belly. "I want my baby to live in a free country."

"How admirable,"

"Thank you. By the way, is your friend okay?"

"Yes. Ebrahim nearly dropped you when he saw an eye on the ground."

"Oh no!' she said. 'The same officer hit an elderly priest before he hit me.[4] The baton broke the man's spectacles. The White policeman was like a wild beast. Every blow struck at someone's head including mine."

A pale Ebrahim rejoined the group in the kitchen. He fumbled with a wrapper before he chewed vigorously on the fresh strip of gum.

The man served them tea and biscuits. "I think we all need a cuppa," he said. "The noise outside has subsided; I can drop all of you off in my car if you wish."

"'We live close by, so we'll be fine," said Pat.

"Thanks," said the woman. "My husband is on duty today. He's an ED nurse so I expect they'll be busy today."

Pat and Ebrahim took their leave after they expressed their thanks to their host. The woman gave them both a long hug.

"Thank you so much." She patted her belly. "We'll never forget what you did today."

Pat liked the way she called herself 'we'.

"I'm still feeling really shook up," Ebrahim confessed after they had left. "Every time we experience such police brutality, I'm convinced we have to do more. They don't listen unless the reaction to their violence is as violent." His frantic gum-chewing had eased off.

"We discuss more action whenever an event gets our blood going. We chant 'Amandla, ngawethu', wave our black power salutes, throw our stones. What have we achieved in ten years? Today's event was another call to arms. Our greater involvement is overdue."

The couple walked hand in hand down the empty street.

"I'm keen to see what's on at our UWC (University of the Western Cape) campus. There's bound to be action there. What do you think?" asked Pat.

"I don't see why not, unless there are major road blockades."

"We should be able to steer clear of the blocked main streets. Let's go!"

They collected Ebrahim's car from Pat's place to drive via the backstreets where people milled around aimlessly. They passed fires, mainly from burning tyres, vehicles, and a few government buildings.

"There's a lot of shit going on. Damn! I doubt any marching group will reach Pollsmoor prison today." Pat punched the dashboard.

"Please don't damage my car." Ebrahim's Cortina had two cracked side windows from stone-throwing. Even his Black Power fisted salute had not helped at times. "I hope my car does not add to today's smoke. Are you sure we'll reach UWC?"

"Don't know. Relax!" Pat lit another cigarette, inhaling deeply. "See how I do it?".

They drove through Hanover Park, Manenberg and Bonteheuwel, arguably Cape Town's most impoverished Coloured townships. The gunshots, vertical bands of smoke on the windless day, with many military vehicles bore testimony to widespread township violence.

"It feels weird to drive through Modderdam Road when there are hardly any other vehicles," said Ebrahim. "It's already been an eventful day. What awaits us at the end of our trip?"

"We'll see." Pat's exhaled stream of smoke soon dissipated in the rush of air from the open car window. *I hope we have no more excitement today.*

CHAPTER 5: MANDELA'S POLLSMOOR MARCH DAY, GUGULETHU

28 August 1985

CURTIS WALKED THE FEW kilometers from Bishop Lavis to Gugulethu at a rapid pace. He wanted to join the Pollsmoor march from the African township where he anticipated there would be more action than in Bishop Lavis. His Three Star in his pocket was like having his father with him.

With two Police Academy recruit hits to date, Curtis hoped he would use the knife again today. He allowed himself a smug smile instead of the inner rage he normally used to feel when his route took him past the police station. He glowed inwardly, knowing that since he'd begun his lone campaign against them three months earlier, there were two empty police recruit bunks at the Coloureds-only Police Academy. Because of the nature of his attacks, the township newspaper, *The Cape Herald,* had nicknamed the unknown assailant, the 'Armpit Assassin'.

Curtis noticed how police recruits now walked around in groups of three or more since his last strike three weeks ago. *The Herald* reported how a special task force had been established to investigate the killing of the recruits, yet Curtis had seen nothing different in the area to suggest that the police were there in numbers to find him. *Things would've been so different had the damned recruits been White.*

From the horizon upwards, the early morning sky glowed a broad band of brilliant orange, yellow and blue, all more intense than normal. Table Mountain and Devil's Peak were visible, though the daily city haze would obscure them by mid-day. Curtis dug his hands deep into his windbreaker pockets with his shirt collar pulled up above his jacket collar. He strolled past the King David Country Club, where he caddied. Located close to the airport, the enigmatic golf course was like a green island oasis alongside the Cape Flats' worst slums.

Like Modderdam Road, the Settler's Way major route was clear of traffic except for several military and police vehicles. He headed towards the main street, NY1[5], into Gugulethu. When he saw the flashing lights of the police blockade on NY1 in the distance, he chose a southerly sandy track almost smothered by bullrushes over a length of 100 meters. Early morning workers commonly used the route, but there were none around today. In the distance there were already signs of trouble ahead. Thick fingers of dark smoke rose skyward. Sporadic gunshots went off; his pulse quickened.

Curtis knew his way from the two years he had lived in the township with a girlfriend. His dark skin colour allowed him to blend in easily in the African township whose two square kilometers were home to tens of thousands in a mix of informal shanty homes interspersed with municipal structures. Breeze block council houses stood cheek by jowl with metal *pondoks*. Tarpaulin sheets covered tree branches shaped like beehive structures resembling the traditional Transkei huts without the mud walls. Metal shipping containers had morphed into barricaded shops with grilled slots in the locked doors to serve customers. Crude hand-written signs displayed the limited wares available at the makeshift stores which often doubled as windowless housing.

He headed along NY111 towards NY1. The shanties disgorged somber-faced people who all headed towards NY1. The normally troublesome *tsotsi* gangsters were nowhere to be seen. A few women had toddlers strapped on their backs in the traditional Xhosa style with wrap-around blankets. In what would be the biggest protest ever in Cape Town since the historical 1960 Langa march, all ages were there to demand the release of their leader, Nelson Mandela.

The early sun cast long shadows on the wide NY1. The central gathering point of the march was much further along the already busy street. Close by, Curtis heard gunfire which sounded like rubber bullets, pistols, shotguns, and tear gas. He had heard enough of all of them over the years.

With his tongue feeling like cardboard, Curtis crouched behind a containerised shop on the corner of NY1 and NY111. He watched as people in the distance scrambled away from a group of charging policemen who smashed their cudgels, clubs and batons onto bodies, limbs, or skulls that came in their way. Curtis clenched his fist when he saw a grey-haired woman struck down from behind with a baton. With the ring around his index finger, his closed Three Star was firmly in hand.

A slightly overweight man of about Curtis' age, came running towards the corner. Sweat streaked the hard lines twisting his taut face. His knock-kneed run looked almost comical. The untied laces of his basketball boots flapped about in all directions. *Shit! Will he trip on those laces?*

From behind the shop, Curtis watched as the man turned into NY111. The distressed runner glanced over his shoulder at a White police officer who rounded the corner with his pistol in hand. Blood streamed from the officer's fresh facial wound. The lone policeman was an uncommon sight because they never separated from each other like this.

When Curtis took off after the law enforcer, he flicked open his Three Star to a thrusting grip, ready to strike with the knifepoint directed forward. Could he strike him from behind? Into the armpit, maybe the neck? After about 100 meters the policeman knelt in the middle of the narrow street to take aim at the fleeing figure now less than 50 meters away. He fired just as Curtis' knife struck him in the exposed right armpit from behind.

The force of Curtis' perfect thrust pushed the knife tip through the top of the police officer's shoulder. With a firm grip, he sliced through the tissues which were no match for the keen blade; the gun dropped from the officer's paralysed arm.

With an agonised scream the policeman jumped to his feet. The bloodied limp arm flailed around his waist. The officer faced Curtis, who struck forcefully again at the other armpit, with similar precision.

The stunned officer shrieked. His blue eyes bulged in disbelief at his useless, bleeding limbs. He groaned, his nostrils flared. Shock lined his smooth face with the well-groomed, thin moustache so beloved by Afrikaners. His cap had fallen off to expose his cropped, spiky blond hair. He backed away from his attacker with stark disbelief in his blue eyes.

The man's wide eyes darted from his wounds to Curtis. He blubbered, "*O my God wat het jy gedoen?*"

"Oh my God, what have you done?" Curtis mimicked his victim.

Blood soaked quickly into his clothing. The next stab to the right groin had become a critical part of his routine. The clinical attack was over in minutes. The blood-soaked officer dropped onto one knee before falling onto his face in the middle of the street. The blood on the road had already started to gel.

Curtis hovered over the softly groaning officer then stooped to wipe the knife on the man's camouflage uniform. He stepped backwards to survey his handiwork with an intense inner glow at a job well done. *This one's for you Dad.*

He turned to run off when two other young men rounded the NY1 corner at speed. Curtis continued along NY111 following the fresh blood drops from the fleeing man. Blood trailed the way ahead to where a narrow street headed off to the left.

Before Curtis turned off NY111 he glanced back towards the fallen policeman, where he saw the two youths stab at the body of his latest success. He watched with grim satisfaction how one of them used the policeman's gun to fire two shots at the body. The other attacker dragged his associate away before the two disappeared between the nearby houses.

Curtis ran on, his face flushed as he fisted the air. Ahead of him the portly figure of the runner waved at him from the corner. Curtis followed the stumbling blood-stained figure along the alleyways to a lean-to shack. The man fumbled at the door lock before he staggered in to collapse onto the double bed, which virtually filled his *pondok* home.

Curtis closed the door behind him before he pushed up the sleeve of the man's sweatshirt to check the injured left arm. Arterial spurting came from an area above the inside of the elbow. *Shit, he looks so pale.* There was less bleeding from the exit wound where the bone felt intact. Curtis put his fingers across the spurting wound to compress the bleeding artery against the underlying humerus. The stranger's pallor troubled Curtis.

His Boy Scouts training flooded back. In the absence of a pressure bandage to stop the bleeding, Curtis had to rely on direct pressure first to stop the arterial spurts. He squeezed until his fingers were numb, before swapping hands without any further squirting.

The house did not look like the kind of place with any dressings. Beside the bed were a couple of book-laden boxes beneath a desk. There were books everywhere. An oil lamp hung from an exposed roof beam with rusted corrugated iron roof sheets above. A Primus stove stood on a shelf with a few kitchen utensils in a plastic bowl.

Curtis looked at the wounded man who had short curly hair, full lips, prominent ears, and a conspicuous scar across his furrowed forehead. A groan indicated the man was coming round.

"Don't move! You have a spurting artery here," Curtis said. "I have to press hard to stop the bleeding. What's your name?"

"Yours's first," muttered the injured stranger.

Curtis noted the man's caution. They seemed to be on the same side, so Curtis gave him his real name. "And yours?"

"Thembani."

"Ahh, Thembani - Hope. What do you hope for?" asked Curtis, blinking his eyes a few times.

"Freedom. Democracy. Peace. Right of domicile. The vote. That's just for starters. You?"

Curtis watched him through narrowed eyes. "About the same, I suppose.."

'For how long have you been pressing?"

"At least half an hour. What we need is a pressure dressing followed by a doctor."

"Check in the box over there." Thembani pointed. "I have two crepe dressings from a sprained ankle a few months ago. I think they're clean."

Curtis slowly released the pressure on the wound. The pumping of blood had stopped. He wrapped one of the crepe bandages firmly around the wound. With the second strip, Curtis fashioned a looped sling from around the neck to the wrist to support Thembani's arm.

"Where'd you learn the first aid?"

"I was a boy scout years ago." Curtis sat on the side of the bed. "I don't understand why the policeman came running after you. They never move around alone like that." The eyes blinked again.

Thembani chuckled. "From nearly 50 meters away the rock I threw struck him in the face. He went ballistic, so he ran after me. I saw how you stabbed him, Curtis. Did you kill him?"

"I don't know," Curtis lied. "But the two men after me must have. I saw them getting stuck into him with their knives before they shot him twice with his own gun. I'm impressed with your 50-metre throw," Curtis smiled, although he was worried; Thembani had seen him stabbing the officer.

"Hey, I know your smile," said Thembani. "Don't you caddy at the King David like I do?"

"Why, yes. I thought you looked familiar. Your laces are never tied. I live across the road in Bishop Lavis. I grew up there."

"Ahh! So, you are the Bishop Lavis Armpit Assassin?" The question sounded more like a statement of fact.

Curtis's heart skipped a beat. His brow furrowed while sweat beaded his lip. "You've been reading the *Cape Herald*. I never go near the paper." *Fuck! He's smart.* Curtis glared at Thembani.

Thembani persisted. "They reckon two police trainees have died in three months. The main media said nothing about them. Every week I read the *Herald* just to see if there's been another attack by the Armpit Assassin. It's hard to believe you are my rescuer." Thembani scratched the side of his nose, smiling.

"Oh fuck, the blood is soaking through the dressing." Curtis again applied firm finger pressure to the area. Thembani grimaced with pain from the applied force.

"Just relax." Curtis preferred silence. "You need a doctor, but we have to control the bleeding first or you'll bleed out." Thembani groaned with the force Curtis applied to his arm.

The walls of the shack seemed to press in on Curtis. His stomach had never felt more knotted as darkness threatened to overwhelm him. Here he was in a cramped *pondok* in Gugs (Gugulethu) when the first person he meets realises he is the Armpit Assassin. His head reeled. Could he trust the stranger? Curtis wanted to leave.

"What's with all the books? They're everywhere."

"I love reading," Thembani looked animated. "I buy them at the second-hand bookstalls on NY1. Anything goes - plays, westerns, romance, history, politics. It's a world in which I can hide," he grinned. "I hope to do my arts degree one day if things ever settle."

"My science degree is also on hold." Curtis looked around the room. "I don't see any clothes. Do you have any?"

Thembani laughed. "I have another pair of black jeans somewhere. Also a few tees and sweatshirts. Plus, two pairs of basketball boots. These ..." He pointed to his feet. "... and another pair, somewhere."

Curtis laughed. "I'm surprised you can run with your untied laces. I was worried you would trip on them."

"I'm lazy, and they don't affect my running."

"You call that running? With those knock-knees of yours?" They both gave a half-suppressed laugh.

"Where's your family?" Curtis asked.

"They live on the other side of Gugs. Our home was a bit crowded, so I moved here. What about you?"

"I live with my family. My father was killed by the bloody police on his way home from work in '76. He wasn't even demonstrating." Curtis paused, lost momentarily in the painful memory. "I worshipped him." He compressed his lips with his jaw clenched firmly.

'I'm sorry to hear about your father. My Dad was another one of those shot in '76," said Thembani. "It took him months to recover. He limps from the police bullet injuries to the abdomen and hip. My Mom lost an eye to a rubber bullet in the same week." He pinched his nose.

They lapsed into silence as a smile highlighted Thembani's features.

"What's so funny?" asked Curtis, frowning.

"It's funny how apartheid works. You are classified Coloured, yet you are so much darker than me."

"It's why Black Power will work, brother."

"Yes, you're right. Those classifications are the rubber stamps of our denigration. By the way, what's with the eye blinking?"

"Ah, it's when I'm excited." Curtis maintained firm pressure on Thembani's arm.

Thembani grimaced from the pressure. "How much longer?"

"Not much, then we'll make tracks for a doctor. The bleeding seems to be under control again. Try not to move the arm too much as you've bled enough already."

"We can't go to Gugs Clinic - they often arrest injured people before they're treated. Dangerous conditions may force them to close during periods of rioting, especially on a day like today."

"Do you think you can walk to the King David? I'm sure we can flag a lift to our family doctor in Elsies River who'll help."

"Rather there than the Clinic," Thembani replied. "Listen to all the shooting outside." Thembani closed his eyes and groaned.

With a wrinkled brow, Curtis watched Thembani. *Shit! I hope he makes it.*

THEMBANI SUPPORTED his injured arm. Despite his sling, the through-and-through bullet wound ached with every movement. It intrigued him to have the Armpit Assassin as his rescuer. Thembani decided not to pursue the issue any further because Curtis looked shocked when Thembani had identified him as the infamous assailant.

Curtis padlocked the door behind them. They were not far from the bullrushes leading to Modderdam Road near the King David Club. They chose one of the paths where the tall growths allowed them to walk upright along the narrow pathway. The rushes hugged in on the two and forced them to walk in a single file. The acrid smell of the fires reached them from the columns of smoke. Shouts, shots, screams and dog barks in the distance came from the direction of NY1 where frustrated marchers had taken on the armed police with their stones.

Thembani's world spun. He had to fight to hold onto consciousness. The stabbing pain in his arm exacerbated with every step he took. He did not want to faint. Thembani gritted his teeth until his jaw hurt.

They worked their way undercover to a point where the rushes gave way to scattered wattle bushes to further shroud them from the troops a few hundred meters away on NY1. They crossed an unusually empty, dual-carriage Settlers Way. Curtis called a halt a few meters away from an equally quiet Modderdam Road. Thembani felt his head spin more than before. He did not want to faint.

"Let's check what vehicles are passing by. You look so pale, Thembani. Damn, you are bleeding again."

Thembani did not reply. He staggered. Everything blurred. His head swirled with nausea, saliva filled his mouth. *Oh no!* Thembani let go the painful arm. He stumbled before lurching forward towards the gravel at the side of the road. From behind, Thembani felt Curtis grab hold of him before he hit the ground.

"Oh boy," muttered Curtis, who carried Thembani to the middle of the road. Thembani felt himself slide along Curtis' body onto the street. Waves of pain swept over him. Before he collapsed, he saw Curtis waving frantically with both hands towards a light blue Cortina approaching them from the west.

CHAPTER 6: MANDELA MARCH AFTERMATH

28 August 1985

WITH THE BLOOD-SPATTERED Thembani in his arms, Curtis stood in the middle of Modderdam Road, relieved when he saw the Cortina slow down to pull over beside them. Within minutes the driver and his passenger helped Curtis and Thembani into the back of the vehicle.

There were no questions asked, except, "Where to?" from the driver, while his passenger lit a cigarette.

Curtis, already pressing on the arm, called out. "Head across the field here towards Elsies River. Follow the track. I know all the streets. The police will have sealed off the main roads to the area. Take the first road to the left ahead, followed by a right at the next junction," looking down for a second to survey Thembani's condition. "Damn, the blood is oozing through his dressing again. He's already lost a lot of blood from the bullet wound to an artery."

Curtis was astride the legs of an unconscious Thembani, who lay sprawled across the length of the seat. Curtis' fingers were sticky with blood, not his favourite sensation. His fingers were soon numb from the pressure he applied until the blood stopped dripping through the dressing. He alternated hands to relieve his fingers.

The front passenger turned towards Curtis. "You two must be part of the action in Gugulethu. We came from the aborted

Pollsmoor march in Athlone where the bastards beat and shot people. We were on our way to check out the action at UWC because we're part-time students there. What happened to you?"

A cautious Curtis chose his words. "I was passing by when this guy came running along. I'm glad you arrived when you did. It's the second time he's collapsed from blood loss." Curtis' eyes blinked excessively.

Thembani moaned as he stirred.

"Don't move your arm," Curtis told him.

Thembani's eyes flickered. "Okay. Where are we?" he groaned.

"In Elsies River. These two men came by at the right time. We're on the way to the doctor I told you about."

"Thanks," mumbled Thembani who again lapsed into unconsciousness.

"It looks like he's lost a lot of blood. By the way, my name is Pat," said the passenger. "The driver is Ebrahim, who gets the horries at the sight of blood," he giggled.

Curtis did not respond. Should he tell these strangers his real name? He instructed Ebrahim where to turn. The route included a couple of grass-covered fields, all well away from the main road.

They passed by stragglers rushing to home or safety. Youths on the prowl carried stones, knives, and sticks. There weren't many women on the roads. Fewer fires were visible in the distance with less shooting than in Gugulethu.

"I'm Curtis," he finally said. Thembani could eventually disclose his name if he wished.

"Who's the doctor?" Ebrahim asked, chewing slowly on the gum in his mouth.

"Dr Stanley Gershon. He normally stays open when the action is at its worst. He's our family GP," said Curtis. "We're almost there. Around the next corner, you'll see his surgery on the left. There should be parking in front, close to the door."

They carried the stuporous Thembani into the waiting room while Curtis maintained pressure on the arm. From his previous visits, Curtis knew nurse Desray Daniels who took them straight through to the procedure room. A group of injured patients in the waiting room all looked on with concern.

Stanley arrived to quickly assess the immobile Thembani while Desray organised a drip into the non-injured arm.

"What happened here Curtis?" Stanley asked as he inflated a blood pressure cuff to act as a tourniquet to the arm.

A relieved Curtis let go the arm, shaking his numbed fingers. "Thanks Doctor Gershon. The police shot him in Gugulethu, where I came across him. There was a lot of action there today. The wound was spurting blood, so I applied a dressing as well as direct finger pressure over the area to control things, but the bleeding keeps starting again."

"Yes," said Stanley. "Arterial injuries can bleed a fair bit; it's no wonder he looks so pale. You can wash your hands in the basin over there, Curtis. The space here is limited, so two of you will have to go to the waiting room."

"Thanks. I'll stay here if I may," said Curtis as the other two exited the room.

Thembani stirred. "Are you the doctor?"

"Yes, I'm Dr Gershon. Most people call me Stanley, except Curtis. Now I need you to keep your arm steady. After injecting you with local anesthetic, I'll see if I can fix your bleeding artery. Okay?"

"Go ahead. I'm in your hands, Dr Gershon. I'll be like Curtis."

Curtis tugged on his shirt collar before he held Thembani's free right hand. He felt a sense of relief when his fellow combatant squeezed his fingers.

Stanley soon exposed the damaged brachial artery with a linear hole extending halfway across the vessel, the arm's main blood supply. With nurse Desray to assist him, Stanley was soon able to place thin silk sutures across the hole. He seemed satisfied that all was well when Desray released the pressure in the cuff. After placing the last skin stitch, Stanley applied a pressure dressing over the area.

Thembani stirred. "Will I live doctor?"

Stanley laughed. "Yes, you will. The hole in the artery is closed. You are fortunate there's no damage to the main nerve alongside the artery. You need to take things easy over the next few weeks."

Stanley smiled as he turned to Curtis. "I presume your sister has been well."

"It's over a year since she last saw you, doctor. You said she would get over her asthma."

"True. Right, Thembani. Ideally, I should see you in the next week; return sooner if you think there's any infection."

Curtis responded, "I live close to him, Doctor, so I'll check on him in the next few days. What do we owe you?"

Stanley waved his hand. "Just make sure you heal, Thembani. Your friends did well to bring you here when they did. You're fortunate as you would've bled to death. We'll keep you another hour in the waiting room to be sure the bleeding has stopped." Stanley applied a more traditional triangular sling to the arm.

"Thank you, Doctor Gershon. The arm already feels much better."

Curtis and Thembani joined Pat and Ebrahim in the waiting room, where patients discussed the morning's action in the township. Most of the injured patients said they were passers-by caught up in the police shooting to disperse marchers.

"The government won't listen," said a neatly dressed woman who nursed a severely bruised cheek from a rubber bullet impact. "They should know they can't hold on the way they have all these years."

Her bald husband added, "In ten years these bastards haven't been able to stop us."

"It's no longer only students they're dealing with," chipped in a man with a forehead bloodied from a baton blow. "Look at us here in the room. Us parents have responded to the students' calls to join them, and now we're beaten, shot or detained along with our kids." With an exasperated tone, he threw his hands in the air.

A student cut in. "Today I marched to release Mandela, *our* leader. We will succeed no matter how long we take."

The emotions on display were raw, reflecting the greater Black togetherness forged over the previous decade. Curtis felt pleased at the revolutionary sentiments expressed in the waiting room by mainly older people.

THEY RETURNED VIA THE backstreets to Bishop Lavis. Clusters of people scurried along, most seemingly headed home, a few seemed aimless.

"Do you live together?" Ebrahim asked, chewing hard on the gum in his mouth.

"No, I'm in Gugulethu," Thembani replied.

"It may be better if you stayed at my place tonight," Curtis suggested, "Getting you into Gugs today will be difficult. My Mom is a fabulous cook, so she'll prepare us something tasty."

Thembani pinched his nose before he responded. "I like the idea, especially the food. It's probably the blood loss as I'm very hungry. I'm sorry about your car Ebrahim. It's a mess here on the backseat."

Ebrahim waved a hand. "Don't worry. I'll add the cost of cleaning to your tab." They erupted in laughter. The pent-up tension found an outlet in their exaggerated mirth.

"Turn right over there, then stop," said Curtis. "Can you walk a short distance, Thembani?"

"I should be okay," Thembani replied.

Asbestos-roofed council housing lined both sides of the narrow street, now devoid of people. Ebrahim pulled over as he popped a gum bubble through pursed lips.

"Can I phone one of you for a chat in a few weeks?" Pat, cigarette in hand, half-turned to face the rear.

Thembani remained silent.

"Yes," Curtis responded. "We needed a phone because my sister has asthma. What do you want to talk about?"

"Mainly, we'd like to know you are both well," said Pat. "Afterwards, we'd like to arrange a meeting to discuss a few activist issues with you. It's inappropriate to go into any detail now."

Curtis gave Pat his phone number before he exited the car to join Thembani who thanked them again. Curtis pointed ahead to where they could access Modderdam Road. As the Cortina headed off, the two ambled their way towards Curtis' home, a block away.

"Do you think we can trust them?" asked Thembani. His expressionless face manifested his concern.

"I'm not sure, though there are few people who would drive from Athlone to UWC on a day like today to check on the action. Either they're keen or committed. I suspect they're both. We'll have to see what they want. I can always contact you if you aren't away throwing stones at policemen again," he laughed. Curtis had warmed to the guarded Thembani.

Thembani grinned. "The best time is in the evening. My lamp stays on till late when I have a decent book to read." Thembani put his uninjured arm around the shoulder of his saviour. "Did you say your mother cooks well? I'm starved."

The violent aftermath in Cape Town continued for a few days. Over 30 people died in the townships during or after the attempted peaceful march to Pollsmoor prison. The violence related to the demonstrations was a sinister portent of things to come on the Cape Flats as would be the case throughout the country.

CHAPTER 7: MATERNAL CONCERNS

29 August 1985

CURTIS WATCHED HIS mother cover Thembani with a blanket where she had made his bed on the sofa in the lounge. After patting Thembani on the shoulder, his mother pushed Curtis towards the kitchen, closing the lounge door behind her.

Curtis' mother scowled at him while she spoke in a loud whisper. "So, was your friend in trouble or were you? They could've shot you too. It's tragic how we lost your father in '76. I don't know what I'll do if I lose another member of my family. All I have left is you, your baby brother and your two sisters. The thought of losing any of you kills me every day."

It pained him to see his mother's face so drawn. Life had been tough since his father's death. "But Mom, when he ran past me I saw he needed help. A police stray bullet caught him in the arm. Dr Gershon said he was lucky to survive. It's the first time I've ever saved someone's life. My boy scout training came in handy to control the bleeding from an artery. He's a bright, nice guy. Until today I had never met the man."

"So, what were you doing in Gugulethu in the first place? I told you to stay away from Mandela's march. I admire the man, but I didn't think they would release him from Pollsmoor just because you knocked at the prison door. According to the radio news, many people died today. Probably it's more because they always lie about the numbers of dead. There may be more deaths tonight. Listen to all the shooting still going on with buildings and cars on fire all over the show." She pointed towards the kitchen window.

Tears flowed from her eyes - she looked much more than in her late forties. She repeatedly untwisted or twisted a tea towel when not dabbing her eyes.

"I can't go through another loss. I'm so nervous about all of you. You are the main one who causes me grief. It's like you have a fire raging inside you. I'm so afraid you'll explode one day." She threw her hands in the air. "Losing your father was the worst day of my life. I can do without losing you too. Promise me you won't do anything stupid. Please." Her fingers dug deep into his forearm.

Curtis wrapped his other arm around her. Her head barely reached his chin as her shoulders heaved with sobs. He looked through the barred kitchen window to where the kitchen door light shone on their minuscule garden patch.

Curtis blinked hard to control himself. All he could do was kiss her on the forehead while holding her until the moment passed. There was no way he could promise her what she asked. He preferred to stay quiet rather than lie to his mother.

"Please Mom, don't cry. I'll be alright." He held her tight as his heart ached like never before. *How horrified would she be if she knew I am the Armpit Assassin.*

THEMBANI PROVED TO be an engaging guest who enjoyed Mrs Fouche's breakfast treats. He slapped his belly after eating. "I'll miss you, Mrs Fouche. I enjoyed your cooking."

"Our door is always open to Curtis' friends Thembani. I'm sure your mother worries about you in the same way I do about Curtis."

"Too true Mrs Fouche. Our mothers are indeed the keepers of the nation."

After breakfast, Thembani set off for Gugulethu with Curtis. "Your Mom's cooking made my shooting worthwhile. I could not help overhearing your mother's concerns about your safety. My parents are the same."

They crossed Modderdam Road and Settler's Way before taking the shortcut through the bushes.

"At least there's no shooting to be heard so far," said Thembani.

At Thembani's place, the door was ajar. A rotund woman wearing a black eye patch with a bright floral print apron emerged from the tiny house. There was no mistaking Thembani's mother. She paused in front of him before she threw her arms around his neck to hold him to her chest. There were no tears, though the intensity of her hug, and her deeply creased face spoke volumes.

Thembani held on to her with his uninjured arm. When they separated, she stared at Thembani, who tried to hide his tears as the impact of the past day's trauma and his narrow escape from death finally hit him.

"I was worried when you were not here at breakfast time. They killed so many people yesterday, so I decided to check on you." She sighed deeply. "I let myself into your house with my key. You can't imagine how I felt when I saw the blood in your room. Ay! At least I didn't find your body here. You don't look right though, you're too pale. What happened?" She pointed to the arm.

"A stray bullet hit me yesterday. Curtis saved me, Mamma. Because of the bleeding, I stayed the night with Curtis after the doctor fixed the arm."

"Thank you so much Curtis. I haven't seen you around before." She extended her hand to Curtis.

"I'm from Bishop Lavis, Mamma." Curtis bowed his head while he respectfully touched his right wrist with his left hand. She briefly held on to his hand with both her hands. "I was walking past when I met your injured son. Once the doctor had fixed him up, we thought he should stay the night at my place until things were quieter. Don't worry, Mamma. I'll look after your son whenever he's with me," said Curtis.

"Well, I suppose you must be the guardian angel Thembani spoke about two nights ago. He's my favourite, just don't tell him I said so," she whispered to Curtis before she turned to Thembani. "I'm glad you had Curtis to look after you, son. I left you fried chicken alongside your bed. I see you haven't cleared away those books yet as you promised. Ayy! We really must find you a bigger place," She shook her head.

"I do wish you wouldn't worry so much, Mamma. I'm a survivor who will sell his books soon. A bigger place is too expensive, and I'm comfortable here."

"Now I better be off as I have a few jobs to do." She patted their shoulders then embraced each of them before she departed.

They entered Thembani's house, where his mother had cleaned the bloody mess. Sitting on opposite sides of the bed, they hardly had space for their knees. The shanty was pleasantly warm from the bright, sunny spring day. They tucked into the fried chicken with a plentiful supply of chips, which they had placed on a *Herald* newspaper between them.

"Sounds like our mothers are the same," said Thembani with his mouth full of food. "It's not easy for them to carry the emotional scars of our struggle the way they do."

"It's probably the same all over the world. What's with the eye patch?"

"1976. I told you before. A rubber bullet hit her in the eye in the same week my father was in hospital with bullet injuries to his hip and bladder. What happened to your Dad?"

"Again, '76. He died from a police shotgun blast to his back, just days after they changed from birdshot to the more lethal buckshot. The close-range shot made a mess of his back. Us school kids were demonstrating on the opposite station platform when the police went berserk. Once they started shooting, we all ran away." Curtis paused, his eyes elsewhere, far beyond the walls of the room. He shook his head, blinking his eyes. His voice cracked.

"I had to identify his body at the police morgue the next day. You can imagine my horror when I saw the state of his body from two shotgun blasts. They shot him in the back at point-blank range judging by the closeness of the pellet holes with the powder burns on his clothing." Curtis closed his eyes. "I can never forgive them. *Never!* Bloody hell, I was fifteen at the time." Curtis lapsed into silence, his hands intermittently fisted or unclenched at his sides.

Thembani watched Curtis. He had never met a man so full of pain, visible there in his dark eyes, coming from deep within. *So this is what drove him to become the Armpit Assassin.*

"I'm sorry to hear of your father's death. About the same time, I was protesting at Heideveld station to stop people from going to work. At least I saw my father collapse when the police shot at us. My pals and I dragged him from the station then carried him to the nearby Day Hospital. He spent the next eight weeks in Groote Schuur Hospital recovering from his injuries. Two other people lost their lives at the station that day."

"Those bastards must pay one day. It'll be such an injustice if they don't." Curtis' hands were now in tight balls at his sides.

Silence blanketed them. Thembani looked at Curtis, who had dozed off. Though he was somewhat amused to have the Armpit Assassin asleep on his bed, they seemed like such unlikely co-warriors. Maybe his injured arm was a sign that he needed to stop throwing stones. Maybe what he needed was real action. *Like Curtis, will I have to kill to move things along?* He rolled over, seeking elusive sleep. Instead, a throb in the injured arm kept him awake.

CHAPTER 8: A TOUGH DAY FOR A TOWNSHIP DOCTOR

September 1985

DR STANLEY GERSHON often navigated his vehicle along informal streets on his house calls. His body swayed from side to side as his new Pathfinder crawled along the rutted, sandy roadway towards a cluster of shanties in the distance to attend to a sick child.

On the unsealed roads he often had to use high range four-wheel drive to negotiate the wintry mud or the low, dried-out dunes of summer. Elsies River, a designated Coloured township, had a few streets with solid houses like the one he had lived in, but there were many areas of shanty housing whose corrugated iron shacks exhibited different degrees of workmanship or rust. Such was the fate of hundreds of thousands who lived on the Cape Flats.

Over 35 years, many townships became the dumping grounds for 250,000 displaced victims of the Group Areas Act. In addition, desperate jobseekers, from the impoverished rural Bantustans[6], built informal housing there despite regular raids by the police in search of citizens deemed by them to be illegal aliens without a *dompas*.

Stanley parked in the sandy street. Despite the unsavoury environment, he knew his vehicle would be safe because the criminals appreciated his years of making house calls to an area avoided by many doctors.

The sunny spring day would add to the deep natural colour of his exposed forearms. Polo shirts over casual trousers were his preferred dress on warmer days. He ran his fingers through his spiky hair, different from the shoulder-length hair he sported since 1974, when he had started his general practice. A few grey streaks in his dark hair since then, did not bother him, though he preferred to ignore the thinning at the front. With reluctance, he had parted with his dated Hank-Marvin-style spectacles, now replaced by rectangular metal frames. His slim build reflected his ethic of hard work and hard play as he ran, dived or hiked to ease the stress of practising in the Cape Flats slum.

Stanley swung his black medical hold-all on his way through the narrow alleyways where the low shanty roofs almost touched each other. These days there were more tarpaulin-covered shacks than before. The plastic sheets posed a significant fire hazard in areas where there were no fire hydrants, electricity, or stormwater drainage.

He wrinkled his nose at the stench of the bucket toilets nearby while he waved away the flies buzzing around him. Not many could afford the Jeyes Fluid he occasionally smelt; the fastidious few cleaned their loos every day.

Stanley soon reached the rusted shanty he sought. Two years before, he had issued the death certificate of the family's first-born child who had died of gastroenteritis, the slum's main child-killer in summer. He deplored how children's death certificates almost always resulted from State-generated poverty in Africa's most prosperous country.

The mother opened the door; the child's father was at work. Her tears started to flow when she saw Stanley, who held his breath. His last visit had started the same way.

He stooped when he entered the flimsy single-roomed home. A thin shaft of light from the nearly closed door allowed him to work his way towards the child's bed in the far corner. A dark blanket covered the only window, adding to the oppressive heat from the sunny day outside. Already he suspected the diagnosis.

His eyes adjusted to the gloom indoors. The rough floorboards creaked when he crossed the room. Cardboard-lined corrugated iron walls provided no insulation. Indoors felt hotter than outside. The recessing chest with the child's fevered distress told a complicated story with a typical rash. The two-year-old's eyes were puffy-red with a yellow crusted discharge; measles was the most common cause of childhood blindness in the country.

She had a fever of 40 degrees. The cough was moist, her breathing too fast. His stethoscope confirmed she had bronchopneumonia complicating her measles. The girl needed urgent hospitalisation. He would call an ambulance from his rooms.

Measles was another sad barometer of how poverty impacted on the spectra of disease that Stanley faced every day. The measles mortality was ten per cent amongst Africans, five amongst Coloureds with hardly any White deaths from the highly contagious disease. Stanley restrained himself from fisting his hands.

Shacks surrounded Stanley's parked vehicle where empty cans, bottles, paper and plastic lay scattered around the often crudely constructed *pondoks*. He sweated in the hot car despite running the air-conditioner at full blast. Once home, Stanley collected Fay Ismail to go to their weekly afternoon session at the Crossroads Empilisweni SACLA Health Clinic, where his medical and her pharmaceutical skills were sorely needed.

FAY ENJOYED THE HIGH seating of Stanley's Pathfinder, so she normally drove them into Crossroads where tens of thousands of squatters lived. Crossroads' informal housing complex was an eyesore, located incongruously alongside the southern end of Cape Town's main airport. On a recent flight, Fay was surprised to see how much bigger the place was than her last trip two years before. Clearly visible below the landing plane were hundreds of shanties with their mishmash of corrugated iron roofs, and blue tarpaulin covers, surrounded by the ubiquitous Australian wattle bushes. The blighted first view is what most visitors had of one of the most scenic cities in the world.

The low bush-covered dunes of Crossroads had mushroomed into a settlement of over 100,000 African people who were in search of an elusive lifestyle change from the poverty-stricken areas of the Transkei and Ciskei, one thousand kilometers away. In the process of their resettlement, Crossroads had become a battleground of squatter builders against bulldozing police. The thousands who went to prison followed by their forced return to the Homelands[7], returned time after time in a cyclical life of shanty reconstruction until their next rubber-stamping to exit Cape Town. With a populace already in simmering discontent, Crossroads had become Cape Town's biggest pustule on the much-acned face of apartheid.

They drove past the patchwork of shacks on their way to the clinic. Many structures looked like they had been erected overnight with their new blue tarpaulins. More established *pondok* roofs had an assortment of rocks, tyres, or bricks to keep their corrugated iron sheets in place. The lucky few had a communal tap nearby. Many water gatherers came with their plastic or metal containers balanced hands-free on their heads. It was common to see teenage girls walking with a bottle of water standing upright on their heads.

During a quick tea-break in the cramped staff kitchen, Stanley and Fay spoke about recent events with the nurse manager, Thulani.

"It's shocking the way the police often raid people's homes after midnight. I heard of two such patients tonight," said Fay.

"They recently swooped on those who lived in tents under sanctuary in the church grounds where they attacked a frocked priest in the process. The next morning, we had to suture his head wound where they had struck him," said Thulani.

"I had a couple of traumatised children who dreaded going to bed because of these nighttime blitzes," said Stanley.

Thulani nodded. Despite all the deportations, the raids had increased as the State's influx control measures failed. "They need our labour, yet they won't let us live in peace in a slum. Who wants the 99-year leasehold rights they are offering us? How do they dream up such nonsense?"

"It's shocking," responded Fay. "Absolute power has blinded them."

"Ayy! I'm anxious about the tension around us. Though we live in hope in South Africa, we often die in despair instead," said Thulani.

Fay enjoyed her clinic days on Wednesdays when she was able to work in the same environment with Stanley. On their way home earlier than normal, Fay zig-zagged her way along the poorly maintained road, passing a mangy dog lying in a pothole in the middle of the street.

She had only driven a few hundred metres when four men across the road waved at them to stop. Often, they had to give a fisted 'Amandla' (Power) salute before they were allowed to continue, but these gloomy men looked different.

"These characters look surly," said Fay with a twinge in her belly.

"Get out," said a bald man from the passenger side of their vehicle. A reluctant Fay found the instruction unusual.

The car's lights cut a bright path ahead of them through the dark of a street with no lighting. There was no housing near them. She could hardly see the faces of the men who had moved into the murky shadows on each side of the car. The three men on her side stayed put while the balding member approached Stanley on his side of the vehicle. Fay's mouth was like chalk while her heart galloped.

The bald man had his knobkierie (hardwood club) ready with the fist-sized club head resting on his shoulder. He raised the *kierrie* to a menacing height as he waved the club slowly to-and-fro. The man seemed either drunk or drugged.

Stanley shouted at the man. The louder their voices, the more Fay's pulse raced with her stomach now tightly constricted. "Hey, you, leave us alone!" she shouted while she slammed her shaking hands on the bonnet of their vehicle until they stung from the impact.

Stanley handed over his watch and his wallet. The leader pocketed the items before he lashed at Stanley with a forehand swing. As Stanley ducked, the heavy club passed over his head. The following backhand strike glanced off the right side of Stanley's head.

His attacker circled Stanley as blood flowed from his scalp wound.

"Leave us alone!" Fay screamed again with nerves jangling and legs trembling. A direct blow to the head could be fatal. She slammed her fists on the car once more. "Hey! I'm talking to you. Leave us alone!"

Stanley again ducked under the next horizontal swipe while he bobbed and weaved to avoid another strike.

Even though the other men were close to Fay, they did not look too keen about what was happening.

"Hey, you. Stop!" boomed a deep voice. A tall powerful-looking man in his sixties strode purposefully towards them.

Fay recognised Faku, the receptionist at the clinic. The barrel-chested man placed himself between Stanley and the aggressor. "Have you nothing better to do? These people come here to help our people. Shame on you. Hand over whatever you took from them."

The *kierrie* remained in an aggressive upright position. The sullen-faced attacker's eyes narrowed as they darted from Faku to Stanley.

"Hand over whatever you took." Faku's demeanour projected authority. With reluctance the thug dropped the clubhead. He was not keen to hand over his ill-gotten gains.

"Come on. I don't have all night to stand here." Faku's eyes were intense, his extended hand flapped with impatience.

The assailant handed his loot to Faku, mumbled an obscenity before he signalled to his gang members to join him as they slunk off into the dark of the moonless evening.

"These thugs would serve the community better if they used their energy as revolutionaries, not thieving *tsotsis*," said Faku. He handed over Stanley's possessions.

"Thank you, Faku." Fay hugged him quickly before she turned her attention to Stanley who held a blood-stained handkerchief to his scalp wound. Strength slowly returned to her jelly-like legs.

"I'm okay, love. Fortunately, the blow was only a glancing shot. I think a few Steristrips across the wound will do the job. The clinic has closed, so I'll patch myself up at home."

Stanley turned to thank Faku. "Thank you, Faku. I felt a bit dizzy after he hit me."

"It was my pleasure, Doctor. Luckily, I was on my evening walk. I live over there." He pointed to his left. "My action is a small thanks to you after all the work you two have done for us at the clinic over the years."

Fay kissed him on the cheek before they took leave of their rescuer, who stood to the side of the road when they drove off.

Once she parked the Pathfinder at home, a more composed Fay smiled to herself while holding onto Stanley's arm when they entered the house from the garage.

In the bathroom, Stanley cleaned the scalp before shaving a strip on each side of the laceration. "As I suspected, it's only a skin wound," he said. "Onto bone would've needed sutures."

Fay applied Steristrips across the wound. Later they unwound with a glass of wine while seated in their kitchen nook. The distant Table Mountain and Devil's Peak were hardly visible in the dark. Fay closed her eyes as she breathed in deeply. "Thank heavens Faku was around," said Fay. "Let's hope these events don't come in twos or threes." A now composed Fay smiled. "Faku is well recognised in the local community, so I was relieved when he appeared. I must admit I've never been so afraid in my life."

"I suspect the main villain was drunk or drugged. It's funny how we've never felt that we were in danger in Crossroads before."

"Yes," said Fay. "If things ever settle in the country, crime may be apartheid's worst legacy."

"And violence," added Stanley.

"Cheers!" Fay lifted her glass. "Here's to an experience not to be repeated." Whenever Fay was on an emotional high, her most intense feelings always went out to Stanley. She leaned over the table to kiss him. After nearly ten years together, their bond was stronger than ever.

She opened her eyes to sip the berried red wine. After so many years of violence, escaping from their daily tension was difficult. Crossroads was a significant concern with the ongoing tension, social dislocation, and unrest. *How would Stanley hold up?* At least he had not manifested any of the symptoms he had experienced in 1976. After his stress-related overuse of Valium, she always kept a watchful eye over him. With their daily challenges, he did not need the evening's assault to add to his pressures.

CHAPTER 9: BEST BUS RIDE EVER

September 1985

CURTIS CAUGHT HIS BREATH. The unknown beauty boarded the crowded bus to Elsies River station at one of the Halt Road bus stops. She was a captivating image of well-proportioned perfection, tall with her tightly curled dark hair cropped short. Curtis could not believe his luck when she stood right alongside his seat. A hint of floral perfume sent his senses into high arousal. Without hesitation, he stood to offer her his seat.

She paused. "Am I so old?" she asked with her full lips drawn into a mischievous smile to reveal an alluring thin gap between her front top teeth. She had prominent cheekbones, but her most striking features were her mismatched eyes. One was hazel-coloured, the other speckled-green. A cute spray of freckles across her rounded nose added to the cheeky persona she projected. Her light brown skin was flawless. Stunned by her beauty, Curtis was unable to speak.

"But I'm rather ungrateful. Thanks." Her deep-dimpled smile mesmerised Curtis who looked at her long shapely legs in tight powder-blue denim jeans where she sat.

"You're welcome," he managed to stammer. His mouth was dry while his heart pounded in his ears. He was spellbound. She wore a figure-hugging white tee-shirt with no bra. He caught his breath, diverting his gaze.

Curtis deliberately passed his bus stop because he just had to talk to her. She hummed a tune to herself with a hint of a smile. She seemed to have slipped into a world of her own. *How I would love to join her there.*

A few stops further, she rose from her seat. "You can have your seat again." When she moved past him in the narrow aisle, her body brushed against his. Every part she touched sent bolts of arousal through him. Her floral fragrance wafted under his nose. His head spun. He so much wanted to reach out, to touch her, to kiss her, or more. Curtis could not help himself when he followed her. Once they were on the pavement, she turned towards him.

"Oh! You're there. Are you following me?"

Curtis' mind raced. "No." He thought of something sensible to say. Her eyes scanned his face. "Actually, I hoped for a cup of tea," he stammered.

"Really? Where?" Her brow furrowed; her half-smile mocked him.

Maybe the eyes teased? Maybe they dared him? His mind raced. "With you."

She laughed. "You're outrageous! I have three brothers who don't take kindly to strangers. I don't even know you."

"Well, my name is Curtis. Curtis Fouche. I'm from Bishop Lavis." There was a tone of desperation in his voice. "You?"

"So now you reckon I know you?" She snorted as she lapsed into silence. Her eyes narrowed while she studied his face. "Okay," she said. "My name is Tina. Tina Stephens. With a 'ph'. I hate having my name misspelled. Especially Tina. It's with an 'i'. Understood?"

"Yes, of course; 'ph' and 'i.'" Curtis looked her in the eye. "Well, since we know each other, I should be safe from your brothers."

"You hope. Yes. You better hope," she laughed, "They can be nasty, especially my father. He's tough. He beat up one of my boyfriends because he didn't like him. I'm his favourite."

At least he had her talking, "Where do you live?"

"Halfway along Seventeenth Avenue." She pointed ahead. "I was born here in the original house. What about you?"

"Like you, I live at home with my family. Mother, two sisters and a baby brother. I lost my dad in '76."

"I'm sorry to hear of your loss. My mother died when I was still a kid; it's why my Dad is so protective of me." A cloud seemed to pass over her before she continued. "Are you married? Do you have children?"

"No. Why do you ask?"

"Just checking. I can't stand those types. You sure?" Tina stopped, half-turning to look at him. "Now don't lie to me. You'll regret it." Her eyes narrowed again.

"I'm sure." Curtis smiled. His eyes narrowed too. "You afraid of me?" It was his chance to tease her.

She snorted. "Don't fancy yourself." They ambled along the street with their hands sometimes brushing against each other. As much as Curtis wanted to hold her hand, he did not. His insides felt all scrambled with an enchantment that was new to him. He hoped that she felt the same way.

The street was typical of the area with a mix of houses with decades of jaded styles. Most of the homes needed attention. A few had well-tended gardens while others had a weed patch in front or around the sides. There were no shanties in the street, but, across an empty plot, he could see a cluster of them in the next street. The long road ran from west to east, with the snow on the Helderberg Mountains visible in the distance ahead. Table Mountain and Devil's Peak were behind them. The delightful spring day with a cloudless sky was already perfect.

"Just wait here a minute," said Tina who walked through the low gate to a short, curved pathway. She moved with a slow alluring roll of her hips. He tried in vain to suppress his arousal as she closed the front door behind her. The house looked dwarfed in the middle of its quarter acre plot, typical of the earlier properties in the area. A low front wall held a well-trimmed lawn in check. Pruned rose bushes grew on each side of the pathway close to the front of the house. To the right of the house, a bricked driveway led to the back.

Curtis was pleased that she was not put off by his excuse for a cup of tea. He now had to let events play themselves out. Anything else would put him in bonus territory.

"Are you going to stand there all day?" Her cheeky face popped around the corner of the house.

A grinning Curtis followed her along the driveway lined with neatly pruned alternating quince and pomegranate bushes.

"I live at the back of the old house where my ever-busy father built each of us kids a room. All the men are at work today, in the building trade. Now the one with the pink door is mine. Naturally, the three blue doors belong to my brothers."

Tina opened the door to her orderly room. After locking the door behind them, she placed her handbag on a chair beside the bed. She turned to face him with a mischievous expression on her face. He held his breath. Everything she did aroused him, especially when she had locked the door.

She stood upright, her breasts prominent, with her hands on her hips. His erection strained to be released.

"I have water but no tea in the room." The hooded eyes burned into his soul. She stepped close to him. Her fragrance made his head spin. "Would you prefer a kiss instead? I would."

Curtis' head swirled when their lips met. He ran his hands down her back. She followed suit, with her fingers tracing electric lines along his spine. Their hands explored each other. His skin tingled with every touch.

He liked the way she did not force her tongue into his mouth. Instead, she tantalised the tip of his tongue with hers. They broke apart to undress, their clothes soon in piles on the floor. Facing him, Tina looked splendid.

They continued their passionate exploring of each other's bodies as her body heat mingled with his. The bed with a pink satin cover beckoned, but Curtis wanted her where they stood. She was the perfect height. She guided him into her, as both exploded on contact. Curtis held onto her as Tina slowly inclined backwards till her head rested against the door with her eyes closed.

His legs were close to the double bed behind him. With an arm to support himself, Curtis lay across the bed while he held onto Tina with his other arm until she sat astride him with her lips compressed. With her head held back, he was awestruck by her magnificence.

The pace of their rhythm increased again until they climaxed simultaneously. They remained in each other's arms for several minutes.

"Do you still want your cuppa?" Tina asked. "I'd have to go to the kitchen in the main part of the house."

"No. I'm more than happy with my entrée and mains." Curtis nibbled her shoulders followed by kisses to her back. Sitting alongside her lissome beauty, he massaged her from her neck to her lower back. She sighed as she rolled over to lock her long legs behind him. After a protracted period of physical and emotional intensity, they again shared their moment of impassioned release.

Tina lay on her side next to him. He looked at her face with her eyes half-closed. Despite the wonder of the moment, Curtis' thoughts drifted to his secret programme. *What about Tina? Does she have any?*

In the days ahead, he often recalled the best bus ride he had ever had.

CHAPTER 10: GRAVEYARD REVOLUTIONARIES

September 1985

PAT DREW ON THE LAST of the cigarette then flicked the butt through the car's window. He and Ebrahim had collected Curtis and Thembani near the King David Country Club. They now sat parked in the shade of a few pine and Eucalyptus trees in the Modderdam Cemetery, close to the Club. There was no one else around. A few gravesites showed evidence of regular attention. Most did not. Sun-bleached plastic flowers in vases dotted the cemetery. Traffic roared past on the busy Modderdam Road.

"Well, you look better than the last time we saw you." Pat smiled, shaking hands with a solemn Thembani. "It's good to see you too Curtis."

Their muted laughter sounded forced, like their stiff movements, awkward with the body language of unfamiliarity.

"I'm glad to see you all of you today to formally thank you again," said Thembani, who brushed his index finger over his nose a couple of times. "Dr Gershon said I was lucky to survive. I must apologise to Pat and Ebrahim." He addressed the pair. "I deliberately withheld my name from you two. It's Thembani. You may know my name means hope." They exchanged firm handshakes.

"I have often passed by the place without knowing there was a cemetery here," continued Thembani. "Around Cape Town these invasive plants have taken over." He waved his hands at the trees. "There's Pinus radiata from Europe. Like the ubiquitous Port Jackson wattle, the Eucalyptus lehmanii is from Australia. The colonisers needed the straight, long timber of the pine trees, while the wattle bushes were used to control the Cape Flats dunes. Unfortunately, these weeds took over the country in the same way their noxious White human counterparts have done."

"How'd you know those plant names?" asked Ebrahim, who slipped a Wrigley's gum into his mouth.

"Thembani eats books," laughed Curtis. "You should see his room where books are like wall-to-wall carpeting. And he remembers everything he reads! He's a walking encyclopedia."

Pat threw his next cigarette stub through the car window. "If everybody agrees, Ebrahim and I think we need to know each other's stories. Why do we want change? More important, how far are we prepared to go with activism?"

"No problem with me," said Curtis. "Let's talk."

Pat warmed to the quiet Curtis who constantly seemed to need action.

"Same with me," said Thembani. "We must all be a bit inquisitive about each other."

Pat said, "I'll kick-off. In appearance, people think I'm White, but I am a committed Black South African, not a 'so-called Coloured'. I dislike the term. Family oral history indicates Dutch ancestry with slave roots. My motivation to change the country comes from a lifetime of apartheid's indignities. The government's ongoing violent repression has steeled my resolve to bring about transformation.

"I live in an established area in Athlone where anti-government sentiments run high. Like Ebrahim, I attended Alexander Sinton High School. It's still a hotbed of student rebellion. Both of us are part-time students at the University of the Western Cape where I'm in Science, while Ebrahim is doing Commerce. Our studies have been disrupted these past few years."

Pat paused to light another cigarette. He needed a few seconds to compose himself before he continued. "In '76, I spent three weeks in security police detention." He stopped to look away. He bit on his lip; the worst moments of his detention always threatened to overwhelm him. "It's when I 'met' Hammer van Zyl." He fingered the speech marks in the air. "I think we all know what that entails. He fractured my rib, cheekbone, and an eye socket with his knee. I can't drive because of double vision when I look to the sides. My right ear has reduced hearing from a ruptured eardrum. The missing tooth and buckled nose are van Zyl's handiwork." He tapped the scar on his cheek. "The damned swine called the cigarette burn, 'Hammer's dimple.' I have a couple on each foot. I can still smell the moment he burnt me!" Pat drew a deep breath; deep in his brain recesses there was more.

"On his own Hammer provided me with enough reasons to want violent change, especially when I look in the mirror. I can't banish the image of Hammer van Zyl's evil face from my mind, or the stench of alcohol on his breath. I often think that the reason I survived my detention was my resolution to rid the country of these bastards one day. I was fourteen at the time.

"But my most recent experiences during the Pollsmoor march have accelerated my resolve to move towards violent change. Violence begets violence. I've had my fill of police brutality. Now it's my turn!" His voice was firm, his face intense.

"Finally, in case you haven't noticed, I chain-smoke Lexington *with* filters." He coughed as he laughed at the same time. The rest applauded him with soft handclaps.

Ebrahim paused his gum chewing. "My sister, Suraya, thirteen at the time, sustained a bullet wound to the head from the Riot Squad

Police in August 1976. She was on her way to buy a loaf of bread close to our home." Ebrahim closed his eyes, sighing audibly.

"She survived but with residual paralysis from her brain injury. She struggled at school, where she had previously excelled; she wanted to be a doctor. A few weeks after her injuries she developed epilepsy. Her fits used to be monthly, now they've become more frequent. I cry when I hold her in my arms when she has fits. I sing to her, stroking her hair until the attack settles. Every spasm of hers goes through me too as I grind my teeth with her. Every groan is like a knife stabbing through my brain."

Ebrahim brushed at the tears filling his eyes. A distraught Pat listened to his close friend's agony, often shared in their moments together. He rubbed Ebrahim's arm.

"When she finally settles, she sleeps in my arms. I sing *Thula, thula umntwana - Hush, hush little child.* Suraya often settles with the song. Along with enough other reasons to want change, my only sibling is my regular motivation every time she has an attack.

"After years of stewing, the Pollsmoor march day provided me with the extra impetus that I needed to bring me here today. Enough is enough! We need more action than marches or street corner protests." His delicate hands had clenched into tight fists by the time he finished. Light sweat coated his lip. There was a round of muted applause while Ebrahim chewed more vigorously on his gum.

"What a powerful story Ebrahim," said Curtis who squeezed Ebrahim's shoulder from the backseat. Curits' eyes flickered before he spoke. "I'm sure we've all had those childhood moments when apartheid became a forceful reality. My first experience was during our eviction from District Six when I was seven. With our belongings, they took us away on a flat-bed truck, before they dumped us outside a poorly built council house in Bishop Lavis township. Living there fired my teenage determination to bring about change. The past decade of rebellion prevented me from studying at UWC. After nine years, I finally obtained my senior school certificate through correspondence courses last year." Curtis looked reflective as his voice tailed off.

"I have an intense hatred of Whites, especially the unknown White policeman who killed my father in the 1976 disturbances when things were going crazy at Lavistown station on his way to work. We buried him over there almost nine years ago to the day." He pointed towards the distant grave; his voice threatened to break. Curtis turned from the group to look in the direction of his father's grave. Pat saw him blinking as Thembani squeezed his shoulder.

"My dad's death is way ahead of other reasons for what drives me. I had to identify his body in his bloodied work overalls in the morgue. I can still picture the gunpowder residue around his wounds. Like Pat, no teenager should have those experiences. As Pat and Ebrahim said, violence begets violence; enough is enough! I've been ready since my time in the mortuary." He punched the car seat in front of him.

Pat heard the hurt in Curtis' voice. He saw how compressed his lips were, how his dark eyes smouldered. "I'm sorry to hear about your father," said Pat.

Thembani nodded. "1976 was a watershed year for all of us. My dad took months to recover from bullet wounds sustained at Heideveld station on his way to work. A few days later, my mother lost an eye to a rubber bullet when she stood at the front door during a wild day of rioting." His scar added prominence to the deep lines on his forehead. He rubbed the side of his nose.

"The only good thing was how both my parents then became supportive of the students' fight. My father's limp or my mother's eye patch are *my* daily reminders of the need to bring about change. There are other reasons, including last month's near-death experience when I first met the three of you. I'm through with throwing stones at the police. I'm ready to take our fight to the next level."

Thembani Dlamini had his thinking face on again. "I am of Xhosa descent. I was born in theTranskei on the day of the Sharpeville massacre in 1960. I would say my whole life has been deformed by my experiences under apartheid.

"Like Curtis, I matriculated by correspondence. One day I hope to study English literature at university like the one on the slopes of Devil's Peak." He pointed towards the distant mountain-based University of Cape Town. "Right now the nearest university I can go to is more than a thousand kilometers away from Cape Town."

He pulled his Reference Book from his pocket. "Finally, whenever I have to produce my *Dompas* to a pimple-faced White policeman, gun in hand or on hip, it's a violation of myself. Here's the main reason to want change in South Africa. Right here!" An index finger jabbed hard at the *Dompas*. "Every year in our country of 30 million people, they arrest a quarter of a million of us because of Dompas offences." An uplifted finger reinforced his words.

Pat was in awe of the intense sincerity conveyed by Thembani's deep voice and his furrowed brow. Thembani's African township experiences put him well ahead of the rest of the group regarding social denial and police victimisation.

"By the way, my scarred forehead is from a childhood injury." Thembani raised his brow a couple of times, "and my nose rubbing is a tic, not a cold." He pinched the tip of his nose.

Pat lit a cigarette, coughing after the first deep draw. "Well, we all have our reasons to be more radical. My plan of action is about us forming a revolutionary cell. If you belong to any other cells, then that's your business."

After another deep draw, Pat exhaled the smoke forcefully in a thin stream. "So, was there a lesson in our recent Pollsmoor march experiences? Although every bit counts in our struggle, maybe it's time to leave the street demonstrations to the school kids. We can only laud our martyrs who paid the ultimate price. Now we need something with more impact, more oomph. The internal struggle is ramping up. How can we be part of the action?"

CURTIS REALISED THAT he and Thembani were already an unstructured, informal cell of their own. They had never discussed Curtis' attacks, apart from when they first met. *That's my business, the actions of a one-man cell.*

Silence shrouded the group.

"Yes," said Curtis eventually. "I too believe that we need more than stones or Molotov cocktails to bring about change."

"I think people were too stuck on Gandhi's pacifism," said Ebrahim. "But he did say resistance had to be active *and* provocative. I'm sure it's only a small step from there to the greater engagement we seek."

"One of Gandhi's best is 'poverty is the worst form of violence,'" said Thembani. "I also like the way he says people would 'prefer their own bad government to the good government of an alien power'. Even Nelson Mandela took the ANC onto a pathway of violence after the ANC's decades of passive resistance."

The rest applauded their orator. Curtis, though, needed more substance. He pulled forcefully on his collar with both hands. "Look," said Curtis. "I'm a get-up-and-go-man, but I believe in thorough planning. Does anyone have any proposals, anything concrete, any line of action, any plans?" With difficulty, he restrained himself. His manic energy needed to break free as his eyes blinked. The Armpit Assassin's work was only his. He recognised how the caution of the Academy recruits had put the brakes on his attacks. With a four-man cell he could take a collective step towards freedom. *I want more than The Cape Herald headlines by attacking Whites.*

"Well, yes," Pat replied. "And no. Maybe we would all like to have a Kalashnikov under the mattress or a stash of limpet mines or hand grenades in the cupboard. These are big issues we have to work through. Let's say we want a more aggressive approach. If not, we'll all go our separate ways."

Nobody spoke, each was deep in thought. Wisps of cloud surrounded the distant narrow end of Table Mountain, Devil's Peak and Lion's Head. The only noise came from the traffic rushing by on Modderdam Road. A solitary person tended a grave in the distance.

Curtis fidgeted, he wanted to scream. *But where's the action?* He threw down the gauntlet to the group. "Look, whether guns or explosives are involved the final question is, are we prepared to kill when we undertake more radical resistance? On that score, you can count me in!" Curtis half-raised his arm with his index finger in the air.

Pat and Ebrahim raised their hands simultaneously. "Count us in," said Ebrahim.

"I need to avenge Albert Luthuli's death," said Thembani.

"*Luthuli's death?* The ANC leader before Mandela?" Curtis asked.

"Yes!" Luthuli died in 1967 when struck by a train while crossing the railway line close to his home in Natal. He was Africa's first winner of the Nobel Peace Prize in 1960. "I believe that *they* killed him by pushing him under a train." Thembani stared at each of the group with a piercing intensity.

"My tribute to Luthuli, and others like Steve Biko, has to be violent, like their deaths; *they* understand nothing else. Recently someone said to me, 'To kill, I must hate enough.' I've reached that point; now it's my time to hit back." There was a quivering of Thembani's voice. His fist shot up. "*Amandla!*" he shouted simultaneously with Ebrahim.

"*Ngawethu!*" They all responded with power-fists in the air.

They shook hands firmly as a sense of belonging suffused the group, who already seemed more at ease with each other.

"I appreciate how we have all reached such a momentous point in our lives," said Pat. "Welcome!" They high-fived each other.

"We can chat about things apart from strategy," said Pat. "What do you think of discussing Karl Marx's *Das Kapital*, Thembani?" Pat flicked away his cigarette stub.

Thembani whistled. "It'd be a tough one to start with. The ANC's Freedom Charter would be easier to remind ourselves of what we hope to achieve. This year is the Charters' thirtieth anniversary. Like Das Kapital, it's banned, but I'll find you all a copy. Everything's possible in Gugs," he added with a wink.

"What activities have you considered, Pat?" Curtis asked with eyebrows raised while his dark blinking eyes underscored his fiery zeal.

"I'm going to call you Action Man," Pat said with a smile. "Any mission depends on the type of weapons we get." He paused to light another cigarette. "We can use AK 47s to attack a White bus or a supermarket or a major sporting match - these *Boere* (White Afrikaners) like their rugby, even cricket. Bombing electric pylons to cripple factories undermines the confidence of foreign investors in the country. Or we could lob a grenade or two into a tourist bus."

"Have you any weapon sources yet?" Curtis asked. He clung onto every word from the guarded Pat, who looked at him with increasing warmth.

"I have a few leads without a definite source yet. Do either of you know anyone?"

"There are ANC MK (uMkhonto we sizwe) operatives in the township especially in Crossroads," said Thembani. "Regardless of the source, I would caution a need to be thorough about checking the credentials of any arms vendor. The police have used weaponry as bait to entrap freedom fighters, many of whom have disappeared afterwards."

"Too true," Pat continued. "We've heard about such cases. I've been cautious, so my two contacts are tentative. I hope to know more in the next few weeks. I'll keep you informed when we meet up next. It's a slow process, especially with the festive season approaching. In the meantime, we can all check out potential suppliers while thinking about suitable targets. Where should we next meet?"

"I'm okay with the cemetery," said Curtis. "But we need to change venues rather than meet in the same place every time".

"Cemeteries aren't my thing," said Ebrahim.

"Not mine either," said Thembani, who waved a hand at the surrounding graves.

"I chose the cemetery as it's close to you two," said Pat. "Few people come here. However, I had to promise scaredy-cat Ebrahim that today's graveyard meeting would be a one-off session."

Pat turned to light another cigarette. "I'll find another spot by the time we meet again. We can collect you on the southern side of Modderdam Road near the King David Golf Club where there's a Coca-Cola hoarding. Before we finish, Thembani, could you sing the ANC anthem?" asked Pat. "It sounds so powerful when one hears dozens of people singing the song at rallies or funerals."

Thembani beamed, singing without prompting. The group listened respectfully, captivated by Thembani's deep-voiced rendition of *Nkosi sikelel iAfrik* (God bless Africa). Curtis joined him in the chorus as their bodies swayed to the tune.

"Beautiful," Ebrahim clapped with enthusiasm.

"It's a hymn adopted as the ANC anthem in 1927," said Thembani. "It's all about the Lord's blessings for Africa. There's nothing revolutionary in the words at all, so it's probably the only hymn ever banned. It's already the national anthem in Zambia and Zimbabwe."

"Azania next," said Curtis. "I wouldn't mind if we sang *Nkosi sikelel iAfrika* at all our sessions. My father taught me the words. Your deep voice reminds me of him, Thembani."

"I'm embarrassed to say that I don't know the words. I've never been able to find a copy," said Pat.

"Don't worry, I'll organise one or more," said Thembani. "Ebrahim, one final thing before we finish. I admire your Palestinian scarf. Yasser Arafat wears his scarf draped in the shape of Palestine. Can I rearrange your scarf before we depart?"

"Sure, Thembani." A bemused Ebrahim unwrapped his scarf from around his neck.

"It's simple," said Thembani. "Folded into a triangle, I'll drape the scarf across your shoulders so that the tasseled tips are in front, with the real story at the back." Thembani beamed.

"How cool," Curtis applauded. "It's South Africa, our Azania."

"*Amandla ngawethu!*" They high-fived Ebrahim.

"But that's unfair," said Ebrahim. "I'm the only one who can't see it."

"Don't worry. I'll take a photo of you in your scarf later," said a smiling Pat.

"I'll wear the scarf the other way around so I can see Azania," said Ebrahim.

"No, Ebrahim. People will think it's a bib," said Curtis as soft laughter rippled through the group.

CURTIS SAT ON THE GROUND with Thembani behind a cluster of Port Jackson wattle bushes alongside Modderdam Road, where Ebrahim had dropped them off near the Coca Cola hoarding. The honeyed smell of the bushes' tiny golden pompoms filled the air along with the buzzing of bees in search of their nectar spring harvest.

"So what do you make of those comrades?" asked Curtis.

Thembani looked reflective. "Hmm. Not sure. They seem genuine enough. Like us they've had a couple of trials by fire. I've been so cautious in Gugs where your closest friend could be today's police informer."

"Would *you* actually kill someone Thembani? We're not talking stones anymore. It's explosives or guns. I buy into what they propose. I hear you talk of your parents' approach - 'Thou shalt not kill'. You look like a benign soul to me, bookish, smart, meant for higher things. In a liberated country one day I see you as a professor. To me you seem more Gandhi than Che Guevara. Even though you quoted me, do you really hate enough to kill? You know I'm already there. Are you?"

A slow, noisy truck passed on the busy road. Thembani cleared his throat. "The thought of killing terrifies me, yet I believe I'm capable of taking a life. My near-death experience on Mandela's march day has convinced me I can kill. Trust me, Curtis. Mandela took the same step. Why not me, huh? Why not?"

Curtis high-fived him. "It's not an easy decision. My apologies if I sound doubtful. It's because I didn't lightly follow the pathway I chose."

"Talking about your pathway, has there been much police activity after the Police Academy recruit stabbings?"

Curtis did not answer straight away. *How much do I tell him?* "No. Not really. Their promised 'special task force' in Bishop Lavis is an inexperienced junior detective who drives in from the other side of town. He seems more interested in his fancy clothes with a different coloured suit each day of the week. Since his arrival, he seems more interested in sleeping with the local women. The main visible difference is that the trainees only venture forth in groups. It seems they now always carry their guns on them."

Curtis wanted to change the subject. He lapsed into silence.

"Pat and Ebrahim are interesting," said Thembani. "They could be gay. What do you think?" He rubbed his nose with his index finger.

Curtis raised his eyebrows. "What?" He paused; images of their interactions raced through his mind. "Could be, I suppose. It doesn't bother me as long as their politics is in the right place. My younger brother is gay. With time I accepted it, when I saw what a loving relationship he has with his partner. They hope they can be married one day, whereas I need a *woman*." He underscored his comment with a sinuous movement of his hands.

"Hey, remind me to keep you away from my sisters." Thembani grinned, wagging a finger at Curtis. "Do you have a girlfriend? I don't."

"No. Maybe it'll happen one day. Who knows?" Curtis thought of Tina, who was not a steady girlfriend, though she had been in his thoughts every day since they last met; he looked forward to their Lion's Head hike the next weekend. In any event, Tina was his business, not Thembani's.

They soon left their spot of semi-concealment. Curtis had more trust in Thembani than he had ever had with anyone else. They lived in a world where friends or family betrayed each other. What Thembani knew of him was adequate to achieve their goals. They had a unity forged from the convenient meeting of people with a shared dream of freedom. Their firm farewell hug symbolised the rare trust he had in his incidental friend.

CHAPTER 11: DETENTION AND EMIGRATION

September 1985

FAY ISMAIL EMERGED from prison on a pleasantly warm day. The clear blue skies with a soft south-easterly wind did not register with her. When she left the police station with Stanley, she felt cold to her core. Stanley's firm hug when he saw her did not thaw her deep inner freeze. There was no feeling of relief or freedom; she felt suspended, somewhere, nowhere. *My loss of self must end. I must rediscover me.*

Fay was a member of the United Democratic Front. The organisation had started a nationwide campaign demanding improved pay in the country. Her detention, along with tens of thousands of others was under the latest draconian national State of Emergency, re-imposed after the thwarted UDF-organised Pollsmoor marches a month earlier.

Fay clung to Stanley's arm when they crossed the carpark at the police station. Once in their vehicle she held onto Stanley. She felt she needed to, but she could not shed a tear. Her inner knotting had been unrelenting during her twelve days in security police detention. As they drove home Fay recoiled when she saw a following Volkswagen Beetle in the passenger side door mirror.

"Those bastards are behind us."

"Yes. I saw them in my rear-view mirror," said Stanley.

Fay knew rage was there, locked away where she couldn't feel it. Her constant ebullience was non-existent, as she remained benumbed, clenching her hands all the way home. She appreciated Stanley's silence, including the way he reached over to squeeze her hand or her thigh while he drove.

She quivered again when she saw how the black VW Beetle had stopped a few houses away from their home. "I want to walk over there to smash their windscreen with a brick. Their car brings the prison to my home, my sanctuary. How dare they?"

"Try to ignore them." Stanley held onto her arm. "It's part of their intimidation."

When they entered their home Fay rushed to the bathroom to shower. "I need to purge myself," she said to Stanley who washed her back with the firm pressure she wanted. She spent many long minutes in the shower. In prison the taps provided cold water only. Despite the warm water on her skin, her inner chill left her shivering. She felt yet hardly responded to Stanley's kisses on her wet shoulders. There was none of the emotional comfort she always used to feel.

When done she wrapped herself in her dressing gown before she went through to the kitchen.

"I'll burn these clothes later." Fay threw the garments through the kitchen door.

Fay dabbed at her eyes with a tissue as Stanley brought her a warm cup of tea. With alarm she realised how blurred Stanley's image was. A bolt-like tremor went through her. She closed her eyes to compose herself as she slurped at the black tea through bruised lips. When her eyes opened, they flitted around the room, unable to focus on anything.

"They're such bloody swines," Fay said after a while.

"What happened? What did they do to you? Do you want to talk about it? You don't have to, but it's probably better if you do."

Stanley's creased thick brows, more pronounced than ever, highlighted his pained gaze.

From where she sat Fay stared over the six-foot-high precast concrete wall towards the distant mountains. The blue sky overhead seemed to mock her.

"It was horrible Stanley. I would hate to go through it again." She sipped at her cooling tea. Staring into the distance, Fay had trouble formulating her thoughts into words. "Where do I start?" Fay cracked the slim fingers of both hands. She began in a hushed voice. "The security police didn't do much to me. While targeting certain individuals, they seemed to have dropped a net over many trade unionists and UDF people." She pushed the empty cup away from herself. Fay fidgeted with the crumpled tissues in her hand.

"In the distance, we heard the screams of the committee members. They seemed to be the people they really wanted. Later we saw their bruises. We shared the pain when they yelled in their sleep." Fay sucked in a breath through clenched teeth.

"Their interrogations were torture sessions. Hearing those shrieks was the worst part of my time there. Many of us held those women in our arms once they returned to our cells. By proxy we shared their worst experiences." Fay held her hands to her face, grateful when Stanley stood behind her to rub her shoulders.

"It wasn't easy in the overcrowded cells because we always dreaded that we would be next. They hardly fed us, and we were thirsty most of the time. In the crowded cell you had to pee in a bucket. Cold showers were only allowed every second or third day." She stopped to wipe away her tears.

"Even though they were muffled you could hear the screaming in the distance. Whenever those sounds reached me, I sat there wondering, when would my turn come? When they finally interrogated me the security police seemed almost bored. They pushed me around, slapping me often. My lips still feel bruised." Her fingers touched her mouth.

"They wanted to know if I wanted sex. It's awful the way they strip you naked with their eyes. One of them fondled my breasts while he rubbed his erection against me. He wanted to know if I wanted it. The rest of them laughed." Fay shivered, her head bowed low. "He went no further, though the moment hung over me all the time I was there. The threat of rape in those circumstances is ... like being raped."

"How disgusting," said Stanley, his face etched with deep lines.

"I dreaded that Hammer van Zyl would question me. He put in a brief appearance during my interrogation. He stared at me and whispered to his men before he left. They returned me to the cells after a short while. Thank heavens I never saw him again, though we heard from others who had been brutalised by him. He had ruptured the eardrums and fractured the ribs of a few women; electric shocks or water on the hoods seemed to be reserved for committee members or organisers. The idea that he would interrogate me was stressful."

Fay blew her nose. "Look at those blood-stains." She threw the crumpled tissue into the bin. "They smacked me around often, always wanting the names of organisers. Whether they had enough information, I don't know, as my afternoon with them passed quickly. They hardly seemed interested in a few of us." She had to blow her nose again; at least there was no more bleeding.

"The swine electrocuted many, while they deprived several of sleep for days. As soon as a few detainees fell asleep in the cells, the bastards took them away again. Those women were the worst affected. Part of their cat-and-mouse game was to tell a prisoner they were about to be released only to interrogate them again."

Fay stood up, walked to the kitchen window then returned to sit again. She did not know what to do with her hands, so she clasped them tightly with her elbows tucked into her sides.

"They stripped one woman naked, held her across the top of a chest of drawers, then slammed the drawer on her breasts. She was in such agony with her tense purple breasts almost doubled in size from the bruising. They dragged other women across the floor by their long hair. One of them was suspended by her hair before they punched and electrocuted her. A few were stripped naked. Every woman had a morbid fear of rape."

Fay tried to control her shuddering. Her tears started to flow freely. She rocked in her chair. Her intermittent moans came from somewhere deep inside. She wanted to vent her outrage. Her body shook as she clung to Stanley's midriff while she sobbed. She felt Stanley's hands clenched into fists where they rested on her shoulders. Fay's body remained tense while she breathed deeply to regain her composure.

Stanley massaged her shoulders. His kisses on forehead, face, and neck caressed her. *How I need this!* He held her head close to him. Fay sighed. She felt her belly knot ease. She enjoyed this bonding of their souls. After a few seconds she released herself to go to their bedroom, where the late afternoon sun had warmed the room.

Fay turned to face Stanley who had followed her to the bedroom. "Before I change into my clothes I need you to hold me. Please." Fay choked, whispering.

Stanley gave her one of his bear hugs before slowly running his hands the full length of her spine the way she liked. His hands rested on her hips. He kissed her on the neck. She sighed, closing her eyes. Fay's body moulded into Stanley's. She needed his proximity, to smell his aftershave lotion, to feel his warmth, to relax, to be herself. She noticed an inner pleasant stirring.

Fay drew his head towards her more firmly. Her fingers played with his hair. Stanley had not spoken much to her. He knew she needed a tender moment. To her surprise Fay felt herself moistening with his caresses and his soft kisses. She wanted to be even closer to

Stanley to seek the disconnect she needed. Fay's senses tingled as she drew his hands towards her breasts. She took off her gown, while he followed her cue. They did not take long to dissolve into their moment of intense fervour.

Fay welcomed the blurred state of suspension where she was impervious to pain, smothered by Stanley's love. She wanted him again until they lay in each other's arms. Despite the cooling day they were both sweaty. Fay wrapped into him. Here was her sanctuary. Stanley drew the duvet over them.

"It's ten years since we met," she murmured close to Stanley's chest. "One of the first things I told you was I wouldn't emigrate."

"You said you were 'against emigration.'"

"During my detention I felt less certain about my comment from a time when the death of my brother Fah was still raw," said Fay. She faltered, her mind in turmoil. Fah had died as an ANC MK guerrilla fighter on the South African border. "I try to have pleasant memories of our time together before he left. Instead, I wonder about Fah's death as a freedom fighter. Did the border troops shoot him? Was he caught? Tortured? Did he have a decent burial from his comrades, or did the vultures or hyenas get to him?" Fay shuddered.

Stanley held her more closely with her head against his chest. "People talk about closure. I'll never have peace when those thoughts intrude the way they do." Her body shook with her crying.

Stanley kissed her neck while his steady eyes scanned her face. Their arms remained wrapped around each other.

"You are my security blanket." She paused. "Thank you." Her voice was quiet. She pecked him on the cheek.

"We haven't talked about emigration since '76," said Stanley. He had considered the matter then; instead, they had settled on their annual working holidays, alternating between New Zealand and Australia. "Are you having a rethink about emigration?"

"I don't know. I don't know! I'm torn between leaving or staying. Much has gone on in the last ten years. I have watched you brave the traumas in the practice, even shared them with you at the SACLA clinic. I've worried about you ever since your post-traumatic stress issues. My prison experience has been harrowing, to say the least." She could feel herself scowling; her facial muscles pulled tight. "Would I emigrate? Where to? New Zealand or Australia? They already feel like extended homes with our annual trips."

"Let's go to the kitchen," said Stanley. "We both need to eat. We have a bit of left-over curry I can warm for us."

STANLEY HATED SEEING Fay so upset. They put on their gowns and slippers. He held her by the hand, kissed her again before she sat in the rounded kitchen nook opposite the kitchen window. Stanley switched on the gas heater. In the last of the day's light, the shaded lower Constantiaberg range was still visible towards the left of the side-on view of Table Mountain. Stanley removed the heated food from the microwave before he snuggled close to Fay. He kissed her on the cheek before turning to his dinner as Fay nibbled at the food she had dished. Mostly, she pushed her food around on her plate.

"Fay, I can relate to your experience from what my tortured patients have told me. Their abuse has always distressed me, so your experience has been the most traumatic twelve days of my life. I was worried about you every day. They were plain rude or unhelpful whenever I went to enquire after you." He paused to take a few deep breaths; his pain was profound. *How much worse must Fay feel? She's normally so tough, now so fragile.*

"Our emotional barriers constantly need to be reinforced," Stanley continued. "It's why we run, we hike, we dive or we go away a few weeks every year. A huge part of my shield is our love over the past decade. Those same tools will help you to recover," He squeezed her forearm before holding her hand.

"So, do we emigrate or not? Leaving the practice won't be easy. If we leave, would we choose New Zealand or Australia?"

He stared at Fay. He had never seen her look so powerless before. His heart bled at the sight of her vulnerability, at how her effervescence had vanished. He hoped he could soon turn her around from her depths of despair.

"I don't know Stanley. I've not given much thought to emigrating. What if they arrest you? Or me again? Their Beetle followed us all the way home. It's like an invisible octopus tentacle reaching right here into our bloody kitchen!"

"The whole process is part of the conditioning of those swines," said Stanley. "Cower us into submission." He hardly tasted the curried mince he ate. "New Zealand versus Australia?" Stanley continued. "Which country is better?" The New Zealand courts had cancelled the All Blacks rugby tour to South Africa. Their Prime Minister Rob Muldoon had won an election when he allowed the 1981 Springbok tour to New Zealand.

"Is New Zealand the kind of country we want? We'll have the rebel Australian cricket tour here in summer, which neither the Australian government nor the Australian Cricket Board supports."

"But I can't forget my Australian experience in Tamworth when a white Australian wanted to push me off the pavement while his family walked in the opposite direction," said a distressed Fay. She spoke louder, her neck veins distended. Her eyes narrowed when she recalled the only serious, racist episode she had ever experienced outside South Africa. "Yes. On balance, New Zealand seems less imperfect."

"I feel the same way," said Stanley, who laughed softly. "But I'm not ready to leave yet. Our annual breaks over there are a huge tonic. Maybe you should apply to be registered in both countries then we can do locums together. It's refreshing to expose oneself to a different style of work."

"I'll look into it," said Fay, who reached out to kiss him.

After Fay's prison incarceration Stanley was not surprised at the turnaround in her stance concerning emigration. Fay had previously said moving abroad would be a betrayal of Fah's beliefs which cost him his life as an MK freedom fighter.

From his 1976 experience with post-traumatic stress disorder, Stanley knew how delicate the balance was between normality and dysfunctionality. Thanks to Fay, the sneezing, hoarseness, and nightmares of yesteryear had not troubled him again. Most important of all, he had not touched any Valium since then. In the days ahead Stanley had to ensure Fay's recovery. She needed looking after; he wanted the exuberant Fay to return.

CHAPTER 12: TENDER MOMENTS

September 1985

EBRAHIM KHAN LAY ON his left side with his right hand towards a wall heater above the bed. He ran his warmed hand from Pat's neck to the knee. The heater suffused the lovers in a warm orange glow. Both were naked the way they preferred to be in their moments of closeness. The much-needed intimacy was their first in many weeks.

When they lay together, Ebrahim enjoyed the sharp contrast of his darker skin colour against Pat's pale skin. No wonder Pat often said they belonged together, like molten chocolate with whipped cream.

Both men were good-looking. Each had dark eyes with well-formed teeth, although Pat had lost an upper central tooth from his time in prison when the infamous Hammer van Zyl punched him in the mouth. Pat had gained no satisfaction when van Zyl had cut his finger on Pat's tooth.

With his thin trimmed moustache, Ebrahim's mother had often commented on his resemblance to her favourite Indian actor, Raj Kapoor. He used to accompany her to the Sunday Indian movies at the Athlone cinemas. Their favourite had been the epic hit, *Mother India*.

"Must you always smoke?" Ebrahim asked Pat.

"As the Lexington advert says, it's my 'after-action satisfaction' my dear."

"You should chew gum the way I do. You'd smell better."

"No, gum's not my thing. It makes me too hungry after a few minutes of chewing," he laughed.

Pat De Bruin's birth certificate said Mixed Race, changing to Coloured at the time he obtained his compulsory Identity Card in his late teens. He was somewhat pimply, with smooth black hair like Ebrahim, except he preferred not to part his hair the way Ebrahim did on the standard left side. There were times when his pale skin embarrassed him, especially at school where his nickname was 'Whitey'. Both men despised the name.

Pat rolled onto his right side blowing a couple of smoke rings away from a vigorously chewing Ebrahim. The rings hovered overhead, changing shape until they faded away in the thin beam of sunlight crossing over Pat's bed from a high narrow window.

"At least our love lasts longer than those rings," said Pat. "Your soft hands drive me crazy. I feel I want to make love all day when we're together like this."

"I like the way you say, 'make love'. Sex sounds so crude. Screwing is worse. Yes, I prefer to make love. It's like a melting of the souls when we climax together the way we do. Yet you always have your eyes closed all the time. You hold your head like you're looking into the distance or the future. Do you ever open your eyes?"

Pat smiled. "No. With my eyes closed I see heaven in the distance along a bright pathway before ... before I disintegrate. I crumble from within to let the moment take over, to smother me in the all-embracing sensation."

"It's called love," said Ebrahim.

Pat had finished his Lexington. They kissed, their lips nibbled, their hands constantly caressed. Each touch was exciting while each stroke of a digit fanned Ebrahim's flaming emotions. Their wandering hands added to the magic until they again melted into each other.

"See, your eyes were closed again," laughed Ebrahim, curling further into Pat's warmth.

'Why do you watch me? Are you a perve? Have you tried closing your eyes?"

"Yes, I have, but your face enthralls me, so I have to look again after only a few seconds. It's when you're at your most beautiful." Ebrahim traced his fingers around Pat's face as Pat pursed his lips to kiss Ebrahim's soft palms.

"I wonder if our parents will ever accept our relationship?" Pat asked. "It took a few months before my Mom supported me, though my Dad refuses to talk about it. My brothers and sister understand. At least they don't call me a *moffie* (faggot). I hate the word."

"Me too. Like your dad, both my parents won't go there. I think Mom sighs her life away when I'm around her. It's awkward with Dad. My relationship with you is the elephant sharing the space in the garage where we work on his import-export business. At least he allows me time off whenever I wish. My sis has a greater understanding of our relationship. You know she's the other love in my life since long before the police shot her. No one else holds my hand the way she does when we walk together."

"Why do people seem to fear gays?" asked Pat. "Do they think it's all about anal sex, or we'll contaminate them by our presence? Most of us aren't brown queens."

"Homophobia is such a threat to us," said Ebrahim. "The State's religious zealotry is designed to give gays hell on earth."

Ebrahim shuddered. "Wrapped here in your arms is my escapist cocoon where I feel like me. Though I must say I prefer you clean-shaven. Your two-day growth gives me a rash." He rubbed Pat's chin. "Your stubble is too prickly."

"Hey, you are the one who hardly shaves. It's a waste of blades when you do." They laughed. "But I do like the after-shave you use." Pat nuzzled into his beloved's neck, inhaling deeply.

"I'm glad you like the lotion I had specially mixed at the Rylands store close to home. They use sandalwood, and musk mixed with rose oil from India. Of course, I put a drop or two in all the right places."

"Yes. I noticed." Pat massaged Ebrahim's shoulders, followed by finger combing Ebrahim's sleek black hair with no parting visible. "There you are, perfect." Pat twisted the hair around his fingers.

They lay back, holding hands. Ebrahim's slim thumb stroked the backs of Pat's thicker fingers.

"Like Cadbury's chocolate your skin is so sensuous. I can eat you all day." Pat playfully nipped Ebrahim's shoulder.

Ebrahim closed his eyes, reveling in the emotions enveloping him. The two had been friends since their primary school days. Their intimate relationship had been a slow process of development against traditional societal norms. Their romance started during their senior schooling days.

Their tender moments were magical, even though something always held Pat back, dating back to his days in security police custody before their affair started. *Part of him always broods on his detention.*

Ebrahim pulled a face as he waved his hands at Pat's cigarette smoke. He was worried he and Pat seemed stuck in first gear, unable to advance their activist plans. Maybe a cell of four could move things along, yet Ebrahim's main concern was whether he was ready to kill. The most he had ever done was slice through a fowl's neck at home when he did not like the sight of blood. There were times when he believed he could pull a gun's trigger to kill or drop a bomb or stab someone, especially whenever Suraya had a seizure, or after the Pollsmoor march experiences. Maybe more was needed to get him to cross the line. He knew Pat was already there.

"Now, Ebrahim. I have to spoil our fun, but our mission beckons. Of our two weapons' sources, I trust one guy more than the other. Today's meeting may push me all the way with one of them."

Ebrahim did not know who the potential weapons' suppliers were because Pat was too secretive about any developments. Ebrahim watched his lover dress; he disliked the way Pat had to leave.

Pat and Ebrahim walked in the direction of Ebrahim's place. A group of noisemakers huddled around a burning tyre on the corner of Thornton and St Simon's Road. The burning rubber smell was their winter trademark. The imprints of burnt tyres past scarred the pavement.

"Must be too cold," Pat said. "There's only a few comrades out today."

"I can't see one placard or any stones either. Maybe they need something to activate them."

Ebrahim braced himself, the wintry Cape north-westerly wind always found a way through the thickest of clothing. They greeted a couple of the regulars when they walked by.

Further on, Ebrahim looked lovingly at the closest friend he had ever known. "I do wish we could hold hands or kiss like other couples do when they walk."

"Not in our country," said Pat. "We'd probably spend a month in prison after one kiss in public."

The lovers parted with a brief hug when they reached Belgravia Road. Pat dug his fingers into Ebrahim's forearms. Ebrahim returned the squeeze before heading home a kilometer to the east. He brushed away a tear on his cheek. Whenever they separated, part of Ebrahim always seemed to go with Pat.

Ebrahim hoped Pat's negotiations would lead to the more decisive action they planned; meaningful change in the country needed more activist intervention. They had to add to the flames of insurrection in Cape Town, yet an element of doubt always niggled at Ebrahim. He trembled within, popping a gum bubble he had managed to blow. *Am I really ready to kill?*

CHAPTER 13: THE GOLF COURSE DOMPAS SAGA

October 1985

THEMBANI IGNORED CURTIS whenever they caddied at the King David Country Club. They would talk later, on their way home.

To Thembani the Club was an enigma. Of course, the members were White, the caddies Black. Cape Town Jews had established the course because they felt other clubs were antisemitic.

"It's part of the merry-go-round of racist bigotry in the country," Thembani told Curtis one day.

"You know how members of the National Party did prison time after supporting the Nazis during the war, so there's no surprise to have anti-semitism rear its ugly head in golf as well."

"In the past two years, people of colour have been playing here at the Club including one of my uncles. He looks a bit like me. He's a tight-fisted businessman who does not tip well, so you must beware of him," warned Curtis with a smile. "I heard Club membership numbers are low. Allowing in people of colour could be more about money than fairness."

"I'm lucky I have a regular client," said Thembani. "Mr Goldberg pays me well. He's given me a few radical books. He's a bit of a lefty who whispered when he told me he's a Trotskyite, but I tend to keep my chats with him neutral. I like the way he calls me 'Mr

Dlamini'. One day he said to me, 'South African apartheid is social engineering gone wrong. Like Nazism, apartheid must be eradicated.' Mr Goldberg's hand was clenched tight when he spoke. It's so like the man to offer to assist with my fees if I ever reach university. It's still my goal." Thembani flicked his nose with his finger.

"Mr Goldberg sounds like a rare individual in a country where golf puts into sharp relief South Africa's master-slave relationship. Listen to the way a few of them talk to us. I don't caddy for those people." Thembani raised his nose high. "It's beneath my dignity."

Curtis laughed. "I'm the same. I once left a guy at the third tee because of the way he spoke to me." They high-fived each other followed by a hearty laugh.

Thembani stood around with the other caddies until their regular Saturday morning golfers arrived. A handful of new caddies tried their luck with the players who needed their assistance. He hated the look on the caddies' faces when five or six of them, were not the lucky ones chosen for the round of play after crowding around golfers in need of a caddy. Thembani watched Curtis sitting on his own in deep thought on a bench where he awaited his player, who normally started later. He smiled at the way Curtis tugged at his shirt collar.

The strengthening south-westerly wind blew colder. Thickening clouds had built up. The caddies were well-covered against the mid-spring crisp snap. The smell of many self-rolled cigarettes hung heavy in the air.

The screeching of vehicles around the bend broke the early morning quiet. Two police vans came to an abrupt halt in the car park. Six White policemen rushed at the caddies, many of whom charged off between the parked cars to melt into the surrounding bushes. Three officers chased them with batons and *sjamboks*. The regular caddies looked on because their runaway colleagues did not have a *Dompas*.

Thembani's lips twitched, as he ground his teeth. He knew of people arrested in their outdoor toilets from where they were not allowed to fetch their papers, inside their homes. Here was the ultimate festering abscess. Nothing else made him feel more helpless. The hollowness in his stomach made him want to vomit. *Damn them!* He clenched his fists.

Mr Goldberg a lawyer, had organised Thembani's *Dompas*. Thembani was supposed to be his gardener. Although Thembani's papers were in order, there was always an anticipation of the unexpected whenever he waited while a pimply, armed White police officer checked his status. *What if …?* He knew they could search him, maybe beat him with a sjambok or baton if he were deemed insolent or too slow to respond. Avoiding eye contact was a well-practised survival ploy. Thembani made sure he was on his toes to take evasive action if needed. To strike at an armed Afrikaner policeman still in his teens was not the correct option. People had paid with their lives by doing less.

The policeman checking his Pass Book looked at Thembani, amd said, "The photo does not look like you."

"Well, you can see from the date, there," Thembani pointed. "It's nearly ten years ago. *Ja*, I was thinner then. Of course, my hair was longer, Afro style *jy weet mos* (you know)." Thembani managed a quick lip smile with narrowed unsmiling eyes. He averted his gaze to look at his feet. Mentally he boiled while he struggled to maintain an outward calm. *Relax!* Despite his past experiences his pulse hammered. The bit of Afrikaans seemed to do the trick with the constable; a tremulous Thembani pocketed his *Dompas*.

Thembani turned to see how Curtis had produced his ID card to another policeman. He did not need a *Dompas*, but Thembani knew he always carried his card. He caught his breath. Curtis' slit-like eyes did not waver from the policeman's face. *Look away Curtis, please.*

Instead, Curtis scowled. His face twitched, his lips thinned from the pressure against his teeth. *Oh no he's blinking his eyes.* Thembani could almost feel the tension in his friend. *If they only knew who you really are.*

"You are Coloured? A *Hotnot*? (Derogatory racist term to describe a person classified Coloured)." The policeman watched Curtis from below the visor of his hat as he tapped Curtis' plastic ID card on the nail of his thumb. "You don't look like a *Hotnot*. You are the blackest person here. The *Kaffirs* here all are lighter than you." He waved the card at the other caddies.

Curtis stood upright. He was taller than the mustachioed officer. He slowly clenched his hands. "Must be my slave ancestry. My grandfather was French. Can't you read? Look there, on the card. Fouche!" He pointed. "See there, *F, O, U, C, H, E*!" Curtis pointed to every emphasised letter in turn. His eyes never moved as he returned the policeman's stare.

Curtis' eyes were insolent, even arrogant as he extended his hand to retrieve his ID card. There was an awesome contempt about him. An admiring Thembani quivered for his friend's safety. Thembani almost wet himself when Curtis spelt his name the way he did. Everything else blurred as he fixated on Curtis' dark, fierce eyes.

The officer wavered. "Ja. Whatever. Here."

The flicked ID card missed Curtis' open hand, falling instead to the ground. The two of them continued to glare at each other. Curtis' eyes were almost shut. The officer's eyes mocked with his mouth pulled to one side in a smirk. He seemed to challenge Curtis. He raised his right hand to rest on the butt of his undrawn gun. His friend dropped his right hand to his side flexing his fingers repeatedly. *Please Curtis, leave the bloody knife in your pocket. Take your damned card, man.*

Thembani's breathing quickened. His mind raced with his mouth as dry as a cork. Curtis seemed frozen, apart from the constant flexing of his fingers. A sweating Thembani rushed over to pick up the card.

Thembani faced Curtis. "Is the card yours?" He pushed the card into Curtis' hand.

"Yes." Curtis pocketed his ID Card. His narrowed eyes never left the policeman's leering face. His feet shuffled, almost on his toes with left foot in front of the right. *Damn, he still looks like he wants to take out his knife.*

The noise of the returning policemen broke the tension. Thembani had never been so relieved to see them before. They swore at three of the runaway caddies, two of whom had bloodied wounds on their faces. One bled from the nose, the other from an extended cut to the forehead, while the third man had a black eye.

All three cried in anguish from the unprovoked baton or sjambok blows raining onto them until the lawmen forced them into one of the vans. The police then drove off with their human cargo at high speed. The laden van braked frequently on the sloped access roadway to the carpark. Thembani heard how the prisoners bounced around inside the truck like loose golf balls. The policemen's raucous laughter grated on his ears.

The remaining caddies tempered their relief. Those in the car park looked disconsolate with their soft, barely audible curses echoing the sentiments of many.

"One day they'll pay," said one of the regulars. "We have to ensure that it can't last forever. *Mayibuye iAfrika!* (Come back Africa!)" The refrain passed like a wave around the car park. Their fisted salutes were low, their voices subdued, though the call was more visceral than Thembani had ever heard before.

CURTIS MET THEMBANI under a gnarled pine tree where the two sat on the ground. A pair of startled turtle doves flapped their wings when they took off in search of a quieter tree. Curtis inhaled the smell of the pine tree resin seeping from wounds in the tree bark. With an upright bushy tail, a grey-brown squirrel disappeared behind the tree trunk. The developing misty shroud blurred all distant vistas. A hunting grey heron paced along the stream close by the two men.

"At least we had no rain today," said Thembani. He handed over a can of Coke to share with Curtis.

"It was cold enough. I hate the cold combined with rain. By the way how's the arm?" Curtis swallowed two mouthfuls before returning the can to Thembani.

"It's almost normal except for a bit of pain with certain actions. Dr Gershon said exercise would prevent stiffening from any scar tissue." Thembani flexed his left arm with vigour.

"Those police in the car park were something else," said Curtis.

"It's been ages since they pulled off that stunt at the Club," added Thembani. "There's so much real crime they can attend to in the townships. Instead, they come here to make criminals of those seeking an honest day's labour. The *Dompas* will be their undoing. Humiliation, embarrassment, indignity, shame hardly describe how I feel, except if you roll them all into one. Every time it's like a slap in the face. Worse yet, it's an emasculation. Murderous thoughts come to mind whenever it happens to me.

"On the subject of murderous thoughts, were you going to stab the Whitey? I was ready to hide. All hell would've broken loose there, you know. You looked like you wanted to kill him. All I could see on your face was murder. Ja, sheer bloody murder."

A broad smile crossed Curtis' face. "Stab the White bastard? No. All I wanted to do was throttle the bloody sod. Slowly. Slowly. Like this." His fingers tightened gradually into a two-handed throttling grip while his eyes blinked forcefully. "You spoiled my fun, thanks. I'm not sure where the confrontation would've ended. Anything was possible when he said *Kaffir* and *Hotnot* the way he did." His eyes blinked forcefully.

"Well, I'm glad you didn't.' Thembani shook his head. 'So, is there any news from our men in Athlone?'

"Yes. Pat contacted me yesterday. They want to meet us in the next few weeks. He'll confirm a date when he can. They'll collect us past the Club at the Coca-Cola hoarding where they dropped us off the last time."

"Can we trust them? What do you think Curtis? I've finished reading the banned Che Guevara biography given to me recently by Mr Goldberg. Che warns how freedom fighters can trust no one. Not even their shadows. Stalin said the same thing."

"I'm always cautious, but the two seem genuine enough to me," said Curtis.

"If you're comfortable, so am I," said Thembani. "Che concerns aside, let's meet with them. Keep me informed."

"Yes. I look forward to our session with the two of them. When he called from a public call box we talked about meeting at the hoarding, without using the Club's name. We keep our phone calls brief." Many people in the country were under phone-tapping surveillance.

Curtis felt significantly comfortable whenever he was with Thembani. They hugged each other before he watched Thembani rush off before the rain started to fall. Despite the trust he had in Thembani, the less Thembani knew of him, the better. Che Guevara's words resonated in the Armpit Assassin's head.

CHAPTER 14: FATEFUL LION'S HEAD WALK

October 1985

CURTIS NEEDED A BREAK from the events in the township, so he and Tina were off for a hike up Lion's Head, one of his favourite tramps. Like many locals, Tina had never hiked any of the Mother City's emblematic mountains before.

They took a train from Elsies River to the city, followed by a bus ride from the city centre to the top of Kloof Nek Road. On the way they snuggled together, kissing often. Their shared closeness was a first in his life. Apart from their colours, her eyes continued to amaze him; they were like enthralling pools of merriment. Curtis adored Tina's cheeky take-it or leave-it style. Expressing love was part of her brazenness. Although reserved at first, Curtis soon learned to reciprocate her audacity, while relishing those moments of intense emotion.

They accessed the Lion's Head hiking trail after a brief walk north along Signal Hill Road. They would take about an hour to reach the summit of the 700-metre peak. Lion's Head's attraction was the unparalleled views along the corkscrew pathway, winding its way 540 degrees to the top.

Both wore tracksuits with beanies to protect them against the early morning cold. Curtis had nibbles in his much-used army reject haversack, in sharp contrast to Tina's new multicoloured backpack.

In the beginning the pathway was wide, enabling them to hold hands. They were in no hurry during the relatively easy walk, with a bracing breeze to keep them cool. The snow-covered Helderberg Mountains east of them were barely visible through the light early morning mist waiting to burn off later to reveal Cape Town's more distant, eastern splendour. A few other hikers were already on their way back.

Their sports shoes crunched on the gravel of the well-trodden pathway where thousands would have done the same walk over the centuries. The first circumferential spiral took in the full-length view of the Twelve Apostles leading towards the distant Llandudno beach, followed by Table Bay skirted by the snow tipped Helderberg Mountains 100 kilometers away. To the south Table Mountain came into view with a tablecloth whose cloud tumbled lower in a continuous slow-rolling cascade which never reached the bottom.

"I always love the first circuit," said Curtis. "It has to be one of the most beautiful walks in the country if not in the world. I never tire of it."

"So far, it's stunning. Like so many residents, I have taken Cape Town's mountains for granted."

"Now comes the fun part." Curtis pointed ahead. "We have to pull ourselves along with a few chains on those steep rocks ahead."

"Oh, I don't know if I can do it," Tina's unsmiling face creased, "I'm afraid of heights."

"You'll be alright as long as you don't look down," said Curtis. "I'll follow you to catch you," he laughed.

A wary Tina scaled the steep ledges with half a dozen short chains to assist them. After the last of the chains, she hugged Curtis. "I did it, I did it!" she squealed.

"After a few of these outings you may overcome your fear of heights," he said. He had never seen her eyes sparkle so much.

"We'll see," she said. "but do we have to go down the same way?" She pointed to the chains with her eyes bigger than normal.

"No. We'll take the longer, less steep pathway back," he smiled.

High sandstone rocks now squeezed in on them where they walked in single file with the boulders high enough to obscure the view.

They soon reached the summit with breathtaking all-round views of the Mother City nestled amongst the mountains alongside Table Bay harbour. On a flat rock they stood side by side to take in the panoramic sight. Tina hooked her hand into Curtis' arm. While they shuffled slowly through 360 degrees to take in the view with her head on his shoulder, Curtis felt a rare peace within himself.

Table Mountain crowned the Twelve Apostles at the southern end of the lower range of jagged peaks. The turquoise-rimmed Atlantic Seaboard suburbs of Camps Bay and Clifton through to Sea Point sprawled below them. They could see Lion's Head's rump leading towards Signal Hill. The center of the Mother City's sprawl of buildings was to the east. The Cape Flats with False Bay farther south were in a haze awaiting the later clearing winds. The sound of a speeding motorcycle reached them from somewhere at the bottom.

"It has to be Cape Town at its most spectacular," said Tina. She stretched her arms wide towards the view. "I'm glad you brought me here today."

It took Curtis' breath away to see her silhouetted against the resplendent backdrop of the Twelve Apostles mountain chain behind her. He had never had such intense feelings for a woman before.

They found a flat rock in the sun where they sat with their backs against another rock. Sandwiches, fruit and soft drinks appeared from their backpacks while they tucked into their brunch. The warming day melted the light mist to reveal a flat turquoise-blue Table Bay with a clearly visible Robben Island.

"The Island always makes me think of Nelson Mandela," said Curtis. Mandela had spent 18 of his 27-year detention on the Island before his transfer to Pollsmoor prison. "In August I tried to join the Poolsmoor march for his release, when the police baton charge stopped us. There was a lot of shit in Bishop Lavis, with at least four deaths over two days. Did you manage to march?"

Tina frowned, her face clouded over, her forehead creased, her eyes narrowed. She looked into the distance. "No. I was at work." Her voice was flat, almost troubled. Her body seemed tense. "I don't do any political stuff."

"Stuff?" he questioned, his voice louder, his eyes blinking fiercely. "But it's about Mandela's freedom, eventually about ours. Does our liberation not interest you?" His eyes widened.

"Yes I know, but I'm not into these protest things." Although she faced away from him, he could see the hard angles of her mouth as her head moved from side to side.

"Don't you support the struggle to free the country?" Curtis' tone reflected his incredulousness. His dry mouth tasted bitter. His stomach churned, his head spun. There had been hints of her conservativeness when they had chatted before, but how reactionary was she?

"My father thinks the Pollsmoor march was a waste of time. He says you can't trust the *Kaffirs*. They're not educated, you know."

Curtis gasped. "You used the K-name! Never in my life have I used the word." Tina had turned to face him with her face clouded. "If it's what your father says then what do *you* believe?" His dreams of the perfect woman seemed to have crashed onto the boulders way below them. *'Not educated?' What would she think of Thembani, the brightest person I know?* He felt hollow with his stomach more knotted than before as he awaited her reply.

Tina now turned away from him. "We never discuss politics in our home." She looked sullen with her brows all crinkled in the middle, her eyes lusterless. She folded her arms in front of her.

"How different we are. Hardly a meal went by without my father discussing politics until the police killed him. I haven't forgotten or forgiven them. He taught me that 'Black is beautiful,' long before others used the expression. He was way ahead of his times. My father wanted change. So do I. Don't you?"

"Yes I do, Curtis, but not with so much violence. The terrorists are killing us with their bombs, grenades, guns ..."

Curtis' head spun as he gulped, with his eyes turned towards the distant Helderberg Mountains where nothing registered with him. He flexed his fingers to control himself. "But Tina it's the police who do most of the killing by far. I never use the T-word the way you just did. I prefer freedom fighters, guerrillas, liberators. Do you really believe what you are saying, or are you mouthing your father again?" His tone was harsh. To control the intense blinking of his eyes he shut them tight while he shook his head. He could hardly believe what was transpiring between the two of them.

He opened his eyes. Tina looked uncertain of herself, almost unable to face him as she remained mired in her muteness. Curtis' heart ached to watch her, afraid too of the end of their relationship.

Tina stood with her arms folded tight. She remained upright, projecting a vulnerability that stabbed at his heart. Curtis was perplexed, his mind riddled with torment. *How much more don't I know about Tina?* Despite her disturbing comments, seeing her there with tearful eyes brought him close to tears too. With his secrets, he realised they were dealing with potentially insurmountable obstacles to a continued relationship. There was no way they could continue with such opposing points of view.

"My brain is all muddled with your talk," Tina spoke slowly almost lost in thought. "I suppose I do mouth my father, though I can't blame him." She wiped her tear-filled eyes.

"Why?" asked Curtis. He so much wanted to comfort her, to bridge the chasm between them. *Shit! How did we end up here?*

Tina dabbed at her face with a tissue. Curtis needed an answer. *What is she holding from me?*

"*They* killed my mother when I was six!"

Curtis was taken aback. There was an unexpected bitterness and pain in her voice, while her grim face projected her hatred. "*They?* Who?" he asked.

"Them. Two *Kaffirs* stabbed *my* mother to death in the street early one evening when she came from the shop. They stabbed her seven bloody times after she refused to hand them her purse." Tina was stony-faced, her eyes elsewhere with her fists clenched tight.

Curtis sensed there was more. *What is it?* "But Tina, how do you know they were not Coloured *skollies* (thugs)? Look how dark-skinned I am."

Again, she was silent with her upright posture tense with the recalled moment. Her fingers closed into tight balls. Silent tears flowed. "Oh damn your bloody self-righteousness. Stop protecting *them*! I was *there* with my mother Curtis. Damn you, man! I was right there alongside her all the time. They only spoke in Xhosa, man. That's how I bloody well knew!

"They're damned *Kaffirs*! People without souls or mercy despite a begging woman who held me close to protect me while they stabbed her in the back. One of the stab wounds went through her heart. What would you have done? Embraced them afterwards? Embrace them *now*?" With her head bent low in her hands her shoulders shook with her convulsive gasps as she cried pitiably.

The stridency in her voice grated on Curtis. Her tortured moans shook him to his depths. He had never heard such pain or anger before. *How different, yet similar we are.* He felt ashamed of his earlier response to the words she had used. He struggled to contain his tears. The eye-blinking was excessive. His brain scrambled with the intense emotions they had shared over the past half an hour. Curtis had gone from intense love to the bottom of despair. She brushed away his hands when he tried to hold her.

"Leave me alone. Don't you damned well touch me!"

Her words seared him like a red-hot branding iron. He knew her pain. He shuddered as he blinked hard to erase the image of his father's bloodied body. He tried to imagine how Tina, the non-comprehending six-year-old child, had lived with her nightmarish experience. Curtis' mind was raw with guilt at his earlier reaction.

"Tina, to blame all Blacks is excessive when so much of our township violence is from the way people live in South Africa."

"I don't know how you can talk such bloody nonsense, Curtis. What would you know, huh?" She again pushed away the hand that he tried to place on her arm.

"How would I know Tina? I had to identify my father's body at the police mortuary after the police killed him. I know the pain. I know the rage. I know the hate like you do Tina, except my father's murderer was a bloody White policeman! So, my hatred is of Whites whereas yours is of Blacks." He punched one hand into the other before he lapsed into silence. He turned away from Tina.

They stood with their backs to each other. Tina was sniffling while Curtis inhaled deeply to settle his inner turmoil. *Where do we go to from here?* It took minutes before Tina stopped crying. He realised how he had stirred up their old implacable demons.

Curtis turned to face Tina who again turned away from him with her upright stance stark against the backdrop of a clear Table Mountain. Despite his mental anguish, she looked magnificent where she stood. He sensed the inner melting of his earlier heartlessness. He turned to face Table Bay to the west. *Is there any hope for us?* He dropped his head.

After a couple of minutes of a drawn-out painful silence, he felt her hands on his shoulders from behind him. "I'm sorry." She slid her hands lower to hold him by the waist. Her head rested on his shoulder; his hands held onto her arms. Table Bay had never looked bluer or flatter with no wind to stir it. He felt emotionally suspended in a surreal mix of their shared tragic histories with the surrounding physical beauty. Without a doubt, these had been the most intense visceral moments of his life. He pulled on his shirt collar with his eyes blinking again. *Where do we go from here?*

CHAPTER 15: THE LOWS AND LOWS OF A GENERAL PRACTITIONER

October 1985

STANLEY HARDLY NOTICED the mountains where they stood like props in the distant city haze. Mental heaviness diminished the pleasure he generally derived from the peaks. A month had passed since Fay's release from prison. The gut-wrenching experience was unlike any other he had experienced. Fay returned to work shortly after she returned home. They agreed that she needed to keep herself occupied, but Fay did not want to take any sedatives. Stanley needed no reminder of his near addiction to Valium in 1976.

At the time, Fay had suggested he repeat the words, 'Thou shalt not sneeze!' whenever the stress-related sequence of sneezing followed by hoarseness started. Those four words had helped him. Fay chose, 'Thou shalt not dwell on it!' as her constant reminder to ease her way past her prison experience. She combined meditation with yoga; her time with Stanley was invaluable. They hiked often, with a daily run whenever possible.

It seemed to work, because she had regained her boisterous self. He remained concerned at odd moments when he had found her crying to herself, or she groaned in her sleep. She needed more time to recover from an experience that she would never forget.

He noticed how short her finger nails were. "What's with the nails Fay? They're normally longer."

Fay closed her hands. "It's nothing," she cleared her throat, her guilt screaming loudly with the way she deviated her eyes.

"Come on Fay. Are you biting your nails?"

With eyes downcast, Fay slowly extended her fingers, "Yes," she whispered. "The first time was as a kid, when they forced us to leave our beloved District Six. I stopped after a year only to start again years later when Fah left home to train as a freedom fighter. I was able to stop after a few months, then resumed after he died. I only managed to stop when I met you."

"I've not heard of this secret till now," said Stanley wrapping his arms around her. 'Added to the things you tell yourself, you'll have to say, 'Thou shalt not bite thy nails!' Try it," he encouraged, giving her a firm hug.

Their love had grown over the years. Fay had changed from not believing in love to the woman who introduced him to the concept of soulmate-ship. They were content to be partners, now fashionable with unmarried couples. Parenthood was on their backburners. They did not want children with the worsening sociopolitical climate they had in the country.

Besides Fay's therapeutic presence, Stanley had reduced his working hours as regular locums now covered most weekends. Groote Schuur Hospital had finally opened to Coloured and Indian specialist trainee doctors, a few of whom covered the weekends as well as his working holiday trips with Fay to Australia or New Zealand.

The constant cloud in his life was the threat of political violence in the slums where he practised. Stanley's worst experiences haunted him, though they had become less troublesome with time. He recognised how a post-traumatic stress disorder, like depression, lurked in the recesses of the mind, ready to re-emerge whenever triggered by new events. At least Fay had been spared the worst of the security police trauma during her brief period in detention. People released from detention had bruises, abrasions, burns from electrocution or cigarettes. Bones were broken, minds too; a few came home in coffins.

The last patient of the day was one of the worst of Stanley's career. Under local anesthetic, he had to circumcise a mangled foreskin. Stanley was tremulous while he cleaned the mess.

"What happened?" Stanley asked with reluctance.

Mr Lister, a teacher, remained silent with his eyes closed. He opened his eyes again to stare ahead of him.

"During my eleven days in detention the Security Police kept me awake most of the time. On the eighth day they beat me again for many hours. They shocked me everywhere with their electrodes. The pain of electrocution is ... indescribable. The muscle spasms are 100 times worse than any cramp I ever had. They went on through the night.

"Hammer van Zyl came in with the morning shift. I had heard of him, so his appearance caused a bolt of dread to pass through me. He was in a foul mood, and he stank of alcohol early in the morning." Mr Lister stopped speaking with his head angled sideways.

"Hammer lit one cigarette on another. He promised he'd kill me. 'Do you know why they call me Hammer?' he asked. 'No? Because I like tools.' He seemed obsessed with names, while always wanting me to admit that I was an organiser. I was naked when Hammer said I had to be hooded while suspended by the ankles from the bars over the window." The patient's voice rose. He lifted his head.

"I felt like I was a strung-up beef carcass punched by Sylvester Stallone during his training in the movie, *Rocky*. In my inverted position the head covering disoriented me. I didn't know what to expect. A blow? A kick? An electrode? More water? I felt a rib crack when van Zyl kneed me in the chest. Then they targeted the area with their punches, especially one big Afrikaner fellow.

"Once, when I felt fluid on my head, I realised one of them was pissing on the hood. I never imagined being in a situation where I could drown in someone's urine. I still hear their raucous laughter in my ears.

"When they shock you, the pain is most intense at the two points of contact with the skin. When on the eyelids or in the ears or the nose the shock feels like a hot poker through the brain." He quivered.

"Hammer took off my hood to show me a pair of pliers. 'I want you to watch closely because it's my favourite trick.' I'll never forget how his creepy evil laugh filled me with dread." The patient stopped once more. He squeezed his eyes tight, his head dropped lower.

"He proceeded to pull out lumps of my pubic hair. Besides the bleeding, the pain was agonising, yet there was worse to come." The tears flowed through his closed eyes. "I'm sorry."

"There's no need to apologise," added an appalled Stanley. "I'm nearly done here. What happened to the foreskin?" Stanley did not want to know the details, though he felt compelled to ask. His stomach already churned in anticipation of the details of the mutilation. His mouth was dry. Mr Lister's was one of the worst of all the police torture horrors he had seen. He felt nauseated to the point of vomiting.

The teacher gathered himself, wiping sweat from his face with his sleeve. "Hammer stood to the side to grip my foreskin with the pliers. Of course, the pain was agonising. 'Do you know why these handles are insulated?' Hammer asked me.

"The dread within me multiplied to alarm. The swine constantly swallowed a mouthful of KWV directly from the bottle. He leered when he gripped my foreskin with the pliers, and they applied electricity near my anus and on the pliers. The pain was indescribable. My legs with the whole pelvic area went spastic. My bladder contracted painfully, yet I couldn't pee. With the pliers so tight, my foreskin bulged like a balloon with the pressure of the urine from my spastic bladder. I wanted to push everything out; in the process, I soiled myself.

"I thought my penis or bladder would burst. I thought my belly would burst. I almost blacked out. When he partially released the pressure on the pliers with my penis pointed upwards, urine gushed forth like a fountain. Along with Hammer, his cohorts laughed with tears in their eyes. 'It's my favourite party trick,' said Hammer."

Stanley struggled to contain himself. "Short of death, it's the worst story of prison abuse I've ever heard. That Hammer is a psychopathic beast." The constricting band across Stanley's upper abdomen was tighter than ever before. His normally steady hands trembled throughout the procedure.

"At least the mess has cleaned nicely, though I'll need to see you again after a few days. There is a bit of infection, so be sure to take all the antibiotics. I've included sedatives you can use if you need them."

After Mr Lister, Stanley called through to his receptionist, asking to be left alone for ten minutes. He swivelled his chair around to face the distant Table Mountain. The mountains were clear with the sun about to set, yet he found no comfort in the view. He could not stop his hands from shaking. A hollowness overwhelmed him like never before. His tears started to flow while he sat sobbing with his head on the desk. He did not try to stop what was a first after all his years in practice. Between his experience with Fay earlier, and cases like Mr Lister's, maintaining his equilibrium was difficult. Stanley knew that he could not falter because Fay needed him. He had to soldier on. *Maybe she's right; we should emigrate.*

CHAPTER 16: THE TROJAN HORSE MASSACRE

15 October 1985

EBRAHIM'S IRRITATION increased, as he had no more Wrigley's gum. He fumbled with the key before he leaned against the door to stumble into Pat's room where Pat lay on his bed with a book in one hand, and the customary cigarette in the other. His Coke can ashtray was within arm's reach on his bedside table.

"I passed the corner comrades on my way here," said Ebrahim. "Sometimes they look like Rent-a-Crowd with the same noisy mob there every time on the Thornton Road corner. I'm convinced many must sleep there." He raised his hands. "It's such a waste. Most of them should be at school or university or learning a trade. Think of all these kids on the streets around the country. It's another national crime."

Pat squinted at him through a lungful of exhaled smoke. "Most of them are still annoyed about what happened last month at Alexander Sinton School."

"I'm sorry we missed it," Ebrahim confessed. During a police raid, the parents in the community hijacked trucks, buses, and vans to block off the school and the street after the police had crashed through the flimsy barricades to arrest students; then they had to break their way past the barrier of vehicles to get out.

"I hate telling you, Ebrahim, but there's nothing else to do today, so why don't we join the latest comrades' protests over the enforced closure of our school?"

"Well, I'm not keen to be in a street full of smokers. One of you is all I can handle."

"There you go again! You're such a nag sometimes." Pat laughed.

"Have you phoned Curtis yet?" Ebrahim frowned.

"Yes. My call was brief," said Pat. "I had to reassure Curtis things were on the move. He sounded impatient especially when I said we may only meet in early December, and I would let him know the details closer to the time. He always seems like a man in a hurry."

"True," said Ebrahim, "but I suspect he's a deep thinker *and* planner. You have to admit though, progress with your contacts has been damned slow," Ebrahim complained.

"Too true, but despite the snail pace, we're close. You know I can't rush things," said Pat. "So, let's head off to join the protesters."

Once outside they could hear the chanting of the protesters in the distance. They soon reached the noisy crowd on the corner of Thornton and St Simon's roads.

"It's a louder mob today," said Pat stepping on his cigarette butt. They slowed when they were close to the gathering on the corner.

"They seem to have doubled in number since I passed by here on my way to you. They almost sound festive with all the noise."

Dozens of youngsters stood on the corner. A few smoked with their cigarettes held by their thumbs on the palmed side of the fingers, often with their pinky pointed upward. Ebrahim smiled. The hold symbolised defiance. Even revolutionaries had to look cool. One cigarette often did the round of a cluster of friends. Stamped-on stubs littered the pavement.

An occasional smile or laugh belied their more serious intent. Boys and girls held fist-sized rocks in their hands. They were part of the regular group of demonstrators, many of whom waved their hand-painted banners, spelling mistakes included. The noise increased as protesters banged on cars requiring fist salutes of the passing drivers. Occasional shouts of '*Amandla!*' intermingled with '*Ngawethu!*' in reply from those around them. The two friends joined those on the fringes. Pat wanted to move through the crowd, but Ebrahim held him back.

"No, Pat. Let's stand here." Ebrahim wanted to avoid the smokers.

They stood on the low breeze-block wall in front of the first house in the street. A metre behind them was the front wall of the house with a burglar-barred, lounge window. Four steps led to the porch on their left.

Unsmiling mothers with much-rutted brows rushed by dragging wide-eyed children they had collected from the nearby creche behind them.

Thornton Road was normally abustle with traffic. Today the vehicles inched past the rowdy group on the corner. A distinctive yellow South African Railways flatbed truck with closed wooden crates behind, drove by on the opposite less crowded side of the road with its cabin windows closed. Dressed in khaki work jackets, the White driver with his assistant sat in front. A youth slapped at the passing truck door.

The pungent smell of a burning tyre started to fill the air. Teenagers close by extended their hands towards the heat of the crackling petrol-fueled flames and became more raucous with many of them banging on passing vehicles with their fists.

"Did you see the Railways truck?" Ebrahim asked Pat. "It had two Whiteys in front. Where are the Black labourers?" They normally had to sit at the back.

The truck turned right into a side road to reappear minutes later on their side of the road, heading towards them. Surprisingly, the vehicle had not been stoned on the first trip especially for a government truck with only Whites on board. At the street corner three rocks struck the windscreen. In the middle of the intersection, the driver slammed on the brakes. As the truck jerked to a halt the wooden crates came alive.

Ebrahim dug his fingers into Pat's arm. "Oh my God! What have we here? Get down, Pat." His throat went spastic as the packing case lids flew open. From inside the crates a dozen White policemen jumped up, shooting their shotguns from their shoulders.

Ebrahim and Pat dropped straight to the ground while the police directed their quick pump-action fire at the crowd who were only metres away from them; others directed their shots towards the houses close to the corner.

From where they lay behind the low wall they heard screams of pain, fear, and terror. The shrill shriek of a lone female voice cut through the noise as blast after blast of shotgun fire reverberated in Ebrahim's ears. There was no teargas or rubber bullets this time - this was a surprise attack designed to kill from close quarters.

Not even with previous police confrontations had Ebrahim ever trembled this much before. Glass shards with cement fragments fell from the wall and windows above them. A flattened hot shotgun pellet burned Ebrahim's hand. His breathing raced like his heartbeat. His mouth was dry, and his stomach felt like a knotted mess. He managed to find Pat's hand to hold it against his chest.

Within minutes the shooting stopped. Bloodied casualties groaned where they lay. People appeared dazed from where they had sheltered behind vehicles or other low walls.

"Jesus, those bloody bastards," spat Pat. "They ambushed us. Are you alright?" Ebrahim had landed first, partly under Pat.

Ebrahim gave Pat a thumbs-up signal. "Yes. We can crawl around the corner of the house to check things out from there," he whispered.

Numerous holes pockmarked the cement wall of the house behind the pair. Dozens of flattened shotgun pellets and a layer of cement chips mixed with glass fragments covered the area on each side of the wall where they had been standing.

After they shook off all the cement flakes or glass shards from their clothes, the pair inspected each other. An unscathed Ebrahim found only a few skin nicks on Pat's scalp from the fragmented glass.

"Now that was too close for comfort," Ebrahim's voice was shaky. "Look at all the holes on the front wall of the house."

"Oh shit! I hope the people inside are okay." Shrieking emanated from behind the smashed window, now devoid of glass.

Ebrahim pointed. "The woman's crying is so ... so haunting."

From their semi-concealed position, they could see the mayhem around them. Ebrahim's stomach churned while he surveyed the chaos. Many of the injured lay on the road where they had fallen. A few sat on the pavements on both sides of the road. Friends dragged or carried away the injured. The police arrested many, pushing people towards the middle of the road, where they attached plastic cuffs to their wrists. Police vans emerged from nearby side roads where they had hidden. Police officers with shotguns in hand pushed the detainees into the vans before they drove off at high speed.

There was a bizarre moment when a man stopped his bicycle opposite the truck driver's open window to remonstrate angrily with the driver.

"What do you think he's saying to them?" Pat asked. "He's at point-blank range, yet he seems to be scolding them." The side-drama ended when all the police jumped off the truck to detain the wounded.

It was a surprise that there was only one body on the street. The boy's corpse lay on the pavement. With his dark trousers, casual shoes and a broad white sweatband, he looked asleep. His blood-stained orange shirt told the real story. One of the neighbours chased away a mangy dog wanting to lick at the body. Someone covered the corpse with a yellow sheet. Only the boy's feet remained visible.

Ebrahim wondered whose child lay on the pavement. His insides churned at the sight of the body. *I have to puke.* After he vomited behind a bush he closed his eyes, breathing deep while Pat rubbed his shoulders.

Ambulances arrived to collect the more severely wounded. Weeping parents carried their injured children to the vehicles while others hung around looking for relatives or friends. Holes in the walls and windows of nearby houses bore testimony to the many shots the police had directed towards people's homes.

Shrieking continued to emanate from the house where they had stood on the wall. The front door of the house opened, as relatives carried the blood-spattered body of a boy towards one of the ambulances. The woman's lamentation to the dead made Ebrahim tremble. He had never heard such raw grief. Pat wrapped his arms around his friend, who sobbed briefly in the comfort of his lover's bosom.

"Shit! People aren't safe in their own homes from these murderous bastards." Ebrahim noticed how tight Pat had clenched his fists.

"Murderers! These people are bloody murderers," a white-haired woman in a dark scarf shouted repeatedly. She beat her breasts as she staggered stupefied across the street. A drying track of blood from under her scarf reached towards the side of her chin.

Further along the road, police kicked doors open, searching house-by-house, then dragged plastic-cuffed youth to police vans. Relatives, friends, or strangers added wailing lamentations to the turmoil as the screams of victims mixed with the barking of police dogs. A low-flying military helicopter's whop-whop added to the chaotic din.

"We have just had our urban apocalypse-now moment," said Ebrahim, his fists clenched, his mouth resolute. "They must pay."

"Did you see those people across the road from us?" Pat asked. "They looked like a television crew. They're lucky they weren't shot."

Ebrahim put his arms around Pat. They shed silent tears in their sheltered corner, where they huddled in the deep shade of a couple of tall privet bushes. Ebrahim's body tensed, and his muscles quivered; this experience eclipsed his previous worst moments during their 1976 baptism by gunfire at Alexander Sinton High School.

"Have you noticed Pat, that the police are all White? Don't they trust their Black colleagues to join them in the slaughter?"

"I heard how all the police only spoke in Afrikaans. Those boere are such bloodthirsty bastards," Pat gritted his teeth, his hands remaining in tight balls. "Maybe they wanted to avenge their embarrassment at our school last month?"

Ebrahim needed Pat's embrace. He clung to his lover, who held him tight. "Enough is enough! The sooner we have our plans up and running, the better. We must avenge these outrages. Today I crossed the line, Pat. My reservations about killing have evaporated right here on this corner."

"Yes," said Pat. "I suspected you needed a nudge to cross the line, to really commit to our plans. What we'll do is for our martyrs. Today we have a few more to add to the list."

Later, they heard that the dead boy in the house was fourteen-year-old Shaun Magmoed. The body on the pavement belonged to twenty-one-year-old Jonathan Claasen. The shotgun-pellet-riddled corpse of eleven-year-old Michael Miranda was found at the local police mortuary.

THE TELEVISION CREW was from the American CBS network. Within hours the videotape of the tragedy had been smuggled overseas. Here was a rare example where a foreign television crew had caught on camera some of the township barbarity perpetrated by the police. Dubbed the 'Trojan Horse Massacre,' the fatal ambush was televised around the world, but not in South Africa.

State censorship meant that the leading evening newspaper, the *Cape Argus*, had a downgraded version of the event on the inside pages. There were no photos. Despite global condemnation, the police used the murderous stunt elsewhere in the country. Overnight a spray-painted message, 'Remember the Trojan Horse Massacre!' appeared on a wall close to where the slaying had occurred.

CHAPTER 17: TOYI-TOYI - THE WAR DANCE

December 1985

THEMBANI'S DEEP VOICE echoed around the fifteen meter deep Woodstock Cave on Devil's Peak. He stepped from one foot to another while he addressed his three comrades where they sheltered from a hot summer's day.

"Presently, it's a bit like the *Tale of Two Cities* in South Africa, with the best of times for some, but the worst of times for most. Are we in a season of light or darkness, our spring of hope or a winter of despair? Charles Dickens' words probably cover the situation around the country." He half-turned to look towards the cave mouth before he again faced his co-conspirators. With his wide stance the early morning sunlight behind him cast an imposing shadow inside the low cave. His voice, like his face, projected earnest animation.

"The government bans, imprisons or kills us. White emigration is sky high, while immigration is rock bottom. Their job laws prove obstructive to modernisation because they enshrine job exclusivity. A witches' brew of social conditions cripples the country, so we must strive to move events along at a faster pace."

Thembani held the attention of the group with his oratory style. An occasional punching of the hands or stomping of a foot added emphasis to his words. Thembani could feel the beads of sweat on his forehead.

He turned to face Pat and Ebrahim. "Were you involved in the Trojan Horse episode?"

"I live around the corner from there," said Pat. "We had a close-up view of the shootings, but a low wall saved us. I may sound repetitive, but we need to repay their violence with violence of our own." Pat punched his right hand into his left palm with his neck veins visibly distended. Ebrahim squeezed Pat's arm.

Neither Ebrahim nor Pat went into detail. Silence enveloped the group briefly.

"But enough of these heavy matters," said Thembani. He pinched the tip of his nose. "Do any of you *toyi-toyi*? I am passionate about it," he declared. With arms outstretched, his feet moved to a silent beat. He clapped his hands together to invite the threesome to join him.

"But why do you dance when you protest or demonstrate? Toyi-toyi looks almost weird on TV," Ebrahim commented.

Thembani froze, his mouth partly open. He straightened his short frame. His narrowed eyes glared as he turned to face Ebrahim.

"Toyi-toyi is far more than a dance. It's a statement. Used properly, it's our weapon, *our dance of war.*"

He pursed his lips. "But first, you must believe. *Toyi-toyi* is part of our arsenal. Physically the dance has beauty, with fear generated in its rhythm, in its actions, in its lyrics." He repeatedly punched his right hand on the left.

"Come on you three, have a go. It's a one-two, high stepping motion. Follow me, open your minds. Better yet open your souls to *toyi-toyi.*"

Thembani had them in line alongside each other before he started stepping while gesticulating to his comrades to follow his actions. At times he bent low with his steps barely audible on the dust-covered cave floor. With his knees partly flexed, his belly wobbled in tune with the beat. The untied basketball laces flipped around in a frenzied tempo of their own.

The others followed Thembani.

"I like it." He maintained the steady high foot-stepping action. "Now the arms are important. You can start with them head high, like so."

They followed his lead without any prompting.

"Turn your head a bit from side to side with each step to add to the beat. With your left arm in front of you at shoulder height, keep the arm bent like you are holding a shield. Lift the right-hand higher, while keeping the thumb up, like a closed hand gripping a spear or a *kierrie* (traditional wooden club).

"You must look like you are ready to attack with your weapon. Those who stand close enough to you will see those weapons. They must feel *their* fear and *your* power!"

He maintained a steady cadence with the firm planting of his boots tapping the rhythm on the dusty ground. The other three, less coordinated, soon panted with the unaccustomed effort.

"Follow the tempo. Listen to the beat. Listen!" His feet now stomped a steady firm pattern. The others started to fall off when he increased the pace, as they maintained the beat with a foot shuffle of their own. Now, Thembani's baritone started low with the song from a stooped stance. His rich voice bounced off the hard cave surrounds.

"My mother is a kitchen girl." His deep voice was almost caressing. His body stooped with his arms low, flexed with shoulders elevated, while his palms faced upwards. He stepped on his toes, with the knees not too high; his tread was soft.

"My father is a garden boy." Now the voice was deeper, and louder as he lifted his shield. Soon the spear was aloft, poised to strike. The knees went higher while he planted his feet more firmly on the cave floor where the boots raised more of the fine dust.

"That's why I'm a communist. I'm a communist," his voice was almost gravelly. The boots maintained the forceful beat with their laces flying around in wild dissonance.

"I'm a communist!" Thembani's voice boomed the final line. He jumped high to land on a bent knee with the shield in front of him and the spear raised above his head ready to strike. Sweat stained his tee-shirt.

"*Amandla!*" The call exploded from an intense Thembani who struck with his spear at the invisible enemy.

"*Ngawethu!*" was the instant reply from the other three.

"Yes. Power is ours!" With his arms opened wide, Thembani held his weapons aloft.

Thembani's performance ended with a high-fist Black power salute, smiles and handclaps all round. He used the damp front of his tee shirt to dry the torrent of sweat on his face.

"I felt buggered after five minutes. You went on and on," said Pat. "It's a two-step with a beat." Pat lit a Lexington then inhaled deeply. "Maybe smoking is why I couldn't keep up." He looked at his cigarette, exhaling the smoke through his nose. "I am intrigued, though. How do your untied boots stay on your feet throughout the dance?" They all laughed.

Ebrahim queried, "But what were you singing? I could feel the power. I had goosebumps." His body visibly shook. "I'm embarassed at my earlier ignorance."

"Ahh! You are learning. Much more important is when you believe, then it's your weapon."

Thembani looked at the group, his thoughtful face creased with his hands on his hips. "About the only thing you had right was the high-stepping action. It's another reason why you need to learn Xhosa or Zulu, Curtis excluded, as he knows Xhosa, although his syntax is awful." He smiled when he looked at Curtis, who responded with a thumbs-up.

Thembani scratched the side of his nose before he continued. "The deep soul of *toyi-toyi* is in the lyrics. They can be sad or happy. You never *toyi-toyi* alone. Voices are needed to echo, to reply, to add volume, to support, to improvise more lines. The harmony reflects our unity, our inner strength while the combined voices magnify our power." A regular punch in the hand emphasised his comments.

"The ANC stalwart Vuyisile Mini was the father of many of our liberation songs. Besides others, he composed *Pasopa Verwoerd, Naants'indod'emnyama - Beware Verwoerd, Here comes the black folk.* After trumped-up treason charges in 1964, Mini sang the song with two others on their way to the gallows.

"One of my favourites is by an unknown composer - *Senzeni na? - What have we done*? Each line is repeated four times. I'll translate the words.

Senzenina? What have we done?
Sonosethu, ubumyama? Is our sin the fact that we are black?
Sonosethuyinyaniso? Is our sin the truth?
Sibulawayo We are being killed.
Mayibuye i Africa Come back Africa."

Thembani paused to wipe the sweat from his face again. "A bit of the meaning is lost in translation, yet every line has deep symbolism in Xhosa. The questions are rhetorical.

"In the right circumstances, our dance creates fear. I've heard Black policemen admit how nervous they become when unarmed people *toyi-toy* close to their shields, helmets, batons, or guns. Most of the White policemen don't understand the words, though they also get the message, they feel our rhythm, our harmony, our power; maybe they see the spears too." He opened his eyes wide looking from side to side to imitate their fearful looks.

"Furthermore, we can push away our anxieties when we confront them. Never mind our stones, knives or petrol bombs. We'll *toyi-toyi* them into submission. To me it's a war dance while others say it's a protest dance. I think it's a bit of both. The banned *We shall overcome* is more of a peace song than a war dance. With all respect to the outlawed Joan Baez version, the music lacks oomph!" He again struck his fist into his hand.

"I agree with you," added Curtis. "*Another Brick in the Wall* is my favourite protest song. We must smash the apartheid wall one day." The song was a favourite with protestors especially after the State banned Pink Floyd in 1980.

Ebrahim laughed. "We'll use the broken bricks to stone them into defeat."

"I prefer Bob Marley or Peter Tosh," said Pat. "*Buffalo Soldier* and *Get up, stand up. Stand up for your rights,* are my favourites" He punched the air while singing a few words from each song as the others joined him.

Thembani agreed, "We're the Buffalo soldiers who'll fight for survival. I heard how liberal Whites have taken to *Sugar Man* as an anti-establishment anthem. Mr Goldberg, technically my employer, always talks about his music when I caddy for him. He loves the lyrics - includes drugs, sex and anti-war sentiments. He says the man's music is more popular than Bob Dylan or Elvis Presley amongst White liberals who listen to bootlegged copies."

"There you go again, Professor," laughed Curtis. "I don't know the singer or his music."

"Neither do I," said Pat. "It's not really known in the townships. Who sings it?"

"A Latino-American called Sixto Rodriguez who has been banned by the SABC," said Thembani. "It's all part of our liberation music. Our not knowing of Rodriguez shows how deeply divided we are as a nation."

PAT WAS IMPRESSED WITH Thembani's effort. He was a worthy recruit who provided them with information about his different township experiences. Pat rubbed his hands. They were sweaty, yet they felt cold. He blew on them, hardly feeling the warmth. He bounced from one leg to the other trying to suppress the desire to smoke another cigarette.

Pat wanted to discuss more serious business. "In 1983 Ebrahim and I joined the newly formed UDF. 'UDF Unites. Apartheid Divides' is their answer to the State's divide and rule."

Pat stepped towards the entrance of the cave. "Come over here to my gateway to Africa." The full cave mouth framed one of the best views of the mountain-based city. Virtually at their feet the hazy city extended towards the distant Helderberg Mountains. The rest of Africa lay beyond the mountain range. He looked at his fellow conspirators while Curtis fidgeted. He had noticed how Action Man became restless when stationary.

"Rhodes Memorial is one hour further along the Contour Path to the right of us. Cecil John Rhodes' statue plaque says *Your hinterland is there*. It's actually *our* hinterland, from Cape Town to the Limpopo River. Cape Town can seem isolated, yet Cape Town established a distinct Black identity with the second highest mortality in the country during the events of '76. We need to add more to the current activity."

"Pat, when we last met, you hinted that you had two possible suppliers. Are there any developments there yet?" asked Curtis with an impatient edge to his voice.

"Yes, you'll be pleased to know that I have one source I believe is the most trustworthy." Pat had to light up.

"But who is the guy?"

Pat exhaled a lungful of cigarette smoke through pursed lips. "As you know, Curtis, potential sources can be difficult to verify." He paused awhile, blowing a smoke ring to slowly dissipate in the windless cave.

"Our man runs a major gang in our area. They compete with a break-away group run by his cousin, so things are heated at times between the two. My fellow has an intense dislike of the police, even though a few of them are on his payroll. However, late last year the police killed his parents during the funeral of his fourteen-year-old sister, who had been shot by Riot Squad police during a school protest. All three were in the wrong place at the wrong time. Their deaths were easy to confirm by asking around. There would be few families with a similar triple strike to their credit." Pat again drew long on his cigarette.

"After a few meetings with the man I've learned to trust him. He bristled with hatred when he told me about his family. He says he's not making any money on the deal."

"It sounds believable," said Thembani. "Do you know what the price will be?"

"He needs to check on availability, so he will let me know about pricing when he has an idea of what we want. I've asked him to focus on AK47's and hand grenades."

"How exciting," said Ebrahim. "Pat wouldn't tell me anything until now."

"It's all about a need-to-know Ebrahim. What do you men think?"

"I'd say let's do it," said Curtis.

"Me too," said Thembani.

"I'd have to admit I'm excited. Yes, I'm in," said Ebrahim.

As they high fived each other Pat's mind was elsewhere. *Which option do we go with? Guns or grenades, maybe both?*

Curtis, deep in thought, ambled across the field towards home after bidding farewell to the other three. He did not feel the arousal he normally experienced when the setting sun's colours outlined Table Mountain and Devil's Peak. He was excited that their plans had advanced towards more collective action as he had been stymied by the cautious approach of the police recruits who now probably all carried their guns when they left the Police Academy. However, his joy with the group's progress was tempered by the persistent agony he felt over his acrimonious break up with Tina Stephens. Curtis thought of Tina daily, often wondering what she would be doing. Could they ever be reconciled? He knew that he could not change. *Could Tina? Am I expecting too much of her?*

CHAPTER 18: HAMMER VAN ZYL

January 1986

EVERYONE CALLED HIM by his sobriquet, Hammer. Most did not know his real name. Why his parents named him Adolphus was a mystery, but it resulted in years of primary schoolyard taunts. He preferred to shorten his name to Adolph. By his senior school days Hammer had muscled his way to becoming the chief bully on the school grounds. His high school cohorts did the Nazi goose-step march when they saluted him with 'Sieg Heil, Adolph!'

The other issue tormenting him from his youth was his curly dark hair. At school his peers teased him because they said that he had hair like a *Hotnot* or a *Kaffir*. The taunt drove him to start boxing at the local gym, where he eventually achieved regional middleweight champion status. His best moments, though, were punching those who had dared to torment him over his hair. At school, everyone learned to steer clear of his fighting fists or references to his hair.

By the time he joined the security police ranks he had transformed his days of schooling bitterness into sadistic interrogational malevolence. His warped psychopathy served him well as the local chief of internal security in Cape Town townships where the State turned a blind eye to his excesses. Over the years, political activists feared him.

KWV brandy fueled him throughout the day. There was a time when the ten-year-old brandy was all he drank, but, over the years, the cheaper five-year-old spirit satisfied him. He had forgotten when he switched to the three-year-old brand. A case of the stuff lasted a week; he had stopped using diluting mixers long ago.

Hammer chain-smoked through the hours with a 50-pack of Rothmans comfortably within arm's reach most of the time. Dull nicotine-yellow stained his fingers as well as his full untidy grey moustache and bushy eyebrows. His hair, cropped close to the skin, was too short to take on the hue. He ran an electric razor over his head every second day. Even though his hair was mostly grey- white, he did not need the curls to remind him of his early tormentors.

A lit cigarette was a useful tool of interrogation. The backs of hands or tops of feet were his favourite spots. The face was an excellent place to stub a nearly finished smoke when a detainee would not break. He took wicked delight when he warned them of their fate before he lit a cigarette. 'Talk to me, or your face will be my ashtray when I finish smoking, so you can interrupt me whenever you are ready to talk." He always complemented the statement with a fiendish chuckle; he believed in using all the senses to drive home his message.

Van Zyl shared his experience with his junior colleagues. "Your prisoners must reach a stage where they believe that you have the power of life or death over them, then they're easier to break."

After a couple of puffs on his cigarette he continued. "I don't waste my time trying to conceal what we do. We're never guilty of mistreating our prisoners. Maybe they slip to their deaths on a flight of stairs, or they jump from high buildings or through windows that are several floors high. We can't watch them all the time, you know. Others have ruptured livers or spleens, probably self-inflicted. Regardless of age, strokes or heart attacks are often the given causes of death from our coroners or magistrates.

"The detainees must suspect that I'm the main killer of those who die in detention in Cape Town. There may be a bit of truth in their concerns," he laughed wickedly, somewhat transformed by his rattling cough. He swallowed the expectorated material, then lit another cigarette on the one he had nearly finished, dropping the stub in an overflowing ashtray. "KWV and Rothmans keep me going. Just watch out, though, both can kill you." He slapped his thin thighs followed by heinous cackling.

"I often tell prisoners that I have more than 30 years of practice to kill them by a dozen painful means. You should see their faces when I ask them if they want to leave here in a body bag. 'Can you swim?' I ask them. We can drop them from a helicopter far away over the sea or maybe into an inaccessible mountain ravine. Of course, the helicopter ride is free with no return ticket." He laughed while coughing; he enjoyed holding forth with his transfixed audience.

"From their eyes I can tell when someone breaks. The eyes are indeed the mirror of the deepest mind."

Long ago he had stopped punching prisoners during interrogation. He had had his share of cuts to his fingers on teeth or fractured digits from striking detainees faces. Despite enjoying the crunching sound or the feeling of a collapsing cheekbone or nose, he was not keen on the bloody spatter from those injuries. Kneeing was a better alternative to punching. A suspect, often naked, was instructed to touch his toes. Aiming from the side, a forcefully directed blow with his knee would fracture a lower rib or two. A painful rib fracture could be revisited regularly, especially during several months in detention. He left punching to his more vigorous junior colleagues. Using his knee, his other target was the cheekbone. Done from the side with the detainee bent forward, he cradled the prisoner's head in his hands to provide him with a stationary target. When done properly cheekbone fractures would also affect the nose or the orbit of the eye.

"One of my favourites is the *klapoor*. To do the smack-ear right, keep the palm flat to hit hard enough over the ear to rupture the eardrum." He would hold his hand flat against the ear of one of his trainees. "We prefer to do the right side. You can do the other side too, but then they may have trouble hearing the questions. If you hit them from behind there's a better chance of a stationary target because they won't see the blow coming. The goal is a one-smack technique. Because they don't see it, they'll always be afraid when you are not in their line of sight." His eyes moved fearfully from side to side, mimicking a concerned prisoner. He grinned.

"If struck properly, the smack-ear will make their heads spin, or they may fall over because of vertigo. Later smacks are less painful, though they bring on intense dizziness or nausea; so that's another reason to stand behind them; I hate any vomit on my clothes or shoes. It's why we keep a bucket handy. It's also the reason I never wear suede like your *veldskoene* (lit. field shoes)." He pointed to his junior colleague. "Mine's shiny leather."

"What do you think about pain?" he asked a new conscript one day.

"Pain is pain I suppose." The vagueness in his voice amplified his uncertainty.

"Pain has to be physical *and* mental." Van Zyl's index finger was in the air. "Enough of both will break any man or woman. To extract the truth from the toughest you must add man's greatest invention - electricity. You can crank the amps low or crank them high. We have wires with clips to connect to ears, lips, eyelids, nipples, penis or labia. Without a doubt a suitable metal rod in the arse is the best. We can scramble their insides like an overcooked omelette!" he chuckled.

"They can break a limb or their teeth with muscle spasms. Also watch out if they shit or piss during or after their treatment. Yes, think of our interrogations as treatment against lying." He smiled.

"It always intrigues me how sleep deprivation is so effective. We all need sleep to rest our brains. You know we have over a dozen of us here, so we can go 24 hours a day to keep the buggers awake. If needed, we can go on forever; just remember, though, a lack of sleep can kill. Sleep deprivation does strange things to people. They'll tell you something they won't even remember. With their mental confusion they forget the lies, and the truth emerges.

"We have one rule for our detainees. 'Thou shalt not sleep'. Cold water, smacks or pain are the means to maintain wakefulness along with our rotating teams. It's when you can practice your boxing skills mainly to target any rib fracture. You have to have your body weight behind the punch which they teach you at the police gym."

"What about drugging them?" asked a fresh-faced junior one morning.

"Of course, we can drug them too, though it's not my favourite. You're never sure of the outcome, but it's one way to really scare them. They'll have an out of body experience when they can look upon themselves from above. Lack of sleep is similar, so it's one of the simplest means of mind-warping." He laughed aloud while he sucked a few times on the cigarette.

"Does blindfolding help at all?" another rookie asked.

"Does it ever!" Hammer paused, while lighting another cigarette to blow a couple of smoke rings with his first draw. "I prefer the hood to add to their powerlessness. They never know what's coming. Where's the electrode going to touch them next? Where will they punch me? Will they target the fractured rib again? Maybe the ear? They need to feel totally helpless. By adding enough water to the hood, you'll take them to the point of death by drowning in no time.

"Suffocation with water-soaked hoods till they faint will snap many, as will strangulation while they wear the hood. Tear gas in the wet hood is brilliant, though you must remember to wear a gas mask. Remember, they need to feel our total power over them, the power to determine whether they live or die; a hood will push them towards the moment of truth more quickly.

"Do you know what really breaks many of them?" Hammer looked at the fresh faces who clung onto every utterance. "The most hardened prisoners can hang in there forever. I admire them. I don't respect those who break within a few days. When you think they're almost ready to confess you tell them they're free to go. Once dressed, you even head to the door with them before you tell them you've changed your mind. Watch how their faces crumple afterwards; many will sign anything then, so it's all about timing. It's the perfect weapon to penetrate the stubborn mind. You can even offer to drop them off at home; instead, you drive slowly past their house before you return them to prison. They'll be *klaar*, finished!" He brushed his hands twice past each other with a smug smile.

"The only people those in solitary confinement will see beside us, are their warders. It's interesting to watch the tough ones sink into madness. On discharge, they can go straight from their cells to Valkenberg Mental Hospital before they return to be tried for treason. If they don't leave in a body bag, then they can leave in a straitjacket. Now there you have two ways to neutralise them."

He hated those who died. Besides the extra paperwork there was no heightening of the senses with a prisoner's death. There was not much left in his life to excite him, though breaking a tough nut was the closest he had to an adrenalin rush.

During interrogations, they passed the KWV brandy bottle around. "The threat with a full bottle is we'll stick the bottleneck into the detainee's arse when empty. It's to create dread in them when they see the bottle emptying slowly. They have a choice - with or without the screw cap in place. Of course, we don't use lubricants. It's one of my favourite truth extraction devices. Many will sing long before the bottle's empty."

Hammer's work had increased with the many detentions under the latest State of Emergency. Though his work enthusiasm was colour blind, White communists needed special attention. They had betrayed the side of justice, with their lack of reason or common sense. He reserved his more malign practices for this select group of detainees, apart from a few Coloureds who had dared to refer to his "*croes hare*". Any reference to his kinky hair always enraged him; the term was popular in Cape Town. He eventually elected the shaved bald look to add to his menace.

For many months, Hammer often rubbed a thickened patch of skin close to the knuckles of his left hand. The police doctor told him he probably had an insect bite or skin allergy. The prescribed ointment had not helped. Maybe he needed to try the other police doctor on the panel. He wondered whether these doctors were even worth consulting. Perhaps he needed to try one of the local doctors in the township. Dr Stanley Gershon had been recommended to him.

CHAPTER 19: SEA POINT SWIMMING POOL

February 1986

CURTIS LOOKED AT A photograph of Tina every day when he could relive her facial nuances, her bewitching eyes, or her dimpled gap-toothed smile. When they last parted after their tempestuous mountain hike they had hugged briefly, while agreeing to let things settle. *For how long do I wait?*

When she finally phoned, he was overjoyed to hear her voice as he could not believe four months had passed since they had parted ways. Their suspended romance was intolerable. He felt numb whenever he recalled every word they had spoken on Lion's Head. Despite their brief relationship there was a significant void in his life without Tina.

Tina wanted to meet because she needed to speak to someone. The distress in her voice was evident, though she would not go into any detail.

"It's better if we meet somewhere else. It's awkward here at home." Tina's voice sounded troubled. He wanted to hold her, to hear the lost joy in her voice.

"I've missed you," was the first thing he said to her without thinking. He meant it. "Where will we meet."

"Well, the weather has been perfect so I wondered if we could go to the Sea Point swimming pool." Sea Point was a Whites-only seaside suburb, one of South Africa's wealthiest. The City Council had become a national talking point by opening the pool to all races, contrary to the laws of the country.

"Sounds like an idea to me. I've not swum yet since summer started, and we finally have a chance to swim *there* after all these years."

More critical to Curtis than the novelty of treading the forbidden ground at the pool was the chance of meeting Tina again. He had to know if their relationship had any hope of continuing or not. His hand trembled when they finished their call. A broad smile highlighted his handsome features. *But what's troubling Tina?*

Curtis gasped when he approached Tina at Elsies River station, where they had arranged to meet. She wore the same powder-blue jeans with a white tee-shirt she had on when they first met. The main difference was the sky-blue floppy sunhat that magnified her appeal. He pulled on his shirt collar. His pulse raced more with every step he took towards her. It took extreme self-control not to embrace her. Her dark countenance masked her vivacity. Her eyes were listless, though she offered him a weak smile with a brief peck on his cheek. Thin dark rings under her eyes intimated her distress or a lack of sleep.

With his hands on her waist his whole being ached to see her. "It's wonderful to see you, Tina."

"I'm pleased to see you too," she said. "It's been a while." They sat on one of the platform benches in the shade of the station waiting room behind them.

Her body stiffness distanced her from him. *What's with her?* Curtis was inconsolable at their invisible barrier.

She rummaged in a well-filled hold-all bag to take out her sunglasses. They spoke about nothing in particular until they boarded a nearly empty train coach, sitting opposite each other on the platform-side seats. He wanted to sit beside her so she could snuggle into him the way she had done before, but there was no point in rushing things.

"You must wonder why I needed to see you." The speeding train blurred the passing headstones in the Maitland Cemetery with the in-focus mountains of the city in the distance. "Where should I start? Your comments on Lion's Head stung me. The most beautiful day of my life became one of the worst. I felt like I had stumbled from the rock where we sat to crash to the bottom so far below us."

Curtis wanted to take off her sunglasses, to look into her eyes, though he wanted more. *Is she remorseful? Has her thinking changed?* His pulse quickened.

"Last October's Trojan Horse episode in Athlone impacted on me in the most unimaginable way." She paused with her hands cupped firmly on her knees. "My kid brother, Lance, my favourite, was involved in the action on his way to visit his girlfriend. Two shotgun blasts made a mess of his chest and abdomen followed by nearly two months recovering from his surgery in Groote Schuur Hospital." Her voice cracked.

"In the beginning I thought he was going to die. In ICU he had tubes everywhere to heal his collapsed lungs with holes in all major organs in his belly. Luckily, they all missed his heart. Over two weeks, he needed surgery twice, and remained critical until they moved him to the surgical ward before he finally came home. He had lost so much weight, though it's good to see that he's starting to move around freely. He wants to return to work - he's a carpenter."

Curtis was ready to rip off her sunglasses. He wanted to see her face, to comfort her. He saw how tightly clenched her fists were on her knees. Curtis extended his hands to place them on her hands; she did not withdraw them. Instead, she gripped his right hand forcefully with both her hands. The electrified intensity of her handgrip extended to his whole body.

"Before the surprise police shooting from a truck, Lance had joined the crowd demonstrating on the street corner. It's so like him to be involved in any protest action. He's the politically involved family member who belongs to the United Democratic Front. Lance is proud to be Black, so he and Dad used to go at each other big-time over the issue."

She stopped to rummage in her bag again. She retrieved a tissue then removed her sunglasses to wipe her nose. Her eyes remained dull, almost lifeless. Curtis looked on with an overwhelming sense of helplessness. When Curtis rubbed her knee, she again gripped his hand with hers. He so much wanted to see Tina's eyes sparkle again.

Tina coughed before she continued. "I reflected on your Lion's head comments. Having heard my father's anti-Black comments from the days of my youth, I had clearly taken on his bitterness. Dad went too far when he said that Lance deserved what he got. Dad can be so spiteful, so we had a big fight because he would not visit Lance in hospital. I was at my brother's bedside every day watching him pull away from death's door, the way his doctors put it.

"Lance was barely home convalescing when he and Dad had another big argument. Lance said Dad was a sellout to the Whites. Things became tense especially when I supported Lance." Tina used another tissue to dab away her tears. "For heaven's sake, my beloved brother had not recovered yet from his ordeal."

"At least he survived," said Curtis. His heartstrings were tight.

"I told Dad us Blacks needed to be more supportive of change in the country. I surprised myself because I really meant it. Of course, my old man went ballistic." She compressed her lips with her eyes narrowed. "Now Dad wants us to leave home to live with the *Kaffirs*. For the first time in my life, I felt so disgusted to hear him use the K-word." Her facial lines were tight, and her clenched hands formed tight balls.

"There's too much tension at home. I can't wait to move out. My two brothers, who share my Dad's racist ideas, used to argue a lot over Lance's political views. None of them visited Lance in hospital. I can't forgive any of them; we're supposed to be family, Curtis. That's why I will soon move in with Lance into a house that he is renovating on 20th Avenue. I can't wait because the atmosphere at home is so toxic."

"I'm stunned," said Curtis. "I hope things go well for you two." Curtis' head was reeling. *Maybe there's hope for us in the new family dynamic?*

The train was about to pull into the central Cape Town station. They stood when the train slowed to come to a halt at the end of the line. She turned to Curtis. "Can you hold me please. I need a hug." Her eyes were tearful, her voice soft. Her appealing distressful tone overwhelmed Curtis.

Curtis gave her a firm bear hug. Her sad story of entrenched family racism was music to his ears. He was close to tears especially when her body started to shake with audible sobbing. His head spun with delight when he felt her body mould into his. Every point of their bodily contact registered with him. Her head nestled against his neck where she kissed him. Like their first bus trip, their present train ride was the best he had ever had.

With Tina's head against his shoulder Curtis hardly noticed the long bus ride to Sea Point from the city centre. At the Sea Point Pavillion Swimming Pool, Curtis was disappointed at the way the surrounding apartments obscured most of Lion's Head and Signal Hill behind them, though there was compensation with the view from the seawater pool. From where they stood holding hands in front of the deeper diving part of the pool, the blue water seemed to extend beyond the pool's edges into the turquoise blue water of a becalmed Table Bay extending to the distant Helderberg Mountains.

"I always enjoy the salty smell of the sea." Curtis inhaled a few times.

"There aren't many White faces visible here today," said Tina. She pointed around her. "It's a massive pool."

"I understand it's an Olympic-sized pool," said Curtis. "It's way bigger than the few pools we have in the townships. It's no wonder everyone from the Cape Flats seems to be here today."

They scrambled to claim a vacated bench on the lawn, well away from the main pool. Both of them stripped to their bathers. Tina looked stunning in her Brazilian style, high-cut, leopard print bather, a stark contrast to Curtis' baggy blue costume.

Children of all colours ran, jumped or screamed with joyous abandon close to the pool. Their shrieks, laughter or occasional tears were common to all.

"Here's what life should always look like." Curtis waved his hands at the children.

"I agree. I'm not sure why the Cape Town Council decided to desegregate the pools, but I like it," said Tina with her face shaded by her wide-brimmed hat.

'They took long enough over the decision," said Curtis. 'Minister of Tourism, John Wiley, says the City Council move is a disgrace. The only disgrace is the way they segregate public amenities in the first place." Curtis frowned. "I understand the mayor has had death threats over the decision."

Tina rolled over onto her back. "Public transport is in a bit of a mess too the way they're trying to desegregate the transport in Cape Town. On my occasional bus trips, the bus conductor seems to decide who sits where these days. Of course, the train coaches remain separated because they are under state control, unlike the buses."

"But I reckon it's time to have a lifetime overdue swim. Are you coming?" Curtis held his hand towards Tina.

"No way," said Tina. "I'd sink like a stone! I'm here to enjoy the lovely sunshine, the scenery and to wear my new bather. The pool's all yours with a few hundred others. Besides, someone needs to mind our things while you're swimming."

He bent to kiss Tina. Curtis was thrilled to see the telltale sparkle in her eyes when they shared a lingering kiss with a slight parting of Tina's lips. He squeezed her hand before he headed towards the pool.

The seawater in the pool was cold as Curtis eased himself in to swim in the less crowded area towards the middle of the pool. When he returned to Tina where she lay on a bright red towel, her eyes were on him, her broad smile dazzled him. Her mind-boggling beauty had emerged from the morning clouds.

"So how was the water?" she asked.

"Bracing."

Curtis towelled himself before he joined Tina. He kissed her on each shoulder. She reached to draw his head into the side of her neck. He knew she loved a kiss there, so he obliged her on both sides.

"I'm hungry," said Curtis, who rummaged in his rucksack to extract a packet of Romany creams with two cans of Coke. He handed a can to Tina. "Yours is diet, mine's regular."

"Thanks. You can have the chicken sandwiches I made. I'm having my favourite Romany creams instead." She held the box against her chest with both hands. "If you behave I'll let you have one." she raised a finger.

Her infectious giggle had Curtis tittering too. He had missed her so much. With all his weighty issues, he needed her in his life. Curtis was already more relaxed than he had been during those interminable months without her. He admired the way she supported her brother despite having the family split apart over the issue of being Black. He looked forward to exploring Tina's new-found mindset, but his secret agenda tempered his joy. The compartmentalisation in his life was part of his survival strategy.

Thembani's words rang in his ears. 'Trust no one, not even your shadow.'

CHAPTER 20: THE GUGULETHU SEVEN FUNERAL

15 March 1986

THEMBANI AND CURTIS were on their way to the funeral of a group of seven martyrs in Gugulethu. Since the news of their deaths Thembani had felt numb, as if time had stopped. From his place a few blocks away, they joined the stoney-faced crowd on their way towards the Gugulethu cemetery.

"Most Whites probably believe the news that the seven who died were ANC MK operatives (uMkhonto we Sizwe) on a killing mission," said Curtis.

"Well, everyone in Gugs is talking about it. No one believes the State's claims that the seven men attacked a van full of police officers on their way to early morning duty. We reckon that the police staged their deaths near the junction of NY1 and NY111."

"Ah, near the spot where you were shot."

'Yah,' said Thembani. "On TV at the book store, I saw how they dragged one of the bodies along the ground with a rope around the body. Hey, these shits have no respect. Every corpse they showed either had a gun or a hand grenade on the body. Everything looked so set up. Who dies with a hand holding the weapon across the stomach like that?" Thembani spat out the last question while he slammed his fist into the other hand. "They executed those men, then planted the weapons on their bodies." He clenched his fingers. "Their ages ranged from sixteen to twenty three. I knew three of them who weren't very political. Things didn't stack up."

"Really?" Curtis asked, his eyes blinked slowly.

Thembani's face felt like a stiff mask. He took a deep breath to gather himself. "The two adults who were with them have disappeared. We think they were turncoat *askaris* (ex-guerillas). The late Steve Biko warned that the most dangerous weapon in the hands of the oppressor is the mind of the oppressed, like these two traitors. *They* recruited the seven, trained them, then provided the weapons. Around the country these bloody Judases work against their own people."

"I didn't see the TV news," said Curtis. "But did you see how the *Cape Times* published those eye witness accounts? The article referred to them as guerrillas though it's against the law to do so. The journalist spoke with witnesses including a school bus driver who was across the road from the killings. They saw one of the men being shot in the head at close range."

"The report seemed more like an attack *by* police, not *on* police!" Thembani lifted his hands. "The families found multiple gunshot injuries in their sons' bodies, especially to their heads. Three of them had black gunpowder residue around their shotgun wounds, but the police insist they fired from across the road. One had half of his jawbone blown away; another had the front of his belly ripped apart; a third had the wadding from the shotgun cartridge embedded in his brain. Those things only happen at point-blank range." Thembani's voice rose with each sentence.

"Are you saying these were cold-blooded executions?"

"Correct! Hey, these bloody people must think we're stupid."

Curtis frowned. "The *Cape Times* article did not mention the two *askaris*. But why would they arm what they call terrorists to attack the police?"

"Because they see it as excellent propaganda," responded Thembani. "With all the guerilla attacks around the country, they needed something sensational to show how they are in control of things. That's why they engineered the whole thing. I'll bet most damned Whites believe all the shit in the media. Already two quick inquiries have cleared the police because they killed 'terrorists'. Damn those murderers! Am I ready to kill? You asked me. Huh, huh? I'd kill right now, Curtis!" His voice was strident as he slammed a fist into his hand.

They continued in silence. Thembani's hand waved across neglected gravesites where there were few headstones amongst many wooden crosses tilted in all directions. "One day we'll have a heroes' acre right here in Gug's cemetery to honour the many who have fallen. *Amandla ngawethu!*" Curtis responded with both of them fisting the call.

They hopped across the plastic-bag-strewn trickle of a stream to enter the cemetery from the Klipfontein Road side of the burial ground. More military than civilian vehicles lined the road. Incongruously there was also a tired-looking horse drawing a cart laden with scrap metal to the local dealer. The cart driver looked more ancient than his horse and both seemed oblivious to all the activity around them.

There were hundreds of armed troops in riot gear around the cemetery. Two noisy military helicopters hovered in the distance, occasionally swooping low across the graveyard. The funeral would be Cape Town's largest ever.

"The families are under strict instructions," said Thembani. "Only relatives can attend; no political speeches are allowed; political banners are forbidden; only the priest can address the mourners in the limited time. ANC flags, tee-shirts, and uniforms are banned." Thembani spat on the ground.

"I hope those bloody police behave today," said Curtis. Over the years since 1976, Black cemeteries had become police killing fields during funerals[8].

Along with others, they entered through gaps in the low one-kilometer-long fence along Klipfontein Road. The dune across the street had many well-constructed *pondoks*. A few painted homes intimated at higher income owners. Mostly, unpainted drab buildings surrounded an occasional bright orange-pink or turquoise structure. Between the shacks stood a multitude of somber-looking locals.

Once inside the kilometer-long municipal graveyard, Thembani and Curtis followed the crowd along firmly packed sand tracks leading off from the wider perimeter paths formed by the wheels of hearses over the years. There was no chapel, paving, or tarred road around the cemetery. A few oleander bushes with a low hilltop cluster of Eucalyptus trees were the only adornments. A poorly maintained ablution block offered privacy. When they passed the toilets Thembani's nose wrinkled at the old urine smell. The sparse wild Kikuyu grass was a dry late summer beige as the cemetery had no sprinklers. The place's only glory was the Mother City's distant mountains looking on the cemetery events through the haze of the day's pollution.

The funeral cortége of thousands started to enter the cemetery on foot. Twitchy-looking armed forces rested atop or alongside their military transporters. The helmeted personnel were mostly unshaven. The go-anywhere Casspir troop carriers were always a threat as well as the 'sneeze machines' - the yellow flat-bedded trucks could pump thick clouds of teargas from a huge trumpet-like device.

"Look at the way they gather, like hyenas for a killing," muttered Curtis.

In the distance, they could hear singing with the unmistakable beat of *toyi-toyi*. Thembani's face flushed as a broad smile crossed his handsome face. Already his feet stomped to the distant rhythm while he bounced from one foot to the other.

"You must join us," he called aloud to Curtis who soon responded by high-stepping in Thembani's wake. Around them harmonious thousands sang their defiance along the narrow cemetery tracks. People held their clenched fists high while their *toyi-toyi* steps raised the dust. Their stomped-out combative messages belied the smiles on many faces.

The two comrades joined in the tribute to ANC deputy leader-in-exile, Oliver Thambo.

"Oliver Thambo,

Speak to Botha to free Mandela.

Oliver Thambo,

Speak to Botha to free Mandela to return to us."

The masses made the sound of barking dogs or gunfire. Here were Thambo's Young Lions, who fired their mock AK 47's while barking at the armed forces a few metres away from them.

"Hey, Curtis now you can feel why *toyi-toyi* is our war dance," said Thembani who smiled broadly with his brow beaded with sweat.

In between the songs there were constant chants of "*Amandla!*" with the inevitable "*Ngawethu!*" in reply. "*Mayibuye!*" with an instant "*iAfrika!*" accompanied the fisted power salutes from thousands. The call to Bring Back Africa never sounded more fitting than right there.

Pan African Congress supporters' call, "One Settler, One Bullet", rang out, especially whenever they passed the White troops. No sticks or stones were visible in the crowd; their weapon was their *toyi-toyis*. They made slow, intimidating progress towards the open gravesites.

The troops stood in the shade of their carriers while others sat on top of the vehicles. Thembani looked on with satisfaction at the defiant mourners wearing the banned ANC or UDF tee-shirts with dated photos of Mandela all over the show. Likewise, there were black, green and yellow ANC flags everywhere.

"Hey Curtis. It's like my skin will burst with joy. Victory will be ours one day. I have never felt such pride in my life."

"Me too brother!" Both men beat their chests with a fist.

A cluster of foot-stomping youth waved their banners overhead. Their "Viva UDF!" "Viva Mandela!" or "Viva MK!" sent inexorable messages to inspire the united masses.

Bright yellow tee-shirts declared, 'UDF Unites. Apartheid divides.' A stiff south-easterly wind ballooned a massive banner proclaiming, 'Oh! You who believe! We have ordered you to retaliate against the crime of murder.'

"Do you see the big banner?" Curtis asked Thembani.

"Yes. I told you no one believes their lies. Yoh, man, here's my favourite." The song's popularity was undeniable, serving notice to the former Prime Minister Verwoerd, the architect of apartheid.

"Africa is going to trample on you, Verwoerd.

Verwoerd careful.

You are going to get hurt."

Thembani high-stepped his knees to his chest, the shield and spear in rhythm along with thousands of others. Thembani's rich baritone resonated with the lyrics of resistance. There was a fantastic harmony with so many in song. The densely packed masses, more than 50 abreast, stretched in all directions. Soloists' improvised lines added to the tunes. The brief verses were repeated often, always directed at the armed troops around them. The *toyi-toyi*-driven mass was like a writhing python muscling its way around the cemetery pathways.

"*Toyi-toyis* are steeped in our history, culture, and politics. Can you feel the heritage of resistance in the songs, Curtis?"

"Oh yes!"

To his pleasure Thembani noticed how Curtis was able to maintain the high-stepping action. Thembani saw the troops, but not their weapons. To be amid a singing foot-stomping mass of many thousands empowered him. There was a oneness in their singing, in their dissent, in their hatred, in their fury. Every foot-stomp was one of defiance. From a metre away, they aimed their fist pumps at their armed oppressors. Together he and Curtis mocked, challenged, or taunted the troops they passed. The experience felt liberating.

Another crowd favourite rolled out.

"The *boers* are dogs.

They have killed Steve Biko.

What have we done? What have we done?"

Despite not knowing who started a song, the mass of people went from one crowd favourite to another in close harmony, always with an undercurrent of anger, contempt or opposition to those in uniform.

In an ANC khaki outfit, a solitary adolescent with a black beret carried a meter-long ANC flag. Behind the flag-bearer a distinguished group of clergy lead the way ahead of the coffins, all covered with a white cross attached to an ANC flag. ANC-outfitted pallbearers' power-fisted their way with their free hands. Close to the graves they rested the coffins on boards supported by easels. The *toyi-toying* stopped. Youth of all races stood stiffly in honour around the last resting place of their martyrs. The solemnness of the hymns was in stark contrast to the uplifting *toyi-toyis*.

A loudspeaker system boomed speeches across the multitudes seated on the ground. Religious leaders' addresses were in English or Xhosa, often translated. The Reverend Lesley Mabuza issued forth. "Again, we will bury our martyrs, who fell to enemy bullets. We have waited too long. We are being killed every day by people who call themselves Christian. We shall become the angry Black elephants of South Africa." His emphatic oratory was palpable.

In the mid-afternoon, a cloudy sky obscured the distant mountains in the west. The wind continued to swirl dust around the masses. Military helicopters buzzed past or hung over the area to add more noise and dust to the scene. The empty graves awaited the martyrs' coffins. A wary Thembani shared the nervous expectancy surrounding them. He hoped the guns would remain silent.

They already had seven martyrs too many.

CHAPTER 21: THE GUGULETHU 7 BURIALS

15 March 1986

CURTIS SHOUTED AT THEMBANI. "Are they spying on us from the helicopters, or are they trying to drown out the speeches? I'm surprised they haven't intervened yet because we have broken every condition imposed on the funeral."

"Maybe there's too many of us."

They watched the pallbearers lower the coffins by ropes into the graves. Forceful chants of

"*Amandla!*" followed by "*Ngawethu!*" accompanied the bodies into their final resting places, dug in the firm-packed grey-white Cape Flats sand. Curtis looked at the somber faces of people who bore the brunt of the country's inequities. His clenched hands shook. Despite the inspirational *toyi-toyis*, his inner tension screamed for release.

Across the road the residents stood outside their homes with silent fisted salutes to the martyrs. In contrast the troops maintained an ominous proximity. Snarling German Shepherd police dogs barked while their dog-handlers in customary fashion barely restrained them.

"I reckon they train those creatures to attack only Blacks," said Thembani. "The dogs are going berserk because we're all around them. I hate those beasts. I've had three police dog bites in my time

- one in the arse in '76, another in the hand in '82. Last year was the worst when I thought the beast was going to rip my left arm off." Thembani shivered as he pointed to the scars on his forearm.

"I'm a bit concerned," said Curtis. "There are more troops positioned closer to us. Most of them are on the ground. They look twitchy, like they usually do before they let go."

He had hardly uttered the words when a loudhailer boomed a message instructing the mourners to disperse.

"How many minutes warning has he given?" Curtis asked.

"Not sure," said Thembani. "There's too much noise, especially from the helicopters. There's never enough time anyway. People are already moving away from them. Let's move to the left. It's close to the church where there will be tables of food."

Curtis smiled. He knew Thembani never refused an offer of food.

Thembani added, "Walk fast, don't run; it's less likely they'll shoot you," spoke the voice of a decade of experience.

Both men bent over double as they scurried towards the fence. None of the sneeze machines was in action; people ran in all directions away from the approaching troops. Curtis had never seen so many police dogs before. Their growling sounded like they were Alsatians from hell.

Hundreds of mourners had already cleared the low fence. Thembani led the way to the church while an unconvinced Curtis followed.

"Napoleon Bonaparte said an army marches on its stomach. He's my man." Thembani patted his belly.

Along with the crowd, the pair jostled their way into the church towards the food-laden tables. Despite the chaos outside, those in the church sanctuary tackled the food with enthusiasm. Their delight was short-lived when the rear doors burst open, and a horde of police entered the holy building. Police swirled their batons and *sjamboks* at everyone in their path. They overturned tables, while battering people, many of whom tried to flee through the front entrance where others, oblivious of the police presence, tried to enter.

The priest of the church approached the troops waving his hands in the air. They felled him with a baton blow to the head; blood streamed from his forehead. The mayhem continued until people outside realised that they had to escape from the situation indoors. Hundreds turned to flee from the church.

After elbowing their way through the front doorway to the outside, Curtis and Thembani charged along with the rest. When they stopped briefly, Thembani still had a cheese sandwich in one hand, with a fried chicken leg in the other. They looked to where people had dissipated, while the police hung around outside the cleared church. Curtis again noticed the weary-looking horse pulling the now empty cart. Despite the turmoil around him the driver hardly lifted his head; his day's business was over.

"Damn the bastards!" said Thembani. "Death has no dignity with these bloody police. There's a lesson there. You and Pat said violence must beget violence. *Right now,* I can kill. Believe me brother. Believe it." He threw away the food he had been so keen to eat only minutes before.

'I believe you Thembani," said Curtis, squeezing his forearm.

Thembani dug his hands into his jeans pockets with his shoulders low. Curtis shared his hurt. It's what fueled their desire to bring about change. He felt ready to burst and his adrenalin surged. *Oh, how I need a knifing target right now!* He looked around, but none were visible.

In the distance he heard dogs barking and it gave him the chills. To Curtis, the distinctive whop-whop sound of the helicopter blades was a harbinger of death whenever they passed by. *Would they shoot from above?*

He led the way around the corner when Thembani's scream chilled Curtis to the bone. He swung around to see Thembani struggling on the ground with his lower leg in the jaws of a huge German Shepherd. It's deep-throated growl made Curtis' blood run cold. The canine clung to Thembani's leg like a wild animal with its prey. Thembani's face contorted as his teeth chattered. The dog had separated from its police handler, who was nowhere in sight. To no avail, Thembani kicked at the hound with his free leg.

His terrified screams filled Curtis' head. The opened Three Star was already in hand for a strike. *But where do I stab a dog? The neck?* The powerful brute dragged Thembani along the ground, shaking the big man from side to side like a ragdoll.

"Curtis do something!" Thembani shrieked, then whimpered uncontrollably while he frothed at the mouth.

Curtis' eyes narrowed. *There's only one thing to do.* From behind the growling beast, Curtis leaned forward. In one stroke he plunged the knife blade deep into the dog's belly, instantly following through with a slicing action from left to right. With a loud whine the injured animal let go of Thembani's leg to crawl a few steps while the animal's precious lifeblood poured from the wound. The hound whimpered where it lay on the ground.

Curtis felt nauseated at the sight of the rolls of intestines extruding through the wound onto the sand where the blood already formed a gelled pool. The dog, whimpering with sad questioning eyes, turned its head towards Curtis; mercifully, death soon followed.

Thembani scrambled to his feet. He pointed, "Look at those damned teeth, man. They would've ripped me to shreds." He hobbled over to kick the dog as it urinated and defaecated in its death throes.

"No Thembani!" Curtis called out. "Even animals deserve respect in death. Otherwise, we'll be like those bloodthirsty troops."

A relieved and saddened Curtis cleaned the knife on the animal's hair. At least his fingers were clean.

"Quick! We can duck in here between these shanties." Thembani muttered while he limped ahead with a string of profanities. They hugged the narrow alleyways of the informal housing area, melting into the murky shadows until they reached Thembani's home. Once inside, they lay on Thembani's bed. A quiet peace engulfed them in the gloom of the early evening. Curtis tried to forget the experience, but he could still see the dog's sad eyes looking at him through the semi-darkness in the *pondok*. He shivered with an inner chill.

"You okay?" Thembani placed his hand on Curtis' forearm.

"No! It's the dog. Those sad eyes seemed to ask me, 'Why?' Uh!"

"Sorry? Not me. I hate those monsters. All I could see in his eyes was death - *mine*! Thanks Curtis. You saved me again." Thembani extended a hand to clasp Curtis' hand where they lay.

"You're lucky I don't charge you." Curtis suppressed a laugh. He sat on the bed, swinging his feet over the side onto a few books on the floor.

"The dog died quickly. Did you stab at the heart?"

"No. I didn't aim upwards. I probably hit the aorta."

"Maybe tomorrow's *Cape Herald* headline will be about the Police Dog Assassin."

They could not stop laughing. The days' drama seemed to find an exaggerated relief in their light moment. Curtis felt comfortable despite Thembani's reference to the Assassin. He was learning to trust his *toyi-toying* comrade.

"Maybe the police dog could smell the food on you." Another extended fit of laughter followed. "Now, enough!" said Curtis, mirthful tears filling his eyes. "We need more light."

Thembani soon had the oil lamp going so they could inspect his leg. His blood-stained, shredded jeans leg bore testimony to what could have happened to his flesh. Fortunately, there were only a few superficial tooth imprints in the skin. Curtis cleaned the wounds with a dash of Dettol in cold water. When done he rinsed his knife in the solution.

"Sticky blood on my fingers is not my favourite sensation. I think we should leave the wounds open to dry. By the way, Pat called yesterday. His call was brief, though he said things are on track. He hopes to meet us soon."

"It's been three months since we last met," said Thembani.

"Yes, Pat apologised so he wants to meet early in April. He sounded enthusiastic."

"Can *you* wait till then?"

"I've learnt Thembani. Sometimes, it's all about timing."

"I feel like meat," said Thembani after a while. "There's a guy a few streets away who organises his *braai* (barbeque) regardless of the weather or the occasion. He often says revolutionaries need meat. He knows how to use chilli, man. The smell is a magnet to all."

They joined others huddled around Thembani's barbeque man. The jovial chef grilled his meat to well-done perfection the way most of his clientele preferred. The tantalising smell had Curtis salivating.

"Trust you to want food after the police dog drama," said Curtis.

"See, I told you about Napoleon. These vendors all have their secret marinades, but my man is king."

They chewed away at their entrée, barbecued *boerewors* (a traditional spicy sausage) in a bread roll with fried onions, mustard and tomato sauce. The spicy, traditional farmer's sausage was a universal favourite.

Their mutton chops sizzled on the grill placed across the coal in a split drum with a Castrol Oil sign on the sides. Marinaded meat lay on a board atop another drum. Hygiene seemed rudimentary. At times, the chef waved a strip of cardboard alternately over the coal and over the uncovered meat to shoo away the flies.

Standing around them were a dozen unsmiling people who had all had been at the funeral. The noisy banter of hungry customers was absent, replaced instead by the telling of funeral anecdotes.

"We'll beat them one day," proclaimed one of the youngsters.

A misty-eyed greybeard responded. "Yes we must, though I always pray it'll be during my lifetime."

Another teenager chipped in, "Us Comrades[9] will make sure it's during your lifetime father." He gave a forceful fist pump. "*Amandla!*"

An enthusiastic chorus of "*Ngawethu*" and Black Power fisted salutes followed. Everyone applauded. Unprecedented hope was in the air as Curtis shared in the enthusiasm around him. The greybeard looked on, his optimism probably tempered by the fact that he had similar expectations in 1960 and 1976.

Curtis felt that they could not fail these people. Their four-man cell had to prevail. His fist shot high, way above those of the shorter mourners around him. "

Mayibuye, iAfrika!" All responded with vigour.

CHAPTER 22: CRICKET PRACTICE AND LEMONS

April 1986

EBRAHIM PARKED HIS Cortina off Modderdam Road near Bishop Lavis. The four plotters entered the Parkvale Primary School playgrounds through a gaping hole in the fence, where years ago a police Casspir had broken through to disperse the demonstrating young children. A hobbled horse grazing on the field close by had known better days. The dried grass needed the late autumnal rains to start. In front of the school, a group of children kicked a scuffed tennis ball in the tarred school car park. Two mongrel dogs showed no interest in the horse or the foursome in the distant corner of the playing field.

The four plotters gathered in a silent huddle to pay tribute to the Gugulethu Seven.

"What a funeral," said Curtis eventually. "With so many thousands the *toyi-toyis* had such symbolic power."

"Hey Thembani, you should've seen us man," said Pat proudly. "We managed every *toyi-toyi* and my legs haven't recovered yet. The amazing experience was such a tribute to our fallen fighters."

"I'm pleased to hear you were there," said Thembani, "I was filled with pride like never before. There must have been tens of thousands attending."

"We knew you'd be there somewhere," said Pat. "But, to move on, there are lots of stories about trouble in Crossroads. What's going on there, Thembani?"

"Too true about trouble," said Thembani. "There's a lot of escalating tension between the conservative *Witdoeke*[10] (White Scarves) and the radical Comrades. There may be a bloodbath sometime soon, though I hope I'm wrong."

"It's a major concern, but now we need to focus on our session," said Ebrahim. "At the cave we decided on guns or hand grenades as other explosives were less practical and more difficult to acquire. So today we will practice the hand grenade option. Pat will go into more detail later."

"Excellent," said Curtis, rubbing his hands in anticipation.

The four threw a few cricket balls until they established that Ebrahim was the best of the lot. As he took charge of their ball-throwing, his gum-chewing helped control his inner tension. He popped a bubble he had blown.

"You are the skinniest of us all. How do you throw so well?" asked Curtis, their weakest thrower.

Ebrahim sniggered with raised eyebrows. "My dear muscle-man, throwing distance is all in the hips and legs, not in those broad shoulders of yours. It's a bit complicated; my baseball club coach explained how one needs a late lifting of the hind foot with a sideways hip lunge to power the arms. He said I had natural rhythm. I became the star pitcher of our club for many years. To throw well can be taught, though it's not why we're here. All we want is to develop our throwing muscle memory. If you eventually have only one grenade, your throw must be the best you can deliver."

"I've always been a poor stone thrower," said Curtis. "I thought throwing came from the arms. Thembani, you threw well."

"I must have natural rhythm man," teased Thembani. All four chuckled as Thembani lifted his right foot off the ground with an exaggerated sideways hip movement.

"Hey, you guys, it's time to concentrate. Besides length, one of the big things is accuracy," chided Ebrahim. "It's the main thing you will have to practice in the weeks ahead. Remember, practice makes perfect. Now follow my actions."

They stood alongside Ebrahim before their dummy throws. "Stand somewhat side-on to your target like the bush over there. Hold your hands chest high. Extend the left hand towards the bush then drop the right hand with the ball, behind you so the right arm is in a straight line with the left arm. Like so." They all followed as instructed.

"Ah! The arms are in line with the target," said Curtis followed by the customary closing of his eyes.

"Yes, you must aim before you throw. Think of holding a spear or a javelin with two hands. Hold the stance, now let your left hand almost touch the chest. When you throw with the right hand make sure it's a full swing on the follow-through. Use your natural hand action to release the ball."

"Let's hope I remember it all," said Pat, who puffed on his cigarette throughout the lesson. They had placed him downwind of them. He flipped away the butt.

"I suspect he gave us the basics," added Thembani. "There was nothing about what to do with the wrist, the butt, the hips, the feet or the big toe." Pat and Curtis laughed along with Thembani, who had pointed to all the body parts he mentioned.

"All of you have to be focussed," said Ebrahim sternly. His deflated colleagues lapsed into silence. "You can't go on a mission then ask, 'Now how do I throw the damned grenade?' You make a mistake ... boom! The bloody thing will explode in your face. I suspect the cricket ball is lighter than a hand grenade, but we'll worry about that later. Thembani said today is about getting the basics right. You'll throw better when your technique improves." He paused, thinking.

"'Now I'll be over here. The rest of you step away twenty paces then throw your balls to me. Step five paces away from me each time before your next throw until you reach the maximum length you can manage. I will mark where the ball first lands to measure your distances. Stay at the spot from where you had your longest throw, then we can pace your best distance from there. My windbreaker here will mark the spot to aim at."

With diligent guidance from the fast-chewing Ebrahim, the others plied themselves to the task over the next hour. Ebrahim with a baseball glove on his left hand, flitted from catcher to a position behind the throwers to watch or correct them. They practised throws to achieve the perfect 45-degree trajectory to maximise the length of their efforts. An intense Ebrahim urged them along. Despite the cool late afternoon autumn weather their sweatshirts soon added to the targeted pile of clothing.

When the session finished, they sat on the ground alongside the Cortina, facing the last of the day's sun heading to its resting place behind Table Mountain.

"Well done team, though you need to be better," said Ebrahim. 'We can't have complacent buggers who can't throw during our mission." He popped fresh gum into his mouth after flicking the used bit into the sand in front of them.

"My right arm is painful already,' Pat mumbled with an unlit cigarette in his mouth. "I suppose you'll want us to practice a bit in the days ahead."

"How far can you throw the ball?" Thembani asked Ebrahim.

"I held the regional schoolboy, cricket ball-throwing record of 85 metres. The adult world record is over 100. After all these years my baseball club strike-out record still holds. You threw well, Thembani."

"I've had a bit of practice with years of stone-throwing. I once struck a policeman in the face from 50 metres. It was on the day we all met each other." Thembani sniggered without elaborating. "I liked your coaching because I felt that I improved with each throw. I should've met you years ago!" he grinned.

"My direction was better, though my distance wasn't great," commented Curtis who rolled his shoulder. "Like Pat, I suspect I'll think of you in the few painful days ahead. My muscles are more accustomed to karate training or weightlifting."

"Now we all need to practice." Ebrahim raised his finger when he spoke. "Practice every second day at least. I have a spare baseball glove at home so Curtis and Thembani can keep the glove and the two balls they've used today. Pat and I will do our thing in Athlone. If needed, you can practice on your own. Aim at a target like a stone, a jersey, anything; just make sure to use a different field every time."

"But where are we at with weaponry?" Curtis asked Pat.

"My apologies. It's taken time," said Pat. He lit another cigarette before he continued. "My man has his hands full with his cousin's gang trying to muscle in on his turf. With their low-scale warfare they've shot a couple of guys recently. But my man finally has given me a price. One thousand rands will get us an AK 47 with two clips *plus* four grenades."

"It's a lot of money," Thembani whistled. "I've looked around. Unlike you, Pat, I couldn't find a trustworthy source. Gugulethu and Crossroads operatives are nervous after our seven martyrs' funerals. No one trusts anyone these days."

"The issue is whether we can put together enough money to have the gun or the grenades or the lot." Curtis looked around at his group. "I can chip in a bit from the karate coaching which I do at the

Community centre. My caddying at the King David Country Club will keep me afloat. I can also do an extra day there."

"As an assistant in his business I receive a handout from my dad, so I can manage a donation or two," said Ebrahim. He bit into a fresh gum, savouring the first chews with the more intense mint flavour.

"I teach maths to kids, so I have a bit there," added Pat. "I work weekends at a local petrol station where I can do extra time. Maybe I should stop smoking to help the cause." He laughed as he flicked away another butt.

"The way you smoke we'd have the money within a few weeks." Thembani laughed. He stopped to regain his composure. "I can chip in a bit from the sale of my books. My mother has nagged me to clean my place. I know Curtis will be pleased as he complains there's no place to put his big feet. The local booksellers will repurchase them. As a regular customer I can probably squeeze them for a bit more."

"Well with all those books you could easily bring in a thousand rand or more." Curtis laughed along with the rest. "The only place I can put my feet is on his bed after I've kicked off a few books."

"Brilliant!" said Pat. "Ebrahim and I were scratching our heads about how we would go about things. The AK 47 is much more expensive than the grenades. I suspect a grenade will cost 100 rands each. I think they would have a greater impact on the man in the street, as well as being easier to conceal. Any comments?"

They lifted their hands in agreement.

"Where? When?"

"I suspected you would be the one with those questions, Curtis," said Pat, lighting another Lexington. "Where? There are enough options. I don't favour a church attack. A mall? A sporting match? These *boere* love their sport. Tourists at the airport or on a tour bus?"

"How about a rugby match?" asked Curtis.

"A mall may allow easier escape options afterwards. I prefer it." Ebrahim gripped Curtis by the forearm.

"Black casualties have resulted from other mall attacks," said Thembani. "I would rather target a rugby or cricket match. There'll be separate entrances, separate seating or other separate facilities to target. Finally, apartheid can work in our favour." He looked scornful.

"The rebel rugby New Zealand Cavaliers will be here next month," said Curtis. "I have always been an All Blacks supporter, though the present unofficial team disgusts me by breaking the sporting boycott. When I heard Colin Meads would be their coach, the 'Pinetree' fell with the news. I'd target them!"

"They'd be a perfect target, but we may not have our lemons by then," said Pat.

"Ah *limonkas*!' beamed Thembani. "The revolutionaries' grenade. The Russians introduced those after World War Two. They're the shape and size of a round lemon. The RGD-5 is lethal within three metres. They'll injure 20 metres away, so you need to throw the grenade at least 25 metres from yourself."

"Hey! The stuff you know," Curtis had a broad smile as he punched Thembani on the shoulder. Nervous laughter emanated from the group. "So, what other potential targets are there?"

"It's great the way you want to go to the heart of things, Curtis." Pat rubbed at Hammer's dimpled scar on his cheek. "In the first week of November Kim Hughes will again be here with his bloody rebel Australian cricketers. Their Prime Minister Bob Hawke calls them traitors. Admittedly, the tour is six months away, so we need to put the finances together while my man gets us the merchandise we need. We can look at earlier alternatives when next we meet. By then I'll have a better idea of finances as well as product availability."

"I must agree the test match seems far away though a New Zealand or an Australian match would receive better international news coverage," said Curtis.

Ebrahim agreed. "There are other major rugby fixtures at Newlands in the next few months. Until then we must practice, practice, practice; those were my coach's words to me. When your muscles no longer ache, you know you'll be ready. Like top sportspeople we must peak at the right time. We may only have a solitary throw because I suspect we'll have one lemon each."

Ebrahim felt the sweat beads on his forehead. After all the months of discussion with Pat their plans were close to fruition. He grinned. He could not stop the tremulousness when he spoke. "Remember. This isn't cricket, men. It'll be for real, so you must apply yourselves."

Ebrahim felt a lightness in his chest. They had a mission. All of them were keen. *Explosive lemons sounded perfect.* He smiled, popping a bubble he had blown.

THEMBANI WAS ENCOURAGED by their progress. He pinched his nose tip before he rummaged in his backpack. "Well," said Thembani. "I have the copies of *sikelel iAfrika* - Lord bless Africa. There's nothing revolutionary in the name or the words of the hymn.

"The English translation is alongside. The guy at the bookstore photocopied them. Now, let's sing together."

He held his hands together, waist-high with his eyes closed to sing his favourite hymn. He swayed to the music with his deep voice solemn, the tempo measured.

There was a serenity about their singing. When done, a beaming Thembani high-fived all of them. "Well done comrades. I'm more than pleased."

"I'm a Muslim,' said Ebrahim. "But the hymn is special. Now I can surprise my sis who has nagged me to learn the words. Her Xhosa is much better than mine."

They each pocketed their copies. Thembani's head swirled with the uncertainties of their mission. *What would their target be? Would they succeed? Would they survive?* He would prefer them to be in action sooner rather than later. They had waited long enough.

AFTER SEEING OFF THE pair from Athlone, Thembani and Curtis set off on foot through the nearby bush. They were able to walk side by side on the wide path, with the sun slowly setting ahead of them. Somewhere a car hooted. Muted barking came from invisible dogs. Two disturbed doves flapped their way from one of the wattle bushes they passed. The closer they came to Modderdam Road the louder the traffic noise from the busy highway became.

Thembani had noticed how quiet Curtis had been during their training session. "You okay Curtis? You seem preoccupied." He rubbed the top of his nose.

"I need to ask you something." Curtis nodded towards a Eucalyptus tree where they sat on a couple of thick exposed tree roots. Curtis seemed ill at ease as he continuously moved his limbs.

"What's wrong brother?" Thembani focussed on Curtis as any light-heartedness seemed inappropriate.

"I'm not sure where to start. I'm normally a private person." The eyes flickered a morse code signal of his mental discomfort.

"Yes, I've noticed," Thembani smiled. "Take your time." He patted Curtis on the knee.

Curtis with his brow furrowed, brushed past his face at a fly. His eyes blinked forcefully. "Right. I'll start with a question. Have you ever been in love, Thembani?"

Thembani could not help laughing, "I'd have to admit I haven't. I've been close a couple of times, ..." He shrugged his shoulders with a wry look on his face.

"The nearest for me was with my girlfriend here in Gugs, a few blocks away from you," said Curtis. "She wanted everything - marriage, house, children, a dog, a car - I was not ready for commitment so we broke up after two years." He looked towards the distant mountains. "With Tina Stephens it's different. Here's a photo of her."

Thembani whistled. "Wow! She's beautiful."

"There's more to her. Much more," added Curtis. "I met her on a bus in Elsies River. She's so funny with a great personality, so different from my other girlfriends. I often think about her. She has one hazel eye and one green eye. Look. You can just see the colours on the photo."

Thembani looked closely at the photo. "Hmm, interesting. Deep dimples too. No wonder you're dizzy over her." He chuckled when he returned the photograph to Curtis.

"What work does she do?" asked Thembani.

"Clerical work at Cape Town station."

Curtis shuffled his legs, resting against the tree trunk. He closed his eyes briefly. Thembani could see him struggle with the baring of his soul. "When we met she was politically so reactionary, so we stopped seeing each other a few months ago. I thought of her every day. Now we've reconciled with each other since she became quite pro-Black after her brother's shooting in Athlone's Trojan Horse action. She supported him against their reactionary father who is one of those more-White-than-Black-types. I've not met the man. Tina reckons he would hate me because of my dark skin colour." Curtis rested his head against the tree. 'I love Tina.' His eyes blinked to excess.

Thembani smiled with his mouth pulled to the side. He heard Curtis' drawn-out sigh. "You remind me of Shakespeare, Midsummer Night's Dream, Act 1. 'The course of true love never did run smooth.'"

"Too true Thembani. I'm torn between leaving her or staying. I have my other serious issues in life to sort out. There's no way she can know of these plans. What would you do?"

"I'm probably the wrong person to ask, yet you do have the two options you mentioned - to leave Tina or not. I may be inexperienced in these matters, but I'd say you must go with your heart, Curtis. I know I would if I found the right person."

"Thanks comrade. Maybe your turn will come one day." He tapped Thembani on the thigh. "But it's nearly dark so we better head home."

The friends hurried on towards Modderdam Road, where they parted company. Thembani watched till Curtis turned to wave at him before he disappeared into the bush. The thought of a love-troubled Curtis fascinated him. Thembani had not given females much thought, though he would not have minded having the same problem as Curtis. He smiled at the idea.

CHAPTER 23: HIV AIDS

April 1986

STANLEY REFLECTED ON the six months since Fay's prison ordeal. She had weathered the potential mental trauma related to events like the Trojan Horse Massacre, and the deaths of the Gugulethu Seven, though he had not told her of the circumcision case involving Hammer van Zyl. At least Stanley had no lasting consequences from Mr Lister's case.

Fay's weight was normal now, and the animated smile had returned, but she occasionally still stripped a fingernail.

"I notice you still eat your nails at times," Stanley said to Fay over breakfast.

"I don't eat them. I *bite* them!" Fay's eyes flashed; her voice was harsh. "Most of the time, I don't; it's a damned reflex thing."

"Relax darling. It's merely an observation," said a chastened Stanley. "We know your incarceration experience will take time to settle. At least you manage a sound night's sleep without moaning the way you used to."

Fay finished her coffee in silence. She kissed his fingers when he extended his hand to her. "Thanks. I was unkind."

"Don't worry, I can handle it. Why don't you have your nails done by a professional manicurist?"

"Nail polish? I've never in my life used the stuff."

"Well, think about it," said Stanley. "It may stop you from eating, sorry, biting your nails," he smiled.

Fay looked quizzically at him. "We'll see. I could try clear polish, I suppose. Now, we better go to work. We'll chat again later."

During his drive to work his thoughts were all about Fay. She needed to cross this final hump to achieve a full recovery. Like his own experience, hers would linger there in the deepest corners of the brain where they would lurk forever. He hoped his demons stayed dormant. Sometimes the temptation to take a Valium crossed his mind, but he had promised Fay he would never touch the yellow tablets again.

Stanley did not know the man, though he looked vaguely familiar. He occasionally had White patients attend his practice. He was the first patient of the day. Due to the nature of his practice bookings were impractical, so Stanley kept a few slots clear at the start of the day to attend to those on their way to work.

"I'm Mr van Zyl, Adolphus," the man introduced himself. The penny dropped. Stanley realised the somewhat unkempt wretch who already smelt of cigarette smoke mixed with alcohol, was the infamous Hammer van Zyl. Stanley froze inwardly. He greeted the security policeman with a limp handshake. Medical impartiality was difficult in the presence of a man whose decades-old violent reputation hung over the township. He wanted to ask van Zyl to leave. *But why is he here?*

Over the years Stanley had seen patients with a range of police maltreatments often perpetrated by or under the supervision of van Zyl, like Mr Lister a few months earlier. Van Zyl did not look well. A repulsive fascination drew Stanley on, as if to stroke a Cobra's expanded hood, poised to strike. This snake however, looked vulnerable.

Relating to Hammer was not easy. The barrier was there, so he had to think of the man as 'Mr van Zyl', even 'Adolphus'. To maintain his focus, Stanley had to erase the other monicker from his mind.

"I'm Dr Gershon," Stanley replied with an unaccustomed formality. "What brings you here?" The standard medical decorum lacked Stanley's customary warmth.

"*Ja, nee (yes, no)*, where do I begin," said van Zyl as he rubbed the skin above the knuckles of his left hand. He pulled on his uneven moustache whose irregular ends almost concealed his upper lip. The scraggly growth was sorely in need of the crisp trim sported by many Afrikaners. The man's hands trembled while his bleary red eyes darted around. Already he seemed in need of another smoke or a drink.

"It's my hand Doctor." He stretched his left arm across the desk towards Stanley while he pointed with the other hand. "An area of thickening has increased over the past year. It's painless. Two police doctors have told me it's an insect bite or an allergy. I think they're wrong Doctor Gershon," he said with respect, almost humility.

Stanley noted the servility. Afrikaners knew the pecking order. "What made you come here?" he asked when he inspected the area of concern.

Hammer's face was unsmiling, his dark eyes stared at Stanley. "I have no faith in those free police doctors. There are times when I think they're not worth their licences. I'm lucky if they spend more than a minute or two with me. Before he retired a few years ago, the late CID Detective Adams said you were the best in the area. Those were his words. I'm here to see if it's true." A smile crossed his face while the eyes never wavered from Stanley's face.

Stanley was surprised to hear Hammer was 55 because he looked more like 75. Stanley could see how van Zyl was used to the direct look, though he sensed the man's discomfort. Here was a man more accustomed to asking the questions than answering them. A weak smile flitted across van Zyl's face. He seemed almost cordial. *How will I tell him the diagnosis?*

"What about the other hand?"

"*Ja.* I think it's starting there too, almost in the same place." He placed the two hands on the desk in front of Stanley. "None of the other doctors asked me about the right hand." Van Zyl looked pleased. His mouth pulled to one side with a grimace.

Stanley adjusted the desk light onto the backs of van Zyl's hands. With a magnifying glass he had a closer look at the suspect areas. The left had a coalescent nodular thickening with a faint maroon-violet tinge. The discolouration was barely visible in the tiny patch on the right side.

"None of the other doctors ever shone a light on the area," muttered van Zyl. "Never mind a magnifying glass. You are thorough. I'm the same at work too."

Stanley paused momentarily. "I'm not sure about the comparison," said Stanley, who sat back, looking at Hammer. "But I have a few more questions, Mr van Zyl." Stanley paused while he lightly drummed his fingers on his desk. There was an instant change in his patient, who now focussed more intensely on Stanley.

"Why? What's wrong?" Hammer asked, with a perceptible edge to his voice, now almost demanding.

"Just relax Mr van Zyl. I'm nearly there. I'll be quick. Any fever? What about loss of weight? Coughing? Diarrhoea? Any other skin lesions?"

"Sometimes I seem to have low-grade fevers. I've never really checked, but I have noticed a bit of sweating at night. There's not much of me, but I have lost five kilograms since Christmas. I cough all the time. I know, I smoke a lot, yet lately it's become a bit worse than last year with thicker phlegm than before. Also, no to the last two questions." A brief lull followed. "Any answers? Solutions? You look like you already know what's going on." Van Zyl wiped away the beads of sweat on his balding, shaved head with his folded handkerchief.

Stanley's pause was deliberate. He was impressed at how van Zyl remembered all the questions. His mind was still sharp. Stanley now had to formulate an appropriate response to not impact on Hammer's future victims. "The skin patches are what we call Kaposi's sarcoma," said Stanley. "It's a rare tumour of the skin."

"Tumour? You mean like a cancer?" van Zyl's voice was strident. Stanley nodded. Hammer half-stood before he flopped into his chair. "Is this a good one or a bad one?"

Already the look on van Zyl's face seemed to suggest that all was over. Stanley looked at a nearly broken man faced with the prospect of his mortality. *How many lives has van Zyl destroyed in his time?* Van Zyl looked like a gelatinous blob in his chair. Stanley took no pleasure at the sight of a crumbling man.

"It may or may not be, though there's a second part of the problem to sort out. A dermatologist will need to confirm the diagnosis with a skin biopsy. More importantly, we'll have to do a blood test on you."

"What blood test? I don't like needles." He seemed to recoil from the prospect of a blood test. Sweat beads soon dotted his expanded forehead.

The irony of Hammer with a needle phobia did not escape Stanley. An almost resigned van Zyl was quieter than before. He seemed to struggle with his toothlessness, of a life beyond his control.

"There's a new disease found in Africa and the USA. It's called AIDS." When Stanley spoke, Hammer's eyes seemed less steady than they were at the start of the consultation. Van Zyl looked through the window behind Stanley.

"What's the link between the skin thing with this ... this AIDS thing?"

"Its full name is the Acquired Immune Deficiency Syndrome due to a viral infection. You will be more prone to infections or tumours like the skin sarcoma of yours. They found AIDS in gays in the USA."

"But I'm not a *moffie*," said van Zyl aloud. "I hate faggots. Women yes. I have known more than a few over the years."

"Well, you can get the infection from women too."

"Bloody hell! I don't like the sound of what you are saying Doctor Gershon." Hammer sounded agitated. "Are you sure of the diagnosis?" The tone was stern, he now not only demanded, but he also challenged.

Stanley knew the first reaction to unwelcome health news was often anger. He did not expect guilt would be one of Hammer's responses. "No other condition looks like Kaposi's sarcoma." Stanley spoke firmly, staring at the patient whose body stooped.

"Is there a cure for the tumour? What about the viral infection? Can I take an antibiotic or something else?"

He spoke like a man who was always in charge. Now Stanley had his turn.

"The biopsy is a formality. Presently, neither AIDS nor Kaposi's is curable. You would have one to three years to live, maybe more maybe less. The tumour will spread, while you'll be prone to infections of the chest or gut."

"Oh fuck me!' Hammer exclaimed. The initially polite man shed his veneers, while he bristled with his eyes narrowed. Fisted hands seemed to want something to punch.

"I first heard about the disease from reports in the USA around 1980. Three years ago, they found the virus. The ELISA blood test will confirm the diagnosis."

"Is AIDS common?" Hammer scowled.

"South Africa has recorded 20 cases in the past four years, mostly in White gay men, or intravenous drug users."

"But dammit, Dr Gershon, I'm none of those! I don't understand."

Stanley did not mention contact with blood. If Hammer believed he caught the disease during a violent interrogation, who knows if more lives would be lost in retribution before he died. Stanley slipped on gloves to take blood from an arm vein. Hammer kept his eyes closed tight with a grimace on his sweaty face. "I'll send the blood off to the lab. The results may take a few days. Take this referral letter to a dermatologist. I wish you well, Mr van Zyl."

Hammer mumbled his thanks before heading to the door where he stopped. "Maybe I should never have come here, maybe it was better not to know." He turned to leave the room.

Stanley's washing of his hands took longer than normal. He needed to cleanse himself of his contact with Hammer, to rid himself of the creepy-crawly sensation he experienced. After Hammer left, Stanley sipped on the warm tea Desray had brought him. She had worked with Stanley since day one in the practice, but this was the first time she faced him with her hands on her hips.

"You do know your patient is the infamous Hammer van Zyl?"

Stanley had never seen Desray's face project such lined intensity before. "Why, yes. He's just another patient." He raised his eyebrows, looking at her over his steaming cup. He blew on the tea before taking another sip. "What's your interest in him?"

"In 1976 the swine tortured my niece. The lovely intelligent girl has never been the same since. Only the Lord knows how many people he has killed. He should rot in hell." Desray's face contorted.

"I'm sorry to hear about your niece, Desray. I would hope van Zyl doesn't return."

While Stanley awaited the next patient, he thought of Hammer's diagnosis. Hammer was the first case of AIDS in his practice. He had followed the developments on what was a disease with a significant potential to spread throughout South Africa. He had seen cases of non-virulent Kaposi's sarcoma in his early days at a Zululand mission hospital. With AIDS, the indolent skin tumour became a killer disease. Blood spatter from one of his victims was the probable source of his disease. Tuberculosis was common in the impoverished masses. Hammer may well have contracted both diseases from his prisoners. Stanley saw a poetic justice in both afflictions.

CHAPTER 24 - KOMMETJIE TIME OUT

April 1986

STANLEY NEEDED A BREAK. He had to rid himself of the image of van Zyl. His regular weekend locum covered the practice, allowing him to go snorkelling, his ideal balm. He and Fay had not dived since her detention, so they hoped to bag a catch or two. Moderate south-easterly winds had blown all week to provide perfect visibility at *Kommetjie*. The five-kilometre-long stretch of an inhospitable rocky coastline had crayfish and *perlemoen* (abalone) in abundance. When fish were around, spearfishing took precedence. Their wetsuits allowed them to last a couple of hours in the Antarctic-chilled waters.

Stanley was pleased Fay had suggested they go alone without their regular friends who dived more often. A ten-foot-long Jurgens caravan was their most expensive dive accessory, their ultimate sanctuary. The sound of the ocean with the breeze wafting the sea smell through the caravan park provided the solace they needed. With binoculars in hand, an early morning session of bird-watching preceded breakfast.

Their prize-sighting was a *bokmakierie* with the bush shrike singing its namesake song from the top of a high bush close to the caravan. The song matched the bird's exquisite colours with a yellow belly separated from the chin by a black band across the neck. The colours were in sharp contrast to the grey feathers on the bird's back. A host of other feathered chirpers or warblers added to their pleasure, especially the iridescent, multihued collared sunbirds.

An accomplished swimmer, Fay had started snorkelling with Stanley a few years ago. Part of Stanley's joy was to have her there to share his favourite pastime. After an hour in the water, they rested their arms side by side on the car tube attached to their catch-bag with a bright pink marker buoy. Both pushed their dive masks onto their foreheads. The kelp-covered area they were in gave way to a flat blue sea stretching towards the western horizon. Ahead of them a bush-covered low mountain provided a pleasant backdrop with the *Kommetjie* lighthouse poking a cream head above the rocky beach north of them.

"What a brilliant day," said Fay. Her radiance spoke volumes of her wellbeing. "On days like today, I can see why your diving means so much to you. I'm glad you talked me into snorkelling."

"I'm pleased you enjoy it. We need these band-aids." A smiling Fay's soft laughter was music to his ears. Here was the Fay he loved - joyful, teasing, enticing, challenging, all rolled into one. He leaned over to hug her, but their masks interfered with the kiss he tried to give her. Unrestrained laughter erupted from them before they decided they had enough seafood. They slowly finned their way to shore while partly resting on each side of the tube.

They sat outside the caravan on their deck chairs in the pleasant warmth of a cloudless day. Their haul of crayfish and *perlemoen* was in a basin in the shade of the caravan's awning. They had not come across any fish. From where they faced the ocean, the blue of the sky sank into the darker blue of an almost silent flat sea, fringed by the olive-green-brown band of kelp, in turn, edged by the darker strip of rocks with a narrow ribbon of white sand. The sound of waves rolling into the shore sometimes reached them. No wonder Stanley felt a rare tranquility.

"It was truly a day when we could see forever in the crystal-clear water," Fay confessed. "It's better than our last trip when we had zero visibility."

Stanley watched Fay's sparkling smile while she recalled her moments in the water.

"It's been eight months since your detention,' said Stanley. "You seem to have settled. What do you think?"

She sipped at her diet Coke with a straw as she looked at him with a broad smile. "I suppose I have." She looked towards the sea. "Yes. Gone, but not forgotten." Her eyes remained fixed on the horizon. "Days like today help; your support has been invaluable."

"Do you still tell yourself, thou shalt not dwell on it?"

"These days? Not much."

"I suppose it's a bit of mind over matter really."

"A bit? You mean a whole lot," Fay grunted. "But look at my clear-polished nails." She lifted her hands with a twinkle in her eyes. "See, not one eaten yet! Talking about eating, I'm hungry. What's for lunch?"

"We'll feast like royalty on steamed crayfish followed by my soft-fried *perlemoen* served with our favourite Nederburg rosé. I'm drooling already."

"Me too," laughed Fay. "I love the way the colour of the wine matches the cooked crayfish."

She winked at him with a knowing smile, boding well for later. Fay was back; Stanley's ghosts seemed appeased.

CHAPTER 25: CROSSROADS ON FIRE

17 May 1986

CURTIS DUG HIS HANDS deep into the pockets of his padded anorak. The limited news from Crossroads was not encouraging. On his way to Thembani in Gugulethu, Curtis saw tell-tale smoke columns in the distance. He arrived as Thembani padlocked the door of his home.

"You look upset. Crossroads?" Curtis asked.

"Yah. There's a strong rumour the Witdoek forces are planning a major onslaught on the Comrades today. I'm going over there. Are you coming?"

"Of course. I've heard the stories, but I decided to check with you first."

The police had sealed off the major roads to Crossroads with massive concrete blocks, so they entered Crossroads via one of many bush shortcuts off Klipfontein Road. Smoke columns were evidence of significant conflict ahead of them. The gunshots became louder the closer they advanced. People screaming with dogs barking spoke of a tough day for the community.

"I've never seen or heard the likes before," said Thembani. "It's chaotic."

Curtis surveyed the confronting scenes ahead. His skin tingled and his body muscles tightened. He felt nauseated at the mini-civil war taking place around them. Thick spirals of grey-black smoke added to the drama of the struggle raging around them. Any gains made towards Black unity over the years were under serious threat in the bushes, dunes and *pondoks* of Crossroads.

"Bloody hell, look!" Curtis pointed to the right. "The police are using their troop carriers to transport the *Witdoeke*. Those bastards."

"It's like a bus service for *Witdoeke*," said Thembani. "We have to be extra-careful here with those bloody turncoats operating under cover of police gunfire. Oh no, look, there's a soldier torching the houses with a flame thrower over there."

"You're right. Shit man, they're something else. Let's go to the top of the next dune. Its height will give us a better overall view of the action. I don't know about you, but my heart is racing madly."

"Same with me." Hard lines etched Thembani's face. "Those laughing troops over there are not even trying to control the fighting." They could see how the forces shot only at the Comrades, not at the *Witdoeke*.

"With all these fires they look set to destroy Crossroads today," said Curtis. "Fuck! I would love to have a go at one of those police or their lackeys." Curtis snapped his knife open with an agitated slickness propelled by an adrenalin surge.

The pair slogged their way through the loose dune sand between people's ramshackled houses. Many fled seeking safety or tried to collect a few of their prized possessions from their burning homes. Children clung to their parents. The children's crying cut through the other noise and Curtis' brain. Bewildered dogs with tails lowered, barked or sniffed around the flaming homes. Their eyes projected a pitiable emptiness, like their owners' faces.

Curtis swore. "There goes another Casspir loaded with *Witdoeke*, but they keep saying it's Black-on-Black violence with no troops involved."

"So many of those traitors are armed," Thembani spat.

"The bloody police must also be providing them with guns."

Long tongues of fire blown sideways by the wind, jumped from one makeshift home to the next. Twisting whorls of smoke stretched skywards, while the malodorous stench of burning flesh hung in the air. Flaming lean-tos became pyres as bodies helped to fuel the fiery inferno.

Guns fired sporadically. Mixed in with the smell of burning was a hint of teargas. Dark figures flitted through the smoky haze as they strolled or hastened along, alone or in packs. The combatants carried an assortment of weapons - lengths of metal, Xhosa fighting sticks, assegais, knives, axes, tomahawks, and pistols with an occasional Kalashnikov.

In amongst the fiery mayhem were menacing figures in a deadly game of hide-and-seek. A group of armed Comrades on the hunt for Witdoeke, charged past chanting, "Viva, viva. Ay, ay, ay!" A few wore clothing stained with the blood of earlier battles. Non-combatants headed into the surrounding bush to distance themselves from the marauding *Witdoeke*. Amidst the havoc, Curtis saw the incongruous sight of a couple who struggled with a double-bed mattress on their way through the thick loose sand.

Curtis' head snapped back. "Hey! What are those *Witdoeke* up to?" He pointed to where an unarmed man was trying to protect himself from the blows of an attacker's fighting stick. Several metres away another two men were more interested in a woman. Their intentions were clear as they had already stripped the struggling woman of half of her clothing.

In an instant Curtis flipped his opened knife into a thrusting hold. He struggled through the last few metres of thick sand towards the top. Thembani followed a few paces behind him.

"We must stop them!" shouted Curtis. The loose sand sucked at his feet. The attacked man on his knees, tried to cover his head from the dangerous stick blows. A direct blow to the skull could kill him.

Curtis shouted aloud. The assailant turned to face Curtis, who flicked his knife from a stabbing to a thrusting hold. They warily circled each other. He would need all his fighting skills to defeat the stick-fighter. Curtis, on his toes with his knees flexed, took in the flat-footed stance of his adversary who looked smugly at him.

Curtis watched the offensive stick above the man's right shoulder. In his left hand, his adversary held onto his thinner defensive stick in the middle. A thick shirt folded over the knuckles of his left hand, protected his fingers in a stick fight. They circled each other in different directions as both sought an opening for their weapons.

Curtis feinted with a forward knife thrust before he ducked under the horizontal forehand blow from the hardwood stick. He jumped sideways to avoid the next obliquely angled downward strike followed by a backhander past his jaw. The thick sand made evasive action more difficult. All his senses were ultra-alert in search of a successful hit. His narrowed eyes sought the tell-tale signs of an imminent strike. The opponent's feet or legs often signalled the next blow. Curtis stepped aside before he feinted with another knife strike.

He turned to avoid an upward backhand swing. On the next overhead swing Curtis was a bit heavy-footed, resulting in the hardwood stick crashing onto his partly extended left arm. The blocked blow deflected the stick to his left as a numbing pain shot through his arm. A fast backhand swing missed Curtis, who struck at the exposed right armpit.

The Armpit Assassin was true to his name. The assailant's club dropped to the ground with the limp right arm dangling at the side of his body. Blood quickly soaked into the man's clothing. His opponent's eyes widened as his face contorted when he looked at his paralysed limb swaying by his side. The man's face was ashen, his lips trembled as he glared at Curtis, who now saw fear in the man's eyes. *Where's your smug smile now, mister?*

The defensive stick blocked Curtis's next lunge to the left armpit. Curtis ducked low when his antagonist lashed at him. The *Witdoek* swung his weapon in a hit-and-miss fashion with all the strokes directed at Curtis' head. He easily avoided the blows aimed at him from all angles, though he had to watch the sharp-pointed stabbing end of the defensive stick.

He deflected another blow with an angled left arm. The thinner stick caught the same area already injured and he gasped with the pain. The man jabbed at Curtis' face with the pointed end of the weapon. Curtis ducked under the blow, angling his body sideways before burying his knife into the right groin of his assailant. The man screamed. Curtis' slicing action finished off his strike to the leg. The fighter dropped to his knees. Curtis knew he would not have to stab the left armpit.

There was no time to celebrate, as the assailant's two companions had heard his screams. They let go of the woman to struggle uphill through the sand towards Curtis, whose left arm was painfully numb. He readied himself for battle by flicking his Three Star from thrusting to stabbing mode. The slower of the pair had his fighting sticks ready. The younger man with a long kitchen knife in hand led the way towards Curtis, who stood poised, ready to strike despite the injured arm throbbing like hell.

Thembani jumped in front of Curtis with the fallen Witdoek's sticks in his hands including the folded-over shirt to protect his defensive left hand. A surprised Curtis recognised Thembani's stance as one of experience. Thembani swung the hardwood club head menacingly high.

The first Witdoek reached them with his knife in a stabbing hold. Dried blood on the blade was a sign of earlier conflict. Within seconds Thembani poleaxed him with a blow to the head. The hard edge of the fighting stick crushed the skull bone with a sickening crack on contact.

Thembani, with sticks ready, hopped over his felled opponent The older man was slow to arrive. His offensive stick had a bloodied metal nut screwed onto the expanded end. Like the other two attackers he had his white scarf tied around his upper left arm.

The two circled each other. The *Witdoek* swung and missed with a horizontal blow to the head. Thembani evaded the stick, though his backhand swing caught the fighter on the right shoulder with a glancing shot. The man showed no sign that he had been hurt. They regularly reversed their circling of each other. Their sticks swished through the air with the defensive sticks clacking hard on contact to block or deflect the offensive club strokes.

Thembani was more measured as he seemed to bide his time. His sweating opponent swung excessively; his blows easily blocked. In amongst a flurry of strikes his adversary stabbed at Thembani, the sharp end of the defensive stick piercing the sweatshirt at Thembani's side, scraping his skin.

As the man withdrew his weapon, Thembani feinted at the face with the sharp end of his defensive implement, followed by a quick underarm swing of his club between his aggressor's legs. The man groaned, before he slumped onto the sand even as Thembani's next blow smashed into the left side of the Witdoek's skull. Skin and bone split open, no match against the hardwood club's edge. Blood-stained brain tissue oozed around the depressed, palm-sized bone fragment. The right side of his body twitched before he lay still on the ground alongside his companions.

Lines of sweat streaked Thembani's face who turned away from his bloody work to vomit beside a wattle bush. Curtis realised his bookish friend had just killed someone for the first time. He went over to place a reassuring hand on Thembani's arm. They needed no words.

Thembani nodded. "Thanks," he whispered before he dried his mouth on his sleeve.

'The thanks are all mine." Curtis hugged him. "Just try to relax. Take a few deep breaths."

The attacked man helped his wife to dress. When done, the distressed couple came over to them. They shook hands while they thanked their rescuers.

The wife, Nkosinati was beside herself. Taut lines furrowed the bloodied face of her husband, Dumisa. His gory wounds bore testimony to his narrow escape as he rubbed his wife's hands. She managed to suppress her tears, while tense furrows marred her beautiful face. Once Nkosinati had settled she inspected her husband's injuries.

"But Dumisa, there's so much blood on you." While inspecting each wound, she bloodied her hands in the process. "Ay! It's a mess." Her face became more distorted every time she prodded at a wound as she shook her head.

'Don't worry my precious, I'll live. We'll rebuild from the ashes we leave behind us today." Dumisa spoke forcefully. "It'll not be the first time. Our new baby will have a new home." A year ago, the couple had lost their first daughter, Salizwa, from gastro-enteritis just a few days after she had learned to walk.

"I think we should stay together," Thembani suggested. "My parent's house is about an hour away in Gugs. It'll be better than here." He raised his hands towards the battle zone around them. Looking west from their vantage point, the Mother City's landmark mountains remained obscured by the smoky conflagration from what had been home to tens of thousands of people.

The couple consulted briefly. "We thank you Thembani. I can't think of where to go with everything happening around us. Our house is gone." Dumisa waved a hand at the smouldering remnants. "Only the toilet is left. All we have is the clothing we're wearing.

Because of you two at least we're alive. Our unborn baby is due around Christmas. *Enkosi kakhulu* (Many thanks)."

Curtis led the way with the opened Three Star against his wrist, ready for action if needed. Thembani held onto his newly acquired sticks, whereas Dumisa carried the stick with the blood-stained nut. Eventually they passed the Gugulethu cemetery on the left with the overcrowded Kakaza Trading Company (KTC) informal housing compound on the right. People crisscrossed the road with alarm imprinted on their faces. Many looked wide-eyed towards the fires where their homes had been while clinging to crying children or a few treasured possessions.

Past the Gugulethu cemetery they headed along a relatively quiet NY6 towards Thembani's parents' place. Sensation returned to Curtis' arm. The limb had not fractured, though the painful bruising was substantial. He placed his Three Star in his pocket as they walked in solemn silence while the sound of the conflict behind them reduced yet followed them every step of the way.

The events of the past few hours swirled in Curtis' head. The children had impacted the adrenaline-charged Curtis the most. Besides their crying he could not handle the non-comprehending look on their woeful faces. He grimaced, his jaw clenched tight. *We must make their lives better.* Curtis stopped to wipe the tears from his face.

Thembani placed an arm around Curtis' shoulder. "Stop brother, or we'll both be crying." Thembani dropped his head. In a low voice he continued, "I can hardly believe I killed someone today." He whispered, closed his eyes, and sighed. "You said 'To kill, I must hate enough.' *Now* I understand.

"I had my qualms about our group's action plan. The horrors of the day, the *Witdoeke,* those laughing policemen in the background, their taxi service, the destruction of homes, the wanton deaths ... have all removed my doubts."

"After today Thembani, I'm through with killing Blacks," said Curtis through compressed lips. "Black corpses mean bugger all to them. We need to send a starker message to the government."

"Let the day come, the sooner the better." Thembani hit his sticks against each other, the solitary clack on contact sounded ominous.

They hugged briefly. Curtis could feel the intense energy radiating from Thembani. Curtis' doubts about Thembani's resolve dissipated in their clumsy embrace at the roadside.

"*Amandla, ngawethu!*" Both called in unison before they continued on their way.

"You showed fancy stick-fighting skills," said Curtis." I thought only the more seasoned homelands' men excelled."

"My father was the village champion in the Transkei. He taught me from an early age because he did not want me to become a complete townie. In Gugs, we practised regularly until my mid-teens. After his shooting in '76, he could no longer fight, so he continued to coach me. In our Sunday community competitive stick fights, I did well. The scar on my forehead is from one of those competitions, one of the few I lost. You score with body strikes. They could be painful, man. Broken arm bones were frequent. Head strikes were forbidden; mine was an accident. Killing was not allowed.

"My father taught me the underhand swing. It's not so easy to perform or to defend against. It's important to generate enough force into the reduced arc of the swing. You start with a defensive stick jab at the face with most of the bodyweight on the front left foot. What you saw was my best shot ever. It's all about timing based on long hours of practice."

"I thought of Muhammad Ali versus George Forman in Zaire. Were you trying to tire your opponent?"

"Yes. My father taught me every blow must count so I always try to find an opening. Wild swingers like him give one more opportunity."

"I had heard about stick-fighting, yet I never saw one till today."

'It's an ancient form of martial arts in most of Africa. I've heard Nelson Mandela excelled at stick-fighting as a youth. Like Muhammad Ali, I can dance like a butterfly or sting like a bee. So, watch out." He swung his stick horizontally above Curtis's head. "It's an excellent fighting stick, heavy in the head, with perfect balance."

Curtis laughed. "Yes. I noticed what happens to any skull in the way." Curtis inspected the flat cut, stick head expanded to twice the diameter of the handle. The iron wood's attacking end had a bevelled edge of about 40 degrees to the handle. A band of carved-out, fine diamond shapes formed a handgrip around the stick.

"I prefer this style of *kierrie* to the more common *knobkierie* which looks almost clumsy against this beaut. By the way, Curtis, your Three Star knows how to stop a man. The armpit technique is impressive. So was the strike to the leg."

"Like you said, Thembani, hours of practice *and* timing."

Thembani's brow furrowed. "How's your arm?"

"It seems okay. I needed an angled arm block to deflect the strike. A direct blow at right angles with his hardwood stick would've broken a bone or two." Curtis flexed the arm. "It's painfully bruised, so I was thankful when you stepped in."

Curtis turned to the trailing couple. "Are you two alright?" They waved at him. How he would hate to be in their position. How fearful were they about their future? Yet they looked so serene, holding hands like lovers on a stroll in the park.

"She's pretty," said Thembani who had been staring at Nkosinati. "It's a pity she's married," his face looked wistful.

Curtis smiled as they continued. The distant gunshots, shouting, with the inevitable screams and the barking of dogs receded in the distance. Curtis did not want to look at the columns of smoke. They had survived one of the worst days of fighting Cape Town had ever seen. Curtis hoped there would be no more. Despite the turmoil Curtis felt an inner warmth, reflected in Thembani's face. The horror they experienced had forged a stronger commitment to their planned mission.

CHAPTER 26: CROSSROADS SACLA CLINIC TRAUMA

21st May 1986

FAY ENGAGED HIGH-RANGE four-wheel drive to negotiate a sandy track into Crossroads. Red Cross stickers were prominent on the Pathfinder windows. The main roads to Crossroads remained sealed. She chose an alternative sandy track through the bush to the SACLA clinic.

Stanley had half-flattened the tyres to prevent the wheels from digging into the powdery sand, dry from the lack of autumnal rain. She knew their day would be neither regular nor routine. People told them not to go to Crossroads, but their services were needed more than ever during the current crisis. Even the restricted media headlined the fiery events. Though horrified at the reports, Fay insisted on accompanying Stanley.

With all senses on high alert, she clung to the steering wheel with clammy hands. They were on their way into the Mother City's Armageddon. Fires close by or in the distance fed palls of smoke columns all around them. At least a dozen flimsy homes were aflame on each side of the sandy track.

Parents dragged children and a few possessions along with them. A few lost dogs with their tails down, sniffed around in search of missing owners. Armed and unarmed figures ran shelter-skelter either in search of targets or a way out.

While they drove near a blazing *pondok,* a woman waved frantically at them to stop.

"Please!" The woman's facial lines distorted her attractive features. She slapped at her face where the fine sand stuck to her tear-stained cheeks. She waved at what had been her home, now a wild inferno of flames feeding a skyward column of grey-black smoke. Stanley and Fay exited their vehicle. The fire's heat forced them to stop as the frenzied woman fell to her knees on the sand where she beat the ground with her hands. *What does she want?*

"Please, please!" she screamed as tears coursed watery tracks on her sanded cheeks while her open hands shook at the couple. Fay felt helpless. The woman, pointing at the flaming shack, grabbed at Stanley's trouser leg. "Please! My baby!" She shrieked loudly.

Her screeching sliced through Fay's brain like a hot knife. "Oh no, there's a baby in there!" screamed Fay. "I can hear crying. Listen!" With one hand over her mouth, she gripped Stanley's arm. His frozen face was amplified by the way he shrugged his arms, lifting his hands towards Fay. There was nothing they could do.

The crying soon stopped. All Fay now heard was the sound of the all-consuming flames with the mother's woeful lamentations. Fay had never felt so empty, so useless, so numbed. Her face was awash with tears. She felt Stanley's touch on her arm. It hurt her to see how his slumped shoulders displayed his impotence, the tight fists his anger.

"We must leave," he whispered. "There's nothing we can do. *Absolutely nothing!*" Fay saw how firmly he clenched his jaw as they shared in their vortex of pain, grief, horror, anger.

The mother would not go with them. In the rear-view mirror Fay saw how she rocked on her haunches. Her hands intermittently clutched her breasts where she would no longer feed her baby or shush the infant to sleep. The gut-wrenching image disappeared when they crossed the crest of a low dune. Fay stopped the vehicle with the engine still running.

"Without a doubt that was the worst experience of my life." Fay's hands shook. She covered her face with her hands. Tears seeped through her closed fingers. Stanley reached over from the passenger seat. He said nothing as Fay's right hand clutched at his forearm where she dug her fingers into him. With his free hand, he rubbed her neck, then tilted her head to plant an extended tender kiss on her forehead.

"It was bloody awful!" said Stanley with his voice breaking.

They clung to each other as they shared their distress.

"We must go. Do you want me to drive?"

"No. We're almost there.' Fay sniffed as she put the Pathfinder into gear to edge forward. People ran around with frequent wide-eyed glances in all directions. They crisscrossed each other in what seemed a purposeless lack of direction. The drive to the nearby clinic seemed interminable. They finally pulled into the nearly empty car park behind the white building.

The SACLA clinic staff were surprised to see the couple. "You two were brave to come today,' said the nurse manager Thulani. "Some staff haven't been able to come to work. I slept here for three nights with a few others. The *Witdoeke* accuse us of collaborating with the Comrades. Two staff cars with Red Cross stickers have been attacked, so the staff all feel threatened.

"Now there's lots to do. All trauma I'm afraid. In the past few days, we've handled over 300 patients, most of them shot by police or *Witdoeke*. It's been all hands to the pumps so far. We've had a few deaths. At times it's been a blood bath, especially the patient who died earlier today from his gunshot wound to the groin. We have no blood left. All we have is saline or dextrose infusions. We are living through a nightmare with our eyes wide open."

Stanley kissed a still visibly shaken Fay on the cheek. "It may be a long night." She squeezed his forearm until he left her. Despite the commendable work they did at the clinic, Fay felt more like they were the ambulances at the bottom of a steep cliff.

STANLEY'S PAST EMERGENCY Department experience meant Thulani assigned him to handle the worst of the trauma cases. There was one other doctor to deal with the stream of wounded at the other end of the clinic. Stanley knew Robbie the medical student who was in the emergency section with Stanley. Robbie had also spent three nights at the clinic. "It's been like a slaughterhouse at times," said the student.

There was a steady stream of broken limbs, wounds in need of sutures or those who struggled to breathe after their teargas exposure. Two children had minor bullet wounds.

"It's genocide," said Stanley during a lull in the flow of wounded patients.

"How do you manage?" Robbie asked. "You've been around a while."

"You've probably been taught that you must detach yourself emotionally from your work. Like soldiers at war, doctors can develop post-traumatic stress disorder." Stanley did not elaborate on his past horrors. How did one prepare Robbie to face the extreme challenges of South African medicine? Stanley heard the baby crying; saw the 1976 schoolgirl who died from her shotgun injuries to the skull; recalled a blur of other images, the snapshot recalls of his worst cases. He closed his eyes as he shook his head to clear from his mind those moments of collective past clinical horrors.

"Doctors have awful track records regarding drug addiction, alcoholism, divorce, or suicide. We're only starting to understand non-military, post-traumatic stress. It's why you need physical or intellectual outlets. I run, I dive, or I hike regularly. Reading, music, or engaging friendships are other escapist essentials. I play hard, and I work hard to survive our potentially crippling pressures."

The relative calm did not last long. A woman with multiple stab wounds arrived moribund, gasping for breath. A trachea pushed to the right was a sure sign she had a life-threatening build-up of pressure in her chest from a punctured left lung. There was no time to X-ray a nearly dead patient. While Robbie attached the nasal prongs to administer oxygen, Stanley slipped on surgical gloves before sticking a broad-gauge intravenous cannula between the upper ribs of the left chest without preparatory sterilising. The pressurised air gushed from the thin cannula allowing a steady breathing rhythm to recommence. Stanley soon inserted a formal chest drain under local anesthesia while Robbie sutured her other stab wounds.

"There's no time to lose with a severe tension pneumothorax. Be confident about the diagnosis. You must act instantly without X-rays. If you wait too long, the patient will be dead," said Stanley, finishing off the last stitch.

"Oh, oh! Here's major trouble." Stanley rushed to the trolley they had brought in. A comatose patient had a bleeding right-sided head wound. His left limbs twitched; his breathing was intermittent.

"He's not moving the left side," observed Robbie. "It must be a depressed skull fracture impacting on his brain."

"There'll be more," said Stanley. "Depressed fractures on the side of the head are often accompanied by an extradural haematoma. The middle meningeal artery bleeding causes a fast build-up of pressure on the brain. His respiration is already erratic so he could die at any minute. He has to go to hospital right away."

"The ambulance hasn't returned all day. The patient can't leave tonight," said Thulani who was setting up an intravenous infusion of saline.

"Thulani, let me have one of those surgical packs of ours. We can drain the blood clot under local anaesthesia like I did in my Mission Hospital days. Robbie will assist me. Have a shot of intravenous sedation handy when we need it. We could be done in an hour."

After a quick scrub Stanley and Robbie were soon gowned.

"The wound is probably from a traditional fighting stick," said Stanley. He injected local anaesthetic in an inverted u-shape around the wound before cutting into the anaesthetised area. After folding over the skin flap, he was able to ease out the bone fragments before clearing away a massive blood clot to depressurise the underlying brain.

"At least the meninges are intact. I have an aversion to removing pieces of brain with blood clot."

The patient started to move. "Okay! It's time to move into action with the intravenous Valium, Thulani." Stanley tied off the transected artery to control further bleeding. With much relief he inserted the last suture into the scalp as the patient started to mutter.

"You know they'll be alright when they start to move or talk. Thanks for assisting me, you two."

"Well done, Stanley! I've never seen one of those before," said Thulani. "Hey, we're the SACLA neurosurgery unit of Crossroads." She high-fived Stanley and Robbie.

They started laughing. Amidst moments of high medical drama, Thulani often provided much-needed cheer.

The rest of the night was busy though less dramatic. The injured dragged themselves in all night. Trolleys, waiting room benches, even floors along the walls became overflow beds to accommodate the more severely wounded in their blood-soaked dressings.

When Stanley and Fay started on their way home, the smell in the morning air was a mix of smouldering dwellings with charred flesh. Smoke columns still rose all around them. A few pink-tinted clouds heralded the imminent sunrise. They were usually home well before midnight. There were far fewer people around. Smoking troops awaited another day of passive viewing from the tops of their military vehicles.

"I would like to think we would never have another night like we've just had," said Fay who was driving again. Her voice sounded empty.

Stanley stroked her hand before he leaned over to kiss her cheek. "Some of our worst moments in life are those of fear, horror or death. We experienced all of them last night. We'll relive the episode with the baby. When needed we'll talk about the event. You've seen me go through the same process in the past." He squeezed her forearm.

"It reminded me of my 1976 experience when police killed the eleven-year-old schoolgirl," said Stanley. "The image of her shot-up head regularly reminds me of the worst experience of my professional life. You've now had yours."

Fay dropped her arm from the gear lever to squeeze his leg. "I hope things will not worsen."

He noticed how corded Fay's neck muscles were. With a sharp pang in his chest, he looked at Fay's hard-lined face; her emotional tank looked empty. He needed to watch her tell-tale nails in the days ahead.

THE VIOLENCE IN CROSSROADS lasted a week. Police arrested dozens of Comrades. Hordes of people fled into the surrounding bush or to adjacent townships. The injured who could access the SACLA clinic overwhelmed the facility. More than 30,000 homeless people required emergency aid, tents, or food from religious and non-religious aid groups like the Red Cross. Over 30 people died. Both sides licked their wounds in Crossroads while people in the neighbouring KTC shanty complex expected the worst. There was concern that the township conflagrations were not yet over in Cape Town.

CHAPTER 27: KTC - SHATTERED DREAMS

9 June 1986

DUMISA LEFT HIS PREGNANT wife Nkosinati, at Thembani's parents' house. He had decided to throw in his lot with the Kakaza Trading Company (KTC) residents, most of whom were displaced from elsewhere, especially from Crossroads. The overcrowded precinct was home to thousands in the wasteland of nearly two square kilometers. KTC was another thorn of resistance in the Government's attempts to remove people without a *Dompas*.

People slept in primitive housing made from Port Jackson wattle branches covered with tarpaulin or plastic sheets in the shape of a teepee. How different was Dumisa and Nkosinati's destroyed home in Crossroads. Their *pondok* had been their castle atop a low dune alongside many others where they avoided the winter flooding although a few raindrops always defied the odds to seep through. He remembered how he always had to haggle with the merchant to halve his asking price for every metal sheet used to build their home.

He thought of the first time he and Nkosinati made love in the bed they had bought from the roadside furniture dealer. The night was one of their best in their new home, and he was convinced Nkosinati had fallen pregnant that evening. They had purchased other household goods after weeks of saving. A lay-by payment followed by weekly payments often secured a much-needed item.

A heartbroken Dumisa had watched their treasured home become a fiery inferno within minutes. He could still see the hungry flames stretch like octopus tentacles in search of sustenance. He had never felt emptier in his life since the loss of their first daughter on New Year's day. Salizwa had started to walk before Christmas.

In KTC, informal housing had become another site of protest where the police destroyed people's housing structures on a regular basis. The squatters played a dangerous game of cat-and-mouse as they defiantly rebuilt within metres of where the original tarpaulin-covered shelters had stood. Dumisa joined in the cycle of rebuilding after destruction. Desperate people took on the monolithic powers of the State's enforcement agencies in a relentless battle by burying their dismantled wattle branch structures before sunrise; within hours after the police raids, the squatters reassembled them.

Like in Crossroads, the KTC *pondok* dwellers cocked a snook at the State's faltering razor wire system of influx control by refusing to move to the distant Khayelitsha township. Supportive community groups worked hard to provide rebuilding material, food, clothing, or blankets. Taps were scarce, while bucket sewage or pit latrine systems were rudimentary. The smell of outdoor ablutions hovered in the air much of the time. After a few days, Dumisa no longer noticed the smell.

Troops conducted dawn raids with snarling police dogs, arms, teargas and monstrous all-terrain vehicles whose deep-throated diesel engines heralded their arrival before sunrise. The informal iron houses rattled when the Casspirs passed by their homes. To Dumisa, these were mechanical monsters from hell driven by the servants of the Devil.

Thembani's parents had insisted on Nkosinati staying with them until things were quieter. 'She'll be safer here, especially with the antenatal clinic so close to our house.' Dumisa was not keen to leave

Nkosinati, though he felt compelled to join his people in their struggle. He had patted her stomach before he left. "I miss our daughter. I think the present one will be a boy. His name will be Thembani. What do you think?"

"I'd prefer Curtis-Thembani," said Nkosinati. "Those two men saved us."

"I like the name too." He managed a brief smile while he kept his fearful thoughts to himself before he left.

Adding to the police-inflicted trauma the KTC residents faced was the escalating tension between the Comrades and *Witdoeke*. The *Witdoeke* had warned the Comrades to leave or the *Witdoeke* would flatten KTC. The tension between the two groups continued to escalate despite the KTC Residents' Committee getting a court interdict to prevent an attack on their area. Dumisa hardly understood the struggle between competing committees who controlled ground rentals or allocations in the congested complex.

Adding to the tension were the ANC's MK (uMkhonto we Sizwe) operatives who had found shelter in KTC where even the armed forces were reluctant to penetrate the labyrinth of narrow alleyways in search of the armed MK fighters. KTC had become the city's prime flashpoint as it awaited another eruption of violence.

Dumisa had to come to terms with the anarchy in KTC, referred to by MK Comrades as their 'Beirut', likening their situation to the two-month-long 1982 Israeli siege of Lebanon's capital. He knew of infiltrated MK fighters who had trained at PLO (Palestine Liberation Organisation) military camps.

Dumisa managed to squeeze in with three others in a tiny *pondok*. With no furniture in the room, they could all sleep alongside each other on the cardboard-covered sand floor. They relied on food handouts from community organisations. Huddled together to share their donated blankets, they often listened to the gunshots outside between opposing groups of Comrades and

Witdoeke. Unseen figures urgently called to each other as they ran by their shack in the dark. Dumisa's stick, with the offensive head nut, lay beside him at night. The stick was the only possession he had with him besides a change of clothing.

Thoughts of the baby due in a few months' time kept Dumisa going. Despite his misery, he still hoped to find a place to build another home. He preferred the vacated dune in Crossroads, where razor wire now surrounded their hill with spotlights on at night to keep people away. He hoped they could rebuild there one day to again look over the surrounding rooftops towards Cape Town's distant mountains. These were the dreams to keep hope alive when his spirits flagged, when all ahead seemed stark.

Before sunrise on the 9th of June, Dumisa awoke to the din of more shooting than the regular early morning raids. He ground his teeth with his stomach all spastic. The sun was not yet up. The roar of the diesel engines sounded more numerous than before. Already there were flames in the air. The combined smell of teargas and smoke permeated the area. In the narrow alleys he saw a concerted drive of troops, police and *Witdoeke* approaching, as heavy AK 47 gunfire from balaclava-covered MK Comrades forced the hasty withdrawal of the attackers.

Residents started to flee with their meagre possessions. They knew worse would follow. The few with cars or trucks left, their vehicles laden with people or possessions. People scattered in all directions from the *Witdoeke* who attacked or robbed them. The troops turned a blind eye to the violence occurring within metres of them.

The regrouped *Witdoeke* were eventually able to advance when the police sneeze trucks generated voluminous clouds of choking tear gas with the wind behind the aggressors. There was more covering gunfire than Dumisa had ever heard before. Bullets whizzed through the air around him, often ricocheting off the corrugated iron buildings. Along with others, he fled from the blinding choking gas from the large megaphone-shaped horns atop the sneeze trucks. The *Witdoeke* overran the place while looting and torching hundreds of tightly packed shacks; soon a wind-driven firestorm spread through the flimsy homes.

Close to a few burning *pondoks* lay an injured Dumisa. He did not know if a policeman or one of the *Witdoeke* had shot him. A bullet had passed clean through his chest from side to side. His unused fighting stick lay in the sand beside him. The body of a teenaged girl lay spreadeagled, face sideways, in the pathway close to him. A gaping entry hole was visible in her forehead with an exit wound at the back. Where she lay lifeless on the sand, her bent arms seemed to cradle to her head her lethal pillow of clotted blood.

Dumisa had fallen alongside a shanty with the impact of the bullet. He caught his breath with the relentless pain in his chest. He coughed as he spat another mouthful of salty, bitter blood. Searing pain accompanied the coughing. *It does not feel right. I need more air!* He lay on his side, gasping. Out-of-focus figures ran past him where he lay curled in a ball in a vain attempt to ease the discomfort he felt. *Maybe I should sit up?*

Dumisa smiled through his agony when he saw his daughter, Salizwa, wave to him. He opened his arms. Her face beamed while she stumbled into his open arms, having just learned to walk. With Salizwa's head nestled in his chest he kissed her. She clung to him, giggling the way she always did. Close by he saw a smiling Nkosinati wave, yet she did not approach them. He felt the increasing warmth of the shanty fire's flames coming towards him. He could not move so he curled tighter to protect Salizwa who chuckled where she lay snuggled safely in his arms. Dumisa closed his eyes. Curtis-Thembani would never know his father.

THE WITDOEK'S FIRES destroyed KTC over the next few days. Over 30 people died, and more than 30,000 were homeless, identical to Crossroads. The Witdoeke destroyed the SACLA Clinic in Crossroads as well as the supportive Zwolani Centre of KTC, where two thousand people had sheltered in Red Cross tents. Most of the residents from the two informal settlements fled to the despised Khayelitsha township. The Government had overcome the residents' resistance to an enforced move. Following the worst episode of violence in the Mother City's more recent history, the locals coined the name, 'The Township Fires of 1986' to describe the devastation in Crossroads and KTC.

CHAPTER 28: SECRET AGENDAS

June 1986

TINA LAY IN CURTIS' arms after their first moment of lovemaking in her new home since she had moved in with Lance in April. The long months since they were last together magnified in a passionate explosion, just like the first time they met. Waves of rapture radiated throughout her body. Under the pink satin bedspread, their fevered intensity was like a bonding of their bodies *and* spirits. After months of family squabbles, she needed her moment of unbridled release with her lover.

She was pleased Lance had met Curtis as the two men agreed on most political issues. Tina had had to rethink many of the ideas adopted from her father over the years. The K- and T-words had disappeared from her vocabulary. She felt at ease calling herself Black, not Coloured.

Her years of conservatism challenged her on many fronts while she struggled to come to terms with the significant issues blanketing the nation. Her attachment to Curtis, so new to her, increased every time she met the earnest man whose love matched hers. Tina recognised that he was an intensely private person, though he was open about his deep pain over his father's death. His drawn facial lines had scared her a little when he told her of his experience in the police morgue. His smouldering eyes signalled a soul that was on fire due to a father lost too soon. She shuddered at her own much-suppressed images. Spilt parental blood added to their ties.

"You alright?" asked Curtis who snuggled into her from behind.

"Yes, I have all I need right here." She fondled his soft curls. She appreciated his ability to sense when she needed a comforting word, a touch, or a kiss. He was her considerate gentle giant with his sympathetic, loving nature. No wonder she had hardly noticed his dark skin colour from the moment she first saw him.

'I missed all this,' she held his arms closer to her with his hands to her breasts. She tingled with his touch.

"Me too," He drew her closer. "I wanted to be with you so much. I did not see anyone else during our separation. It was my trial by fire. Now, all I want is to eat you." He playfully nibbled at her shoulder.

Despite Tina's comfort, a hollow foreboding clouded their strengthening bond over confidences not shared. At times her brain was a maelstrom of intense emotions, of concealment, of love, of concern at the pace of a relationship beyond her control. *Is Curtis hiding things from me in the same way I withhold aspects of my life from him?*

His love was the salve Tina needed after the confrontations with her father, who had been so dear to her during his years of widowhood, though he had gone too far with Lance. She turned to face Curtis, peeved because he would not move in with her. "Tell me Curtis. Why won't you move in with me?" Her deliberate coy smile was a tantalising invitation.

"You can't imagine how much I want to," said Curtis with a broad smile. "It's not easy to pass on the chance to look at those dimples or eyes every day. I see myself waking in the morning to a face like yours after having you in my arms all night. You are the stuff of which dreams are made. I would walk over hot coals to be with you, but I need you to be patient.'

"See, you don't love me," she pouted.

Curtis nuzzled her as she flexed her neck to stop the ticklish attack on her senses.

"I do love you," he said earnestly.

"Then move in with me," she pleaded. "I need you here, close to me," she turned to kiss him fervently. "With you around, I feel whole, I feel secure, I feel like *me*! When I need you, you'll be there, every day where I can see you, touch you, do things with you, kiss you, make love to you. Anything. Everything! Please, move in with me. I need you, Curtis Fouche."

Curtis looked overwhelmed. *Will he move in with me? What holds him back?* There was something in his eyes, in his demeanour; his body seemed stiff. "Am I not good enough? Are you ashamed of me? Why?" Her eyes narrowed; her brow furrowed with a fervour in need of an answer. She would do anything to be with him. The strength of her feeling surprised her.

"I can't move in yet. I have committed myself to daily karate classes with my group with their upcoming belt-grading early in August. More importantly, I started a much-delayed painting of the rooms at home. I promised my Mom I would do it in July. Between the two projects, I will be pretty tied up. Let's settle on the second weekend of August. I'll move in then. I promise"

Tina's heart fluttered. She squealed, "Whoopee! I'm pleased. I thought you were about to say no. I was so afraid you would leave me again. Thank you, thank you. I can't wait." She kissed him passionately. In turn he held her so tight she struggled to breathe.

"Wow! I could not breathe."

"I wanted you to feel the love. There's no way I would ever leave you, Tina Stephens. By delaying a month, I can fulfil the promises I made to others, especially to my mother." He kissed her around her neck.

Tina luxuriated in the sensations that his kisses evoked. "To be honest, a month's delay is probably better while I sort out a new job at Old Mutual headquarters in Cape Town."

"What's wrong with your present job?"

Tina turned away from him, curling her body into his while holding his arms closer to her. She knew she could not look him in the eye when she replied. "The station job is a dead-end job. They only move you sideways, never upwards. It's like you're there all your life with no chance of advancement. All the managers are White with not a single Black in charge of anything."

"What's the Old Mutual job like?"

"People of colour have better opportunities there. I'm looking into it." Tina kissed his forearm while he kissed the base of her neck. The drift of their conversation unsettled her. She had let slip her plans, yet there was no way she could let him know all of it, at least, not yet. "When I know more I'll tell you."

"Jesus Tina, now I'm really curious about your new job. Have they offered you a managerial post?" he teased. "Why won't you tell me?"

Tina looked askance at him. "I want to surprise you, so please Curtis, later." With concern she realised she had stirred his curiosity. She would prefer to change the subject.

"But why? Oh, come on. You have to tell me!"

"I don't, you know. It's complicated."

"Oh, come on, Tina. Surely you can tell me!" said Curtis.

"Enough! Let's leave things there." An unsmiling Tina clammed shut as she rolled over to face him. Her furrowed brow eased off before she kissed him fervently. She preferred burying herself in their heated passion than walking the thorny path of duplicity. Besides, the intense pleasure of their lovemaking offered her a welcome suspension of a release from a tangled web partly of her own making. If only life were more straightforward. *What about Curtis?* Without any answers she allowed herself to drift into their shared moment of ardent entrapment.

Is this the emotional escape from the past or the present we both seek?

CHAPTER 29: RUGBY GAME PLAN

23 July 1986

CURTIS SAT ON THE GROUND waiting for Thembani behind a row of wattle bushes lining Modderdam Road, close to their Coca-Cola hoarding pickup point. Laden trucks thundered by from the industrial area past the airport to the east of him.

It was almost a year since their incidental meeting on Mandela's Pollsmoor march day. Curtis had a low-intensity knot in his stomach, as today was potentially their last meeting before their planned day of action. He saw Thembani approach from the west with the distant Table Mountain visible in the afternoon haze behind his friend. Curtis smiled when he saw how Thembani's basketball boot laces flapped around even at his leisurely walking pace. The two hugged warmly before they sat on the ground. They had agreed to meet half an hour before they were collected.

"How have you been, Curtis?" Thembani pinched his nose.

"Excellent, I suppose." Curtis smiled broadly.

"Oh, oh, you must be talking about Tina. You devil, tell me!" Thembani chuckled behind his hand.

With a broad smile on his face Curtis playfully punched Thembani on the chest. "Yes. Things have hummed along neatly since we last met. She's living with her brother now." Curtis paused with his smile broader than before. 'Now she wants me to move in with her.'

"What? Move in with her? Are you serious?" Thembani's brow furrowed, exaggerating the prominence of his scar.

"Yes. I'm hoping to."

"But you can't Curtis! There's a lot at stake with our plans so far advanced, man."

"Relax, brother. Nothing will happen until we are done. I've told her I must finish painting my mother's house first. Tina was disappointed, but she's happy to wait. It's a minor complication. Like everything else, the rest of my life is on hold till we're done."

"Right! We really can't take any risks with our plans so close to completion."

"Trust no one, not even your shadow. Remember? It's how I live from day to day. Excluding Tina, I've told you almost nothing about myself. My commitment to our group's plans is firmer than ever. Tina's huge in my life, but she's on hold till we're done. By the way, your words helped me. I've reached the stage where I want to marry her."

"Wow, marriage! How wonderful," though Thembani's brow seemed more clouded than before.

"You look concerned, Thembani. What's up?" Curtis tugged on his shirt collar as he blinked his eyes.

"I may be having the same issue as you with the widowed Nkosinati. You know she's staying at my parent's place until she delivers around Christmas. Each day I can't wait to see her. I visit my parents most days so I can see her. When I'm with her, my hands are all sweaty when those doleful light brown eyes look at me. It's all so new to me. It's a first!"

Curtis laughed. "They are the symptoms of love, dear fellow. I know it well. From the first time I saw Tina on the bus, I was smitten. I was all weak in the knees at the time. When we're together I feel alive."

"So, how do I advance things with a woman who remains in deep mourning over Dumisa. She hardly seems to notice me. Her talk is all about her late husband. I don't blame her because she'll never see his body to have closure. About the only other thing she dwells on is the baby. Hey, she and Dumisa had decided to name the baby Curtis-Thembani if it's a boy."

"Wow! What an honour. You can be a father to Curtis-Thembani, and I'll be his uncle. I'd like it. Now the best thing you can do is to play a supportive role. Let things happen. You're too handsome, so she'll notice you eventually," Curtis chuckled. " Like you said to me, go with your heart brother. I bet your love will find a way!"

Both of them laughed heartily, as their conversation was interrupted with the hooting of a car horn. The pair rushed through the bushes to the Cortina.

EBRAHIM MUTTERED THROUGH clenched teeth, "Thank heavens. I'm glad we didn't turn right." He chewed more forcefully. He needed a fresh piece of gum.

"Me too," added Thembani.

Pat sneered. "Scaredy cats. It's only a cemetery on the other side." He puffed at his cigarette. The front passenger window was open when he smoked as the majority had insisted. "What do you think Curtis?"

"There's nothing wrong with the cemetery as my Dad would've looked after us. Now turn right into Owen Road," Curtis pointed from the rear seat. They drove past breezeblock four-storey council flats with their unpainted walls adorned only with graffiti marking the territory of violent local gangs. Garbage littered an empty field where children played in a couple of rusted car hulks. As directed, Ebrahim turned right into Connaught Road, where the municipal houses with asbestos roofing sheets formed a patchwork of pink, blue, orange and neglect. Add-on structures of all sorts accommodated expanded generations while a mish-mash of gardens had fences ranging from the derelict to precast, unpainted concrete walls.

Tall Eucalyptus trees lined the street, their shade enjoyed by numbers of unemployed youngsters sitting on the pavements with their feet in the gutters. Here was the breeding ground of township gangs. Widely separated street-light poles stood high to protect against stone-throwing vandals. A scattering of self-seeded Eucalyptus trees stood in the expansive field opposite the houses. There were none of the ubiquitous pines or wattles.

"Turn onto the field over there," said Curtis.

When he stopped the car on the concrete slab of a burnt-out factory, Ebrahim took out a piece of fresh chewing gum.

Once outside, they stood in a silent huddle to pay tribute to the dead in Crossroads and KTC. Wind-driven plastic bags plastered the railway fence in the distance. Ebrahim could smell the burning refuse whose smoke blurred the shanties on the other side of the fence where a pair of staked donkeys nibbled away at the calf-high green grass of winter.

"I must apologise," said Pat, who lit another Lexington. "It's over two months since we last saw each other. So much has happened since then. I like what's happening in the north, where Angola is finally a Marxist-Leninist state; the domino effect will mean South West Africa will soon follow. Namibia - I like the name."

"Azania[11] must be next," said Curtis, fisting the air in front of him.

"With so much happening on the border, freedom fighters with weapons are increasingly infiltrating into the townships,' said Thembani. "It's so topical in Gugs, as everyday people want to know what *our* news is, not *theirs*. But the biggest buzz is the abolition of the *Dompas*. It's hard to believe we will no longer have to carry them from next month." He patted his pocket. "I will frame the bloody thing to hang in the shit house where it belongs." They all laughed. "It's a defining moment, but we want majority rule with truly representative democracy, not the crumbs they're offering us."

"It's heartening," said Pat with his brow tightly creased as his hands shielded the Bic lighter's flame when he lit his cigarette again. He exhaled through pursed lips to blow the smoke away from his critical co-conspirators. "Were you guys close to the action in Crossroads?" He addressed Curtis and Thembani.

"Yes, things became gruesome as thousands fled from the *Witdoeke* who were supported by the police." Thembani frowned. "There were so many burning shacks with several deaths." His crinkled brow was pronounced.

"From Bishop Lavis I saw fires over many days," added an earnest-looking Curtis. "It's a major success of the Government's divide and rule strategy by using *Witdoeke* as the State's proxies. They crushed the defiant Crossroads and KTC residents in no uncertain terms."

Thembani cleared his throat with his hand raised. "I must confess to having had reservations about our plans. The decision to step onto a violent platform was ... a challenge. My heart said yes, yet the brain wavered. However, the Crossroads experience shook me to the core. I was left raw at what I experienced there; in the end, my vacillation evaporated. I am now fully committed to our line of action."

"I've always been comfortable with our plans," said Curtis. His blinking eyes flickered faster; his facial lines deeply etched.

Ebrahim nodded. "Early on, I had qualms about our plans too. Like you Thembani, Mandela's Pollsmoor march day with the Trojan Horse Massacre so close to home proved to be my defining moments. After what feels like a lifetime of protest, I know now that I'm ready to advance with our plans." His voice reflected the strength of his conviction. His chewing was firm with visible muscle lines on the side of his jaw.

"I'm like Curtis," said Pat, flicking away a cigarette butt before fisting the air.

"*Amandla, ngawethu!*" All four responded with beaming faces, while they bounced from foot to foot.

"Viva, Viva! Ay, Ay, Ay!" Thembani performed a quick, high-stepping *toyi-toyi* on the slab. The others followed his lead with their virtual shields and spears held high.

Their warm laughter reflected the intense bond that was built on their shared commitment to their mission.

"Okay, men. It's time to play," said Ebrahim. "I suggest we check our throwing first, before Pat takes over regarding a final decision on our target." Ebrahim's stomach was a mess. He had been like a cat on a hot tin roof all week because Pat withheld all details except to say they were on track. How he hated Pat when he was so secretive. He took the underground cell stuff so seriously. 'The less you know the less the security police can extract from you,' Pat teased one day.

Ebrahim pulled on his baseball glove. "I'll be on the sand patch over here. I want the rest of you to start throwing 20 wide paces away from me. After your throw, step away ten paces before you throw again, until each of you reaches your limit. I look forward to seeing your progress since we last met."

Compared with earlier efforts they all comfortably threw 20 metres. "Excellent!" Ebrahim clapped. He underhanded the ball to them. All of them managed the extra distance. At 60 paces Curtis and Pat could not reach the target. Thembani managed past 70. They looked satisfied with their efforts while admiring Ebrahim's return throws at the longer distances.

"So, how much farther can you throw?" Curtis asked Ebrahim.

"Probably another 100 paces more than Thembani."

"Oh bullshit," said Pat.

All of them laughed aloud, flushed at their success.

To Ebrahim the feeling of relief in the group was palpable. He popped two bubbles in quick succession. At the car they sat on the concrete slab with their backs against the side of the Cortina. Table Mountain, Lion's Head and Signal Hill were still visible through the distant afternoon haze. Tiny wisps of cloud hovered over the Table. The earlier stiff wind had settled to a soft breeze around them. Way over to the right, three young men lounged under a pine tree.

From his backpack Thembani removed a folded sheet of paper which he placed on the concrete. "There is my version of our lemons. Gentlemen I present you with the RGD-5 limonka drawn to about actual size." They spun around his pencilled drawing of the grenade as each wanted a closer look.

Ebrahim fingered the sketch. "I like your diagram. All I need now is to hold the *real* lemon. What's the weight compared with the cricket ball?"

"Yes." Thembani responded. "I weighed the cricket ball at the local shop. It's 150 grammes; the lemon is 300, so all we need now is to throw it 40 or more metres to explode four seconds later. I have four rocks of equivalent weight in my backpack. I weighed them on a street-side vendor's scales after I told him I had a science project to do," he grinned. "We can practice with those before action day.

"The lemon's outer surface is smooth," said Pat. "I thought grenades had crisscrossed grooves."

"Those are the French or American versions. Their surface notches allow fragmentation into deadly missiles along the grooves of the metal. Instead, the limonka just splinters into lethal shrapnel. The surface is roughened; being rounded may make them slippery so you must keep your hands as dry as possible before you throw."

"We have all seen war movies," said Curtis. "Tell us about the ring, the pin thingy as well as the handle." He pointed at Thembani's diagram.

"Hey Action Man, trust you to want to know these things," grinned Thembani. He pointed at the diagram. "The ring is part of the pin passing through a hole at the base of the safety lever - it's not a handle." He looked at Curtis. "You hold the body of the grenade with your four fingers. The thumb depresses the lever against the grenade body before you pull on the ring with the other hand to remove the pin. With the safety lever held down, there's no activation of the timer. When the grenade is thrown the lever pops off the body of the lemon. Four seconds later ... Kaboom! Remember, you don't want to be within 20 metres of the bang."

"Now, what's the target?" Curtis stared hard at Pat.

"Relax man. You should smoke to stay calm." Pat lit another Lexington. With his head held high he closed his eyes to savour the first long drag on the cigarette. Although Ebrahim disliked Pat's smoking he took delight in the way Pat lit up, reminiscent of the way he held his head in their more intimate moments. He smiled.

"Attacking the New Zealand Cavaliers during their tour in May would've been more newsworthy. People like Colin Meads, Ian Kirkpatrick, Grant Fox, Buck Shelford and Andy Haden were my favourite All Blacks. Now they disgust me as they should've stayed at home like David Kirk or John Kirwan did." Pat spat on the sand.

"Instead of rugby we can play cricket. The Australian rebels under their captain Kim Hughes will play a match at Newlands in December. On the other hand, there's a derby rugby match at Newlands on the first Saturday in August."

"The derby is always a big match with a packed stadium," said Thembani. "It'll attract Whites mostly. It's only ten days away. I can't wait until December because Curtis has driven me mad with his impatience of late."

"I prefer the earlier option, of course. Where will we attack them?" asked Curtis. "The rugby player's bus? What about the stadium? 85 per cent of the seating is Whites only. We can toss the lemons over the wall from outside or where they queue at their separate entrances. I like both options."

"At Newlands stadium we may be too exposed," said Thembani." We've never been there, so an attack from outside the grounds may prove tricky. With heightened security at a big match there'll be lots of police around the place.

"There'll probably be less police at Newlands station. I've passed through the station a few times to work at Mr Goldberg's place - I normally caddy for him. The station layout is uncomplicated, so getting away should be easy after an attack. Like all Cape town stations, the northern end is the White end of the station."

"In the panic afterwards, we can mingle in with the escaping crowd," said Curtis, who knew the station as did the others. "After our attack we can head directly west towards the Main Road. I suspect most people would head west away from the stadium half a kilometre to the east. I propose we attack the western platform to escape more easily."

They all agreed. There were smiles all round as they backslapped and high-fived each other. A palpable enthusiasm suffused the group of revolutionaries. After their long wait Ebrahim felt ready.

"Right!" An animated Pat leaned forward. "We need to finalise our plans. We know the northern end of the train always has two Whites-only coaches. The other end will have the cheap third-class coaches. In the middle we'll be seated in the two Blacks only first-class coaches. Does anyone know the length of a train coach?"

"I'd been thinking about the train option, so I paced the length of a coach at Nyanga station the other day; it's 20 metres or 20 wide paces," said Thembani.

"From what we have seen of our distances today we need to have Ebrahim and me in the first of the Black coaches. We'll use the doors at the rear end of the coach. I'll aim to drop my lemons on the platform 30 metres away, around the middle of the White coach. With his longer throw Ebrahim will target the next White coach at 40-plus metres.

"You two," Pat pointed at Curtis and Thembani. "You two will be in the coach behind us where you must be at the *front* doors of the coach which will be about ten metres behind us. Curtis will have 35 metres to the first Whites-only coach while Thembani will have around 20 more. Those distances should be well within our throwing abilities."

"I love it," fired Curtis who blinked forcefully.

"A word of caution," said Thembani with his finger raised. "The coaches will be crowded, so people will push their way onto the platform. We need to avoid being pushed from behind when we throw."

"You're right," said Curtis. "It would be best to move quickly to the side of the exit when we step onto the platform. People generally rush straight ahead so there will be a clearing on each side of the sliding doors; there should be enough space to throw without being pushed. By doing so, Thembani and I will be almost opposite the connection between the two coaches."

"I hope there's no one else there with similar plans," said Thembani with a loud laugh.

"Well done you two," said Pat. "There's a lot of sense in your comments! Now on the day we need to have decent-sized pockets in loose light-weight jackets. I wouldn't try to stick these things in a jeans pocket." Pat laughed.

"I'd hate to see my grenade fall from the hole in a plastic bag," said Thembani who giggled along with the rest.

Pat continued, "We know our throwing distances so we can practice with Thembani's rocks to build our muscle-throwing strength.

"So we have a target, we have a plan, and we even know how to throw explosive lemons. So where are we at with the *real thing*s, Pat?" Curtis' tone was sharp.

"Whoa Curtis! My apologies to all of you," said Pat. "The main problem is the warfare between my man and his cousin's gang. I told him we could afford four hand grenades - with all your donations we've crossed the 400 mark. Thank you." They all applauded, smiling broadly.

"I've not paid him yet because he seems distracted with his gang issues, yet he promised me I will have them by next week. I see no reason why he won't deliver."

"Our attack is in ten days' time which will be rather close to our deadline," said Curtis. "What the hell, what's life without a bit of drama, hey!" They all laughed nervously.

"I have all fingers crossed," said Ebrahim.

"To quote from the Robert Burns poem, *To a Mouse*, 'the best-laid plans of mice and men often go askew, and leave us nothing but grief and pain for promised joy!' I hope he's wrong," said Thembani with the customary flick at his nose tip.

"I'm like Ebrahim with everything crossed," said Pat. "On a lighter note I'll be wearing my favourite white shirt with grey top and pants on the day. Ebrahim, I'll be wearing my black shoes, polished."

"Your polished shoes will be a first," laughed Ebrahim. "I'll be in black with my scarf in an Azanian drape." He gave Thembani a thumbs up.

"Blue, definitely blue. Denim jeans, denim shirt, with my shirt collar up," said Curtis, who tugged at his collar.

"My boots will be tied on the day, with whatever else I can find," Thembani smiled.

"So, on with business. Any questions?" Pat raised his eyebrows at his fellow plotters.

"Will you iron your shirt on the day?" asked Ebrahim after a while. "Please!" They all laughed as Thembani tittered away long after the rest had stopped.

Their faces projected their relief as the long wait was about to end. Ebrahim knew that they would all feel the same gnawing sensation he had with the prospect of their high drama now so close.

"May I suggest we travel by train from Claremont; it's one station stop away from Newlands," suggested Thembani. "In the ensuing uproar we can walk the return distance in about fifteen minutes. There's a Greek fish and chip shop on the side road close to Claremont station in case anyone's hungry afterwards."

They laughed aloud at another moment of much-needed relief from the group's dangerous plans.

"Trust you to think of food," said Curtis with tears in his eyes. "Me, I prefer to return to Tina."

"Tina? Is Tina your girlfriend?" asked an instantly guarded Pat. All eyes were on Curtis.

Curtis fumbled in his pocket to remove his wallet. "Here, check her photo. I met Tina Stephens a few months ago. She's worth returning to."

"Wow, she's pretty. What does she do?" asked a concerned-looking Pat.

"Clerical work at Cape Town station," replied Curtis. "Don't worry. We only talk love man, and she's full of it," he smiled.

Thembani chuckled. "He's a real devil, so I keep him away from my sisters." They all laughed. Thembani handed the photo to Curtis.

"She's the one I'm returning for." Curtis tapped the photograph with a finger before he returned it to his wallet. "But it's time for

Nkosi sikelel iAfrika. I have practised, and I would like to lead today if Thembani agrees." Curtis smiled as he pulled on his shirt collar.

Thembani beamed. "The floor is yours maestro." He winked at the others.

Curtis' crooning contrasted well with Thembani's baritone. Pat and Ebrahim knew the words in Xhosa as all of them hooked their arms during the singing.

When finished Thembani could not contain himself. He hand-slapped his way around the group. "*Nkosi.* Thank you, comrades. The singing was faultless."

"I felt all the energy pass through our circle," said Ebrahim. "Now I'm ready to sing with my sis who'll be pleased."

The light moments with the anthemic prayer were needed as Ebrahim was a bundle of nerves. The drawn faces of the others mirrored his feelings. Curtis rubbed his hands; Pat had both fists clenched while Thembani rubbed at his nose. Ebrahim felt ready to burst. *Would their plans work out?* It would be like a night-time leap into a dark chasm.

The refuse fire in the distance smoked less than earlier. A dying flame from the fire flared momentarily. Like the two donkeys, the three men under the pine tree had moved on. A couple of hidden doves sang their love duet from one of the distant Eucalyptus trees. The four schemers in the Cortina took their radical plans with them towards a better future in South Africa, while the setting sun was tinged like an orange tablecloth over the Mother City's mountain.

CHAPTER 30: FINAL MEDICAL CONSULTATION

30 July 1986

STANLEY LOOKED AT FAY across the breakfast table as he sipped his wake-up cup of coffee. "I'm always amazed at how beautiful you look first thing in the morning," Stanley told Fay.

"And the rest of the day I look worse?" Fay asked with an eyebrow raised.

"Not at all. By the way, I had a letter from Australia asking about next year. They need to know if we're coming over again in the autumn months."

Fay looked towards the clear mountains. "I can't easily forget my racist episode in Tamworth last year. Can we give Australia a miss for now?"

"I don't see why not. They know about the Tamworth event, so they'll understand. They have enough time to find someone else. Will you ever feel comfortable there again?"

'We'll see. Let's do New Zealand instead as we both need time to recharge our batteries. Maybe we could walk the Milford Track."

"Sounds like a plan to me. I also want to fit in more scuba diving when we are in Whangarei. It's two years since I qualified there. Maybe you should enroll. I'm sure you'd enjoy the course." Stanley looked at Fay, who looked somewhat absorbed.

"Yes, I will give it some thought. I miss going to the SACLA clinic. It was cynical the way the State took over the clinic," said Fay. The State had used military medical personnel with guns on their hips before the *Witdoeke* destroyed the clinic under the noses of the police and soldiers.

"Now we're late, so I should be on my way."

Fay lingered briefly in his arms when they kissed. She always seemed comforted there. Stanley ran his fingers through her hair then gave her a squeeze around her shoulders.

"See you later," she said.

"And you keep well."

STANLEY SAT AT HIS re-arranged desk so he could see the distant Table Mountain whenever he looked up. Hammer van Zyl again had the first booking.

"I see you've turned your desk around since the last time," noted van Zyl as he sat on the chair opposite Stanley.

"What brings you here today Mr van Zyl." Stanley was in no mood for pleasantries. Gaunter than three months ago, the man again stank of his addictions.

"Well, you were correct Dr Gershon. No doubt you saw the results. AIDS positive blood test. Kaposi's sarcoma on the skin biopsy. Now extra skin nodules have appeared elsewhere, while the lesions on the hands are bigger." He lifted them to show Stanley. "No magnifying glass needed to see them today. The sputum you sent off was positive for TB. They tell me it's drug resistant, so I'm on the last line of defence medication. Lately I have these new swellings in my armpits. Any ideas?"

Stanley palpated the areas of concern before he listened to the man's chest.

"At least the chest sounds clear today," he said. "These new nodes may be from the Kaposi's, or they could be from other cancers or lymphomas or the TB. Other doctors may want to biopsy the nodes; ultimately the decision is yours."

"How so Doctor?"

"One of three things will kill you. Sarcoma, drug-resistant TB or Aids. Do you want a fourth to add to the list?"

"Ahh. Direct and bright. No wonder I like you," Van Zyl nodded his head with his shoulders slouched.

Neither of them said anything for a while. Stanley drummed his fingers on the desk.

"I've been off work since I last saw you. All I do is watch TV, smoke or drink. Maybe the Rothmans or KWV will cure me, like pickling." He laughed to himself. "The police have been told to wear gloves when they deal with people's blood. Could I have contracted this AIDS thing from someone's blood?"

Here was the area of caution Stanley had avoided on his prior consultation. He watched the eyes whose intensity had diminished as van Zyl averted Stanley's gaze.

"It all depends on how much exposure there was." Stanley did not expand as he preferred to change tack. "Over the years Mr van Zyl, I came across people you had dealt with, physically abused actually. What made you do it?" Stanley leaned forward on his desk.

"Nobody has ever asked me that before. Nobody! Direct, bright, gutsy too." He offered a crinkled smile in Stanley's direction. "Maybe I had a sense of duty. Maybe the communist threat, all the Reds-under-the-bed stuff. I don't know. Like the military, the police follow instructions, I suppose." The dark eyes stared at Stanley. There was a blankness about them.

"Maybe you *enjoyed* it?" There was an accusatory edge to Stanley's voice.

Van Zyl's brows drew together in a frown. He sat upright in his chair, his eyes closed.

"No," he said. "I don't think so." He whispered. His eyes opened; his face was wooden.

"Are you with the *Afrikaner Broederbond?*[12] (Afrikaner Brotherhood) Or are you a servant of theirs?" Stanley felt he needed to see the man react, as if he wanted to hurt van Zyl.

Van Zyl again closed his eyes. "Doctor Gershon. Please. So many questions." He coughed a few times, before he nodded his head with his brow furrowed. "You must have read the book about the *Broederbond* those Sunday Times journalists published." The secretive think tank of cabinet ministers, top academics, politicians, businesspeople, priests, teachers, police, and military commanders had at least one Springbok rugby captain as a member.

Van Zyl placed his hands on the desk. "I'm not religious or wealthy or powerful enough to be in the Bond. Ja, like my maid or my gardener, I'm a servant like you said. The BB control the country. Yes Dr Gershon, *they* control all of us. They're our invisible puppeteers." He moved his outspread fingers to simulate pulling the strings of puppetry.

"So how corrupt are they with all the power they have?" asked Stanley.

"Doctor Gershon, please stop." His brow creased even more than before. "However, it's an interesting question. They could be I suppose. I've never thought of it. Power and money make a gloved hand, not so. Like I said they run our puppet show." A weak smile crossed his face while his fingers again pulled at the invisible strings.

"Mostly I survived each day with my smokes or drink. No questions asked. In different ways we're all victims, Dr Gershon. Us Whites don't even realise it." He stopped. "I don't suppose I'm allowed to smoke here. No?" He smiled when Stanley did not bother to reply.

"You won't know this, probably no one does. My son, an only child from a loveless marriage long ago, lives overseas with his wife where they have two children. She's Black. Since they fled the country, I've never seen them. It's too late now I suppose." A look of resignation clouded his face.

"She was our maid's daughter, and the kids played together at our house whenever her mother came to work. The kids fell in love. I was horrified when he told me he was going to marry her. He was thirteen at the time, she was ten. Imagine!" He shook his head. "Do you know I've never spoken about them to anyone, Dr Gershon. You're amazing!" a faint smile crossed his face as he shook his head slowly.

"While I'm into dropping my secrets, here's another first-time-to-anyone story." He stopped to look at Stanley. He took his Rothmans' pack from his pocket to slip a cigarette into his mouth. "Don't worry Doctor, I won't light up. I'm leaving soon, in more ways than one," he smirked. "Where was I?"

"Another skeleton from your cupboard, I think," said an intrigued Stanley.

"Yes. I started to shave off my kinky hair in Cape Town. People here said I had *croes* hair. I could not stand the term because I had enough trouble at school over my curly dark hair. With the playground bullies I was the *Hotnot* or the *Kaffir* because of my darker skin colour. Since those days, I wear long-sleeved shirts all the time. Am I a darker shade of white or a paler shade of brown?" He sucked on the unlit cigarette.

"What kind of scrambled genes do you have?" Stanley pushed on.

Van Zyl looked at him through hooded tired eyes. He pulled his mouth while he raised his hands in an empty gesture.

"Is this how you became what you are today?" Stanley continued. "A violent servant of the State to prove your credentials?"

Van Zyl's brows furrowed all the way to his shaved scalp. "Violent? You're amazing Dr Gershon. You have me singing like no one else has ever done before. Enough for now. The last time I came here I told you why I came to you. I had wanted to come to you sooner about the time we detained Ms Fay Ismail. I delayed my visit to you after her detention."

"I suspected you would know about her," said Stanley whose pulse raced at Hammer's reference to Fay. *Have I pushed him too far? Are we now playing a cat-and-mouse game? What is he after?*

"It was about the time I considered consulting you with my skin problem. I saw her briefly in the interrogation room when I told my men to go easy on her. We were after the big fish." Van Zyl closed his eyes, lapsing into silence.

"Fay did not enjoy the experience at all as you can imagine." Stanley drummed his fingers on his desk. His insides felt all knotted. He narrowed his eyes as he leaned towards van Zyl. "What do your files say about me?"

Van Zyl smiled at him, looking hard at Stanley, as he sucked on the unlit cigarette to exhale non-existent smoke. "It's confidential, you know. However, you've been frank with me, so I'll be frank with you. We were aware of how you collected funds from your colleagues to help detainees in 1976. We were about to arrest the Macphersons, the couple who organised the collection, when they fled to the UK via Botswana. You stopped collecting after they left so you were off the screen until we detained Ms Ismail. We're not really interested in you or her, Dr Gershon," he smiled.

Van Zyl half-turned his chair to look towards a cloud-smothered Table Mountain. "At least I can watch the big rugby derby next weekend. Do you follow the rugby, Doctor Gershon?"

Stanley, still somewhat taken aback by van Zyl's comments about Fay, reflected on an appropriate response. "No." After a pause he added, "I don't follow segregated sport."

Van Zyl smirked. "Honest to a fault, Doctor. Now I better be off before we both probe too far." He paused. "When I left you the last time I was angry at you. I must apologise as I didn't want to accept the news. Allow me to thank you formally." A tired resigned smile tugged at his lips. "You gave me a year or more, but the way I feel, I don't think I'll survive a month."

"Yes, the TB with those new nodes have sped things along somewhat. I wish you well, Mr van Zyl."

"I doubt we'll meet again, Doctor Gershon." The eyes wavered. Van Zyl's handshake had lost its firmness from the time of his previous visit. Stanley noticed the shuffling of his feet on the way out.

FAY WAS INCREDULOUS. "*You did what?*" Her voice rose with every word. Her hazel eyes were wide open, accentuating the lines on her face. "You asked Hammer all of those things? You poked the lion with a spear you know. You are something else." She crossed her arms where they sat in their kitchen nook. The early winter darkness masked the outside world.

It was the first time Stanley had ever broken patient confidentiality, but he told Fay about van Zyl's consultations because he felt they had indirectly suffered so much from what they had heard about Hammer. Stanley knew the story would not go beyond the two of them.

"Part of the van Zyl experience has been the crumbling of a man who abused his State-sanctioned power. The lives or wellbeing of those he interrogated meant nothing to him. Imagine a man capable of such brutality has a needle phobia." Stanley shook his head. "He needed a greater justice from an invisible virus from one of his victims. He must have contracted TB from one of his detainees too.

There's a definite justness in both diseases." Stanley felt his nostrils flare. His tone was steely.

"Retribution too," Fay concluded.

"Yes," said Stanley. "I suppose it's a relief to know they're not interested in us."

They lapsed into a rare silence, each with an arm around the other. The pounding in Stanley's ears slowly settled. He noticed how long Fay's crimson-red nails were. They matched her lipstick, contrasting well with her knitted black outfit. He kissed Fay on her forehead as she nestled further into him, kissing his neck. Their sighs were inaudible.

CHAPTER 31: MAJOR SETBACK

30 July 1986

PAT HAD COME TO SEE Aggie, the leader of the Achar-Americans, at the gang's headquarters. He made his way across the pleasantly warm main room in a sizeable well-constructed shanty. Aggie lived in an opulent home in nearby Belhar. Pat greeted the gang members with a wave. Most sported gang or prison tattoos on faces, necks, or exposed limbs. A few lounged on an assortment of comfortable chairs while a few others stood smoking or chatting around a Dover No.8 stove with the black chimney stack reaching up through the middle of the corrugated iron roof. On the side of the stovetop the steaming coffee pot aroma masked the smell of cigarette smoke. The hum of a generator somewhere provided electricity to power the lights, wide-screen television and fridge, items not found in the average shanty.

He walked through to where Aggie sat in an annexe with two wrought iron garden chairs with a matching round table. One of the gangsters brought each of them a mug of coffee. Aggie had his gun tucked into the waistband of his trousers as he slurped a mouthful of coffee while Pat warmed his hands folded around his mug before he sipped his brew.

Despite trusting Aggie there was always a dryness of the mouth whenever they met. Their early talks had been exploratory before they tackled the issue of weapons' procurement. They had been at primary school together where Aggie was their soccer team's star striker with Pat as a defender. In their last year together, their team was the regional Western Province primary school champions. Aggie had not gone on to senior schooling.

Aggie's two front gold teeth flashed in the low light interior of the room. Pat drew deep on his cigarette; he needed the calming effect. Aggie did not smoke; in fact, the hardened criminal did not do drugs either. He expected the same of his generals. He told Pat there was no other way to run his business.

"Now where are we at with my lemons?" Pat had given Aggie the four hundred rands a few days earlier.

"All's well," flashed the gold teeth. "I have them in the other room. Do you know how to use them? I have a spare so I can give you a live demo if you like." Pat took another sip from his mug as he looked at the tattooed overweight school-soccer hero of yesteryear. Pat lit another cigarette before answering.

"No, it's not necessary," said Pat, who tried hard to conceal his exuberance, mixed in with more than a touch of anxiety. He was so close now.

"I've used them a couple of times. Despite their size, they make a helluva mess when they go off so watch it when you use them. You don't want to be close to them." He laughed. "I'll fetch them for you."

As Aggie rose from the table a loud crash shattered the quiet of the afternoon followed by the grating sound of metal on metal. Bursts of gunfire followed. A startled Pat threw himself onto the floor.

"Fucking hell, those bloody HighLifers have driven a truck through the gate into our yard!" Aggie shouted. He rushed to the door of the room with his gun in hand, instantly falling backwards onto the floor alongside a wide-eyed Pat, whose heart thumped in his throat where he lay. Blood streamed from Aggie's forehead wound. A hail of bullets passed everywhere through the corrugated iron sheets of the building as Pat hugged the ground. Gang members tried to return the fire from where they were trapped indoors. Within minutes the shooting from outside stopped as Pat heard the vehicle roar off with an equally noisy exit from the yard.

Bloodied gang members with weapons in hand rushed through the front door. In the confusion Pat exited through the side door with all senses on alert. His left shoulder ached where a bullet had struck him before he hit the ground. All was clear behind the building. He dashed through the narrow alleyways where the converging roofs pressed in on him. His knotted stomach with paper-dry mouth all spurred him on to distance himself from the gang headquarters. Curious spectators emerged from the surrounding shanty homes to take in the action. A gasping Pat slowed to a normal walking pace. He did not know the area well, but he used the distant Table Mountain to work his way towards a more familiar street.

Pat's dark anorak concealed his shoulder wound as he applied pressure to the area with his right hand. The injury felt like a superficial wound, but his main concern was the derailment of their plans with their attack due in three days. Finding a quick replacement supplier would be impossible. A gutted Pat was at his wit's end.

Once home he stripped off his shirt. He was lucky there was no muscle injury. He dabbed at the skin wound with a tincture of Iodine, left over from the cleansing of his minor scalp wounds at the time of the Trojan Horse episode. The intense stinging of the Iodine soon eased off. Resting against the headboard, the overhead heater's warmth helped the wound to dry, leaving a brown iodine stain to remind him of his close brush with death. After two cigarettes, he started to settle. *When will Ebrahim be here?*

Ebrahim's customary triple knock at the door roused him from his slumber. Ebrahim poked his head around the opened door. His smile turned into a deep frown when he saw Pat.

"What's up? What's with the wound? Did someone shoot you at Aggie's? Are you alright?" Ebrahim rushed towards Pat. Ebrahim's chewing was in overdrive.

"Whoa! Slow down. I'm fine, just shaken by a flesh wound from a bullet," he pointed at his shoulder. "I have a few more lives to go yet, so relax." He reached to hold Ebrahim's hand, enjoying the sensation of Ebrahim's thumb stroking his hand. With his other hand he drew Ebrahim closer to kiss him in the neck as they clung to each other.

Ebrahim's troubled demeanour did not change. "I hate seeing you injured even if it's minor. Each of us has been spared a serious shooting over the years."

"Come on love, you're the one who's taken three rubber bullet shots over the years."

"Four actually. All were intensely painful. How painful is your wound? Who shot you? The police?"

"I was lucky my wound is only a skin knick. I ended up in a damned gang shootout at Aggies where the HighLifers had a go at the Achar-Americans' HQ. I expect it'll cause an all-out war. Aggie took a shot to the head when he was about to fetch the grenades. He looked pretty dead when I left the room.

"They attacked from the front after crashing through the high gates with a truck. The shooting was all over in minutes while they riddled the HQ shanty with bullets. The place was a mess, with many gang members injured. I was definitely in the wrong place at the wrong time. Shit, I'm still shaking!" He showed his tremulous hands to Ebrahim, who sat on the bed beside him where he rubbed Pat's thigh.

"Well, I'm relieved you're safely home again," said Ebrahim. "What happened to the money? What about the grenades? Our plans are buggered without them!"

"You know I handed over the money a few days ago. Aggie was about to fetch the hand grenades from the room next door when all hell broke loose. Shit, man! Our plans are in flames so we should let the other two know."

Ebrahim frowned, holding up one hand. "Cool it, Pat. Maybe we should just think about it."

"Of what use is that?" asked Pat with his voice louder than normal. "We're stuffed without hand grenades. There's no one else I know. *Do you?*" he glared at Ebrahim.

"Hey, hold on. The critical question is whether Aggie is dead or not?"

"He looked dead with so much blood pouring from his head wound. My main interest was to be away from there!" Pat lit another cigarette on the one he was about to finish. The butt went into the Coke can ashtray. His exhaled smoke was in a forceful thin stream.

Ebrahim stood to pace the floor with his brow tightly wrinkled. "We'll check if there's anything on the six o'clock or later news. We need to know if Aggie is alive or not."

"We'll be stuffed if he's carked it." Pat sucked on his cigarette again. His tremulousness had settled, though his stomach remained a mess of tangled nerves. "Ten bloody months of work has gone down the fucking drain." He slammed his fists onto his thighs. "Damn those bloody HighLifers!"

CHAPTER 32: ELSIES RIVER TIME OUT

31 July 1986

CURTIS WAS DUE TO MEET Tina on the corner of Boston Avenue and Halt Road in Elsies River. She was on her way to work an afternoon shift at Cape Town station. He was early so he strolled westwards towards a staggered five-street junction where the Elsies River diverted to prevent winter flooding towards its lower south bank.

Curtis hoped to own a property on the elevated northern banks of the covered river. From the top, a few low hills gave an unobstructed view of the Mountains over the flat surrounding areas. Tina found the idea appealing when he showed her the area one weekend. They both liked a plot on Riverton Crescent from where they could see the side-on view of Table Mountain with the tip of Devil's Peak poking up behind it.

Finding the wherewithal to purchase would be an issue, but the time had come to find himself a steady job. His senior school matriculation certificate would ensure that he found a suitable position. Tina had encouraged him to apply at Old Mutual. She felt optimistic about the place, while he was pleased to see how excited she was when he promised her he would apply once he moved in with her. Virtually all her savings went into a Trust Bank account towards her first house. Her father always encouraged his children to own property; each brother already had one.

He realised how the plans involving Tina clashed with his more radical agenda. His former life had three linked compartments. He was part of the Group of Four, while he and Thembani were a Group of Two. Finally, there was the Group of One, Curtis Fouche, the Armpit Assassin. Until now the transitions between the groups were smooth, though with Tina he now had to deal with an isolated fourth compartment.

Should he continue along his dual pathway with Tina, and his commitment to revolutionary change? Leave Tina? The thought alone tore him apart. She was so different, under his skin in a delightful way. Should he retire the Armpit Assassin? The arming of the recruits had curtailed his work there. Should he desert his three comrades? No. He was too committed to the group's cause. He would go through with the Newlands station attack before turning his attention to Tina because he loved her too much to let her go.

Deep in his clashing thoughts he ambled along to the Halt Road corner in time to see Tina alighting from the bus. She threw herself into his arms to kiss him. He was now accustomed to her brazenness. A knee-length dark coat covered her work clothes with a furry cap over her ears. Long black boots reached below the knee where her thick skirt ended. Her perfume made his head spin as he held onto her warm hand to gaze into her impish eyes. She touched the tip of his nose with her free hand.

"Stop staring." Her eyes twinkled with mischief. "It's rude."

"All I see is ravishing." He nibbled at her neck. She giggled as she bent her neck to protect the ticklish area.

They held hands when they crossed Halt Road, skipping over the narrow island in the middle. The low Kanonberg Mountains were visible to their left across the railway line where all the suburbs were for Whites only. Railway lines, like major roadways, provided the physical barriers between Cape Town's races.

Curtis stopped before the corner on Consani Avenue. "Whenever I pass the Five Star Fisheries here I always buy their fish and chips to eat with a white roll and a few pickled onions. Do you mind if I popped in quickly? I'm feeling peckish." He tugged at his shirt collar.

"You're lucky it's my favourite too, without the roll or onions. I'll shout you. Next lunch is on you."

With their warm purchases in hand, they made their way towards the station where the Non-White waiting room was empty.

"The smell of the vinegar with the batter-fried fish always gets to me," said a salivating Curtis. "I think the smell was better when they used newspaper wrapping."

"Maybe the newsprint made the fish smell better." Tina's chuckle made him smile again. She had such a joy about her since she had moved in with her brother.

It was nearly noon when they opened their steaming fare on the wooden bench between them in the station waiting room. Curtis split his roll with his fingers to place his fish inside. "There are times when I don't know what's better. The smell or the taste."

"Definitely the taste," said Tina who popped a piece of fish into her mouth with two fingers followed by a chip. She placed a chip into his mouth, holding her fingers for him to kiss. Instead, he sucked at her fingertips. Her eyes twinkled with amusement; the Tina he wanted had returned.

"You're supposed to kiss the fingers, not eat them." She did not attempt to remove her fingers, just wiggled them a bit. Her suggestive gaze locked with his as he struggled to suppress his arousal.

"Is there a fly on my face or something? I'm nervous when people stare at me." She withdrew her fingers to continue eating. There was a sensuousness in the way she slipped a chip or a piece of fish into her mouth. Her full lips glistened with the light coating of oil from her food.

"I don't know what's better. The taste of my lunch or my company. No, you by far." He leaned over to kiss Tina.

"No! Keep away from me. I'm not a fan of pickled onions. You can peck me on the cheek instead.' Curtis obliged her.

With a gleeful chuckle she stole his biggest chip while she covered hers. Most of the time they spoke about inconsequential matters. Curtis enjoyed these moments when he could suspend the weighty issues of his life. Maybe the one-man assault force he had become was too much for him? Was this part of the attraction of the Group of Four? A common goal united them. Why not forget the cell of four? Build the house on the Riverton Crescent hill with Tina. The idea appealed to him.

They finished their hurried meal when Tina's train came into view from around the distant bend. "Now duty calls. I enjoyed our time together. Thanks." She kissed him on the lips, her tongue briefly teased his. "We should do lunch again sometime."

"Yes, we will," said Curtis.

"I know we agreed we would not talk about your moving in, but am I allowed to quickly say *I can't wait?* I'm counting the days." Tina drew her shoulders together as she smiled broadly.

"So am I. My Mom was surprised. You two should meet soon as she's rather curious about you. Someone must have spoken to her about you."

"Oh no. What did you tell her?"

"It's private. Maybe I should meet your Dad too."

"I don't think you should. Remember the boyfriend he beat up? My father hated him because he was too black, and he had a lighter skin colour than yours. So, no!" Tina waved a finger at him.

"Well, your train's here," he laughed.

The train came to a stop with the customary screeching of metal brakes on metal wheels. They kissed again before Tina boarded the train where she stood inside the door waving at him until the doors swished close. When the train pulled away from the platform, she blew him a kiss which he returned with two hands. He watched the train head towards Table Mountain as his heartbeat settled over several minutes.

CURTIS ENJOYED THEIR informal lunch, though he also had to go to the Halt Road shopping precinct with its tired Third World look. He went to Maboys, the quality discount clothing store where he often bought his clothes. Three walls had clothing stacked high on shelves. Dresses, jackets and trousers hung on wheeled racks in the middle of the shop. A full-length window faced onto Halt Road.

Curtis soon found a suitable dark blue jacket. He tested the side pocket with his cricket ball; it was a comfortable fit. The light fabric would not impede his throwing. There was only one barely visible defect on the sleeve. The wrinkled store owner, who seemed to have been there forever, pinged the sale on an equally time-worn National cash register. The blue baseball cap was free.

Curtis sat alone upstairs to enjoy the view on the bus trip to Bishop Lavis. The added appeal upstairs was the absence of any apartheid signs telling him where he had to sit or stand. White clouds dotted the blue sky. Cape Town's mountains were clearly visible. Here was the view he wanted from the lounge or the kitchen where he and Tina would spend their free time. Now he had to focus on their bombing mission in two days. He punched the bus seat in front of him. With just a day left before their planned mission, life felt perfect.

CHAPTER 33: TRAIN RIDE

2 August 1986

EBRAHIM HAD NOT SLEPT well the previous evening. He suspected none of them had. Years of suffering, with nearly a year of planning had brought them to a critical point of no return.

They collected Thembani and Curtis from their regular spot on Modderdam Road. There was an air of expectancy amongst all of them. Ebrahim's stomach was like a tight ball. He felt nauseated. Licking his lips did not alleviate the dryness. How quickly the months had passed since the Trojan Horse Massacre. *Will we survive today the way we did then?*

While Ebrahim drove to Claremont, Pat told the other two about the gang shootout. "I thought everything was kaput when I left Aggie with his bleeding head wound. Fortunately, the lucky bastard only had a glancing bullet injury with no damage to the brain. By the time they reached the hospital, he had come round. Fortunately, he only needed sutures to the scalp so he went home the next morning." Pat stopped talking to light another cigarette.

"Not another one! You've not stopped smoking since I picked you up."

"Never mind the smoking Ebrahim. What happened then?" asked Curtis, his eyes wide.

"You can imagine how relieved I was to hear of Aggie's survival. I had already paid him a few days before. I went to see him the next afternoon, but the police were there, so I could only conclude the deal yesterday morning. Your lemons are in my haversack there on the floor between the two of you. I was so relieved to take possession of them finally. Ebrahim and I already have our fruit in our pockets."

"What a story," said Curtis.

"It's no wonder you're smoking so much today," said Thembani. "I'd be smoking too after your experience," he chuckled.

"Forget today. You should've seen him the last two days," said Ebrahim. "He was a non-stop chimney!"

"I'm glad you kept us in the dark about those problems because Curtis would've gone ballistic with the news," said Thembani.

After fumbling with the haversack Curtis handed Thembani his hand grenade.

"May I hand you your *limonka*, sir." Curtis extended the weapon towards Thembani with both hands.

Curtis soon had his thumb on the safety lever with his fingers wrapped around the body of his grenade. "It's a snug fit in the hand." He put the index finger of his other hand through the ring of the pin. "Just one pull on there; four seconds later it's kaboom time!"

"Please don't put your finger in the ring Curtis. You're making me nervous," said Thembani.

"It feels like the weight of the rocks we practised with," said Curtis. He slipped his lemon into his jacket pocket. "Now, finally comrades, I'm ready."

"I see we all have appropriate tops, and, with our caps, we'll blend in with the other spectators," said Ebrahim. "So how did your day start?"

"I went to my parents' house. They're always pleased when I have breakfast with them," said Thembani. "They expect me to caddy at the King David Country Club today. I held on to my Mom for a bit longer when I kissed her goodbye. She wanted to know if I was all right because I seemed troubled.

"Of course, I told her that I was okay. It's just like mothers to notice these things. By the way comrades, if I seem to limp it's due to the fighting stick down my trouser leg." Thembani smiled. "How did your mornings go?" With raised eyebrows his gaze flitted to each comrade in turn.

Curtis responded with unease in his tone. "I had my typical noisy breakfast at home with the family who also think I'm caddying today. I brought my Three Star along with me in case I need it." He winked at Thembani. "There's no knowing when it'll come in handy. In ten years, I've never been without my knife. It's like having my father with me all the time." Thembani gave him a thumbs up.

"One day, you two must tell us about the Three Star and the stick." Ebrahim could feel the light sweat on his upper lip. "I had to excuse myself from my father after breakfast. I hardly ate. My stomach has been a mess since the gang shootout. My father grumbled because he wanted me to help with an order that he has to send off today. Once again, my mother wasn't pleased I was leaving to join Pat on an outing."

Ebrahim smiled. "I spent a few precious minutes with my sis last night when we walked around the block close to sunset. I can still feel her soft hand here, in mine." His eyes were teary. "On the bench outside the local corner store Suraya teased me when I cried after we sang *Nkosi sikelel iAfrika*. I gave her an extra bar of Kitkat, our favourite chocolate. I must return to nurse her again whenever she has her spasms." He brushed away a few tears.

Pat squeezed Ebrahim's leg before he flicked a cigarette butt through the car window. "I only saw my mother briefly before I left. I didn't feel like breakfast, so I left after a hasty cup of coffee. I was concerned that I would cry if I stayed longer. The rest of the household always sleeps late, so I had a brief chat with them last night. My baby brother is a Michael Jackson fan. I told him I would buy him *Thriller* for Christmas."

They drifted into silence until they pulled into the car park in front of Claremont station. Thembani broke the silence. "I have a bit of Shakespeare to recite if I may. It's King Henry before the Battle of Agincourt from Act 111, scene 1. It's so relevant to us today." Thembani cleared his throat. His deep voice filled the car.

Once more unto the breach, dear friends, once more;

Or close the wall up with our English dead!

In peace, there's nothing so becomes a man,

As modest stillness and humility.

But when the blast of war blows in our ears,

Then imitate the action of the tiger;

Stiffen the sinews, summon up the blood!"

They remained silent. There was no need to add to Thembani's recital. Curtis applauded softly.

"Word perfect again, Thembani," said Curtis. "I studied King Henry for my matric exams. Yes, I'm ready, my blood has always been up. Finally, it's time to go to battle."

"There's the Curtis we've come to know," said Ebrahim. He smoothed his South African-draped Palestinian scarf, contrasting well with his black clothes. "I'm ready too."

Thembani started *Nkosi sikelel iAfrika* as the rest joined in. The quiet version was the most visceral song Ebrahim had ever sung. He stretched his arms to embrace the others in a tight ring of solidarity in the Cortina's cramped confines. Their handgrips were firm. Ebrahim sensed the shared flow of hope and tension through the ring. *Will we survive? Will we all be in the car later? Will we sing our anthem of freedom again?*

"Now, I would like to finish off with a brief *dua* for our safety. The prayer is in Arabic, of course." Ebrahim held his open hands in front of him. The rest followed his actions. He completed the brief supplications by wiping his face with his palms, followed by the rest.

"Thanks, Ebrahim," said Curtis. "What does the prayer mean?"

"'I seek refuge in the perfect words of Allah from the evil of what He has created.' I thought the final bit is so appropriate."

"Agreed," said Thembani. "You must teach me the verse some time."

They each had a limonka. Ebrahim's sat heavy in his pocket. Each of them wore a light top with pockets, as Pat had advised. With their baseball caps, they would blend in with the spectators on their way to the big game.

PAT WAS REFLECTIVE when he spoke up. "You have all impressed me with your perseverance in the slow progress towards today. It's been almost nine months since we had our first meeting in the cemetery. There were times when I thought we would never reach our goal, especially in the last three days. Now here we are, all set to go." He slowly flexed his fingers before he continued.

"I'm sure the rest of you are nervous too. I recently saw a graph showing how an ideal performance requires us to stay on the plateau of tension rather than slide down the other side towards panic. Let us be on the optimal level to achieve the best possible result today. Let us use our lemons well, and may we all return to our mothers, our families, and our loved ones."

In the awkward confines of the Cortina, they shook hands before they hugged each other. Pat held onto Ebrahim briefly as the lovers kissed each other. Curtis's hug with Thembani was brief. They needed no words. Curtis tugged on his upright collar, blinking his eyes.

From the car they could see Whites head towards their waiting room at the northern end of the station. The rugby match was a big one. Ahead of them the other waiting room looked full.

"At least the coaches are still segregated," said Pat as he looked at his watch. "The train will be here in ten minutes. Good luck!' They fisted each other before they exited the Cortina.

"I do intend to drive back; this is just in case!" Ebrahim placed his car key under the mat on the driver's side. "And I need a fresh Wrigley's before we start."

They separated from each other on the way to the station. Pat walked close to Ebrahim drawing on his freshly lit cigarette on their way to an area between the White and Black waiting rooms where they expected the first of the Black coaches to stop. To their right, Thembani was close to Curtis.

He and Ebrahim worked their way past people in the Non-whites only waiting room. Most of the festive crowd wore the colours of their favoured team. Pat reflected on how people of colour could view a Whites-only game from a segregated stand; he snorted in disdain.

Pat made sure he stayed close to Ebrahim. His mouth was like parchment while an emptiness gnawed away at his belly. The same sensation probably affected all four of them. The main thing was to keep his throwing hand dry. Then, a few hundred metres away to his right, the train rounded the bend from Harfield Road station into the straight towards Claremont station. Ebrahim winked at him. Pat nodded. He noticed how an intense Curtis and Thembani also watched their approaching train of destiny.

The first two coaches were for Whites only. Pat saw the filled seats, without any standing passengers. *Oh shit!* The third coach also had Whites only signs, not the script they had written. *Will we be close to our coach doors?* He noticed a few empty seats in the last White coach.

The last five carriages were jam-packed with Blacks. *Will all of us get a place on board?* Despite the churning of his stomach Pat resented how relatively empty the White coaches were.

Pat sighed with relief when the train drew to a stop with the rear-end doors of their coach right in front of him. After a final long draw on the Lexington, with regret he threw his half-smoked cigarette onto the platform. People pushed to board the already over-crowded coaches. Once inside Pat elbowed his way to stand next to Ebrahim. They held on to the overhead rail with one hand. Hemmed in by other standing passengers they stood close to the right-hand side of the double doors. Pat was relieved to see the other pair enter the front door of the coach behind them. They were all in position as planned.

Sardined in where they were, Pat and Ebrahim's free hands brushed past each other with every jolting motion of the moving train. Ebrahim squeezed Pat's fingers. Pat was overwhelmed by the most intense feeling of love towards Ebrahim.

Each click-clack of the train's wheels was a metronomic countdown to their destiny. More than ever, Pat needed a smoke. He could see Ebrahim chewing away. Pat sweated. *Will things work out?* Doubt had plagued him since they had formulated their plan. Because of the protracted sourcing of weapons, he had almost given up. To have four of them in position for the climax of their lives was unbelievable, while the weight tugging on his right-hand pocket was a reality check. *Soon, all I have to do is throw the bloody thing the length of a train coach!* He dried his right hand on his clothing whenever he could.

Despite the knot in his stomach, he tingled with every touch of Ebrahim's. Having this moment of high drama shared with the only person he had ever loved was so special. He knew Ebrahim would feel the same way. He desperately wanted to hold his lover in his arms. With his eyes closed he mentally kissed Ebrahim. An unintended tear squeezed through his eyelids. He opened his eyes to brush away the tears with his free hand. Ebrahim looked at him; tears moistened his cheeks too.

The slowing train was no match for Pat's heartbeat which pulsated in his ears; his mouth felt like parchment. The passengers in the crowded coaches buzzed with excitement in anticipation of the afternoon's entertainment. Those standing all turned towards the coach's exit doors. Many rose from their seats. Table Mountain and Devil's Peak hovered ahead of them, above the blurred rooftops of the buildings or trees they passed. The noise of the raucous supporters of the opposing teams faded to a background hum. Pat managed to squeeze Ebrahim's soft fingers. *Will we be together again?* Their unsmiling eyes locked onto each other until the train stopped.

CHAPTER 34: ON NEWLANDS STATION

2 August 1986

THEMBANI WATCHED CURTIS rub his right hand on his jeans pocket. Thembani did the same. He knew the Armpit Assassin could control his hands when hunting as he had once referred to his secret work. *But could Curtis, their weakest thrower, toss his grenade 30 metres?*

Thembani wondered briefly whether he would ever be a lecturer one day, maybe a professor, like Curtis had said. Instead, he now had to concentrate on throwing his *limonka* 50 metres before joining the fleeing crowd. To ease his nerves, he smiled at the thought of Curtis and Tina, so reminiscent of his hopes regarding Nkosinati. A heaviness had tinged his quick goodbye to her. He wanted to hold her in his arms while he quoted to her the lines from Shakespeare's *The Tempest* - "I would not wish any companion in the world but you". Instead, she was her normal shy self with her melancholy eyes when he left his parents' home. How he wanted to kiss those well-shaped lips of hers. *You should've told her you loved her.* He berated himself.

He felt a certain comfort from the fighting stick tucked under the waistband of his jeans, reaching to his left knee. He clung to the overhead rail with his left hand. His right hand was ready to grab the grenade once the train stopped. From the corner of his eye, he noted

Curtis had a similar stance. They were close to the right-hand exit door. He prayed the excited crowd behind them would not impede their throwing.

The train stopped with a jolt, rocking him to and fro. The doors whooshed open as he put his right hand into his pocket. His fingers curled around the grenade body while his thumb was already on the safety lever. His limbs tingled. The dryness in his mouth made him lick his lips to no avail.

A surge of pressure from the passengers behind him propelled Thembani onto the platform. When he stepped from the coach, he slipped on the wet platform which had been hosed down before the train arrived. He did not fall. Curtis was ahead of him in the clearing opposite the gangway connection between the two coaches. Curtis' hand concealed his grenade. Thembani moved closer to Curtis to draw his weapon from his pocket. He saw Pat and Ebrahim let fly with theirs. As Curtis threw, he slipped on the wet platform, and his grenade flew high into the air.

Thembani had more than enough space to release the pin. Many hours of practice went into his throw. He watched how the safety lever sprang free in the air from the arcing *limonka;* he expected his grenade to land on the platform 40 metres away as planned. People around the throwers screamed while they scrambled towards the exits, creating more space around the pair. With alarm he saw how Curtis' lemon had not cleared ten metres. Instead, the grenade landed on the platform close to Pat and Ebrahim.

Thembani's heart thrashed below his chin. His breath rasped in his dry throat. Time seemed suspended. A wide-eyed Thembani watched with horror. In those interminable seconds after Curtis threw his grenade, Pat and Ebrahim, alert to the danger, flung themselves onto the platform. Their arms covered their heads turned away from the deadly missile rolling a lethal path towards them.

With intense nausea, a wide-eyed Thembani watched the *limonka* roll past them over the edge of the platform to instantly explode under the train. In quick succession he heard the other three hand grenades go off. There was pandemonium at the Whites' end of the platform, where already a few bodies were visible on the ground where injured people staggered around. Many ran or pushed their way towards the Whites only exit.

With a look of relief on his face, Pat was on his feet in an instant. He reached to help Ebrahim. As they clasped hands, gunshots rang out. Ten metres away Thembani froze when he saw his two comrades fall in a tangled heap onto the ground. Blood flowed from their head and chest wounds. The visible part of Pat's ironed white shirt quickly turned red. His body stilled after a final twitch. Ebrahim's Palestinian scarf had an ever-expanding bloodstain in the middle of South Africa. He lay face down; a piece of chewing gum lay on the platform beside his open bleeding mouth. His hand held onto Pat's fingers, almost stroking them with his lifeless fingers as was his wont. To a heartbroken Thembani the lovers already looked at peace.

CURTIS, WITH HIS OPENED Three Star in hand, rushed towards the gunman where he hovered over his comrades' bodies. The extended right arm with a gun in hand, provided Curtis with a perfect armpit strike. Instead, the Armpit Assassin went straight to the neck. There was fury in the stroke. The knife slash onto bone, went from ear to ear. Blood pumped in twin jets from the major arteries on each side of the neck. The gun dropped as the bleeding shooter fell alongside his comrades' bodies on the platform. Curtis' stomach churned at the sensation of sticky blood on his fingers. *Now I have to leave. Where's Thembani?*

Curtis half-turned to the left to head towards the crowded exit a few metres ahead of him. In quick succession he heard four gunshots.

Simultaneously, four bolts of intense agony struck him in the lower back through to his belly. Curtis fell with a searing pain in his stomach. His cap fell from his head as the Three Star dropped from his hand. Blood quickly seeped through his fingers from two bullet exit wounds in his stomach. He gritted his teeth with the pain. *Oh shit! I don't feel too good.*

He rolled over from his side to look upwards at the gun pointing at him. Behind the gun a familiar face looked at him. There was no mistaking the mismatched eyes.

'Tina? *You?*"

"Oh no, not you. Dear Lord. No, no!" She shrieked.

"You're a policewoman? In plainclothes?"

Out of the corner of his eye he saw Thembani approach them. His friend had his fighting stick held high. Thembani swung the stick at Tina's head. Curtis screamed, "No, don't! It's Tina!"

The stick missed Tina's head. Instead, the hardwood club struck her extended gun arm. There was no mistaking the sound of her forearm bones breaking. With an anguished scream she dropped the gun as she clutched at her injured arm to support it.

Where Curtis lay, he was torn between giving Tina or Thembani his attention. *But Thembani had to leave.* "Go, man. Save yourself. I love you brother. Leave now. *I'm done for!*" he shouted.

Thembani's face projected great sorrow when he lifted Curtis' knife as well as the Glock 10 police-issue pistol from the platform. "I love you, Comrade!" With a mournful look Thembani turned to join the frenzied tumult ahead, where people jostled their way towards the exit.

Curtis turned his attention to Tina. The noise of the panic-stricken crowd faded into the distance. His vision narrowed to a tunnel with Tina's face the centre of his attention. While he looked at the enthralling face with the gap tooth, the dimples, the freckles and the eyes, Curtis grimaced with excruciating abdominal pain. "I thought you did clerical work," he said.

"I wanted to tell you, but I was so afraid I would lose you. I gave them notice last Monday to start at Old Mutual next week." She sobbed uncontrollably with her fractured arm resting on his chest.

Curtis extended his right hand towards the only woman he had ever loved. With her left hand she clasped his hand to her chest. His pain receded, though his head spun. He struggled to focus on Tina. He wanted to see her eyes.

"The arm looks painful," his voice was soft, almost soothing.

"Never mind me. I want you to live," Tina wailed. "I need you alive. I love you, Curtis Fouche." Her shoulders shook with her sobbing. "Oh, Lord. What have I done? Yesterday I discovered I'm carrying our baby!" She bent over to kiss him repeatedly.

"What? A baby Curtis? I hope the child has your dimples, as well as your eyes." His voice weakened. He tried to smile. His belly tensed. The pain was agonising. *It feels like I don't have much time.*

"I really wanted to marry you. I wanted our house on the hill with a view of the mountains. I truly did!" He closed his heavy eyes.

"Curtis! Curtis! Oh no!" Tina's voice echoed in his head, her sobs filled the air around him. Her voice sounded far away, yet he felt her fervent comforting kisses. Coming from deep within, her wailing was woeful.

To his surprise his smiling father came into view. He held a hand towards Curtis.

Curtis managed to open his eyes. He struggled to smile at Tina. "You are the only woman I have ever loved," his voice was hushed.

With his left hand he managed to wipe at her tear-stained cheek. The weakened hand stopped at her neck. "Please don't cry. I'll always love you. Always!" He whispered. With his failing strength he drew her mouth closer to kiss her.

While they kissed, Curtis' lifeless hand slowly slid along Tina's body onto the platform.

CHAPTER 35: LAST CAR RIDE

2 August 1986

THEMBANI JOINED THE tail-end of the disorderly rush from the platform as passengers pushed to escape. He could not believe the sequence of events as no one expected them to have two plainclothes railways police on board. To have Tina there as one of them was a shock. Curtis' call saved her because his forceful strike to her head would have killed her.

Thembani's head reeled while he relived the contracted seconds there on the station platform. He felt gutted as Curtis' final utterance to him, 'I'm done for.' repeatedly rang in his ears. It was like a dagger twisted at Thembani's insides to have to desert the man who had saved him more than once. Tears filled his eyes by the time he reached the exit.

Gunshots rang out from the White end of the platform. White passengers had started shooting at anyone who was Black. A couple of bullets whizzed past him before intense pain in the bone above his right hip had him pause. He was surprised yet pleased that he could still walk unimpeded. He hobbled his way past the body of a man with a blood-soaked bullet hole in his jacket. The cap beside him with the scarf he wore were in the local rugby club's colours.

Outside the station he went south on Letterstedt Road. Curtis was correct, most of the yelling horde rushed west towards Main Road. Thembani shuffled a bit while using the stick to assist him.

The Glock and the Three Star were in his pockets. Blood stained his jeans, and he pressed directly over the wound, where he felt the bullet sticking in the bone above his hip. Pressure with a folded over handkerchief soon stopped the bleeding. The pain eased off, allowing him to walk more freely on an empty Clarendon Road.

Thembani paused under the Campground Road bridge where he felt totally drained. His mind's eye filled with the blood-spattered images of his comrades as he struggled to stifle a cry. There were no visible tears, as an internal flood threatened to overwhelm him while the buildings around him blurred.

It took Thembani 20 minutes to reach the Cortina. After throwing the stick onto the passenger seat, he put the retrieved key into the car's ignition. Police sirens sounded in the distance. He had never been in such a dark place before. To Thembani, Curtis was more than the Armpit Assassin. In fact, more than a loyal Comrade, Curtis was his closest friend. *He even refrained from using my name there on the station so Tina would not hear it.* He slammed both fists on the steering wheel rim until his hands ached.

With his sleeve he wiped the tears on his face. His jaw ached the way he ground his teeth. He lowered his chin to his chest, his shoulders slumped forward, his hands numb. For a few minutes, he rested his head on the steering wheel.

Thembani roused himself; he needed medical help. After starting the car, he headed to Settlers Way via De Waal Drive before turning off at the Athlone power station. Wide steam columns rose from the twin cooling towers. A thinner, dark column of smoke extended higher from one of the two tall chimney stacks alongside. Thembani stayed within the speed limit. He could not risk speeding as he did not have a driver's licence.

The posh White suburb of Pinelands on the left stood in stark contrast to the Langa housing mess opposite. A railway line with a high diamond-mesh wire fence topped with double strands of barbed wire on each side of the train lines, separated Pinelands from the Langa African township, where over-crowded men's hostels were visible on the other side.

It was mid-afternoon with not much traffic when he passed the Epping industrial complex to reach Elsies River. After stopping outside Dr Stanley Gershon's rooms, he waited till a group of people on the pavement dispersed before he went in to the reception desk. He barely limped when he walked.

He recognised nurse Desray who took him straight to the procedure room where he had been treated before. So much had happened since the injury to his arm. Lying on the couch, Thembani's mind was still in turmoil over the day's events.

Desray freed his clothes to expose the wound. "Stanley will see you soon. Hmm. You're lucky because a bit higher would've been much worse." Desray smiled.

At least he did not have to lie about how or where the shooting had occurred. He appreciated the absence of any records of his visit. Dr Gershon appeared after a few minutes.

Stanley was his normal professional self. "I'm sorry to keep you waiting," he said to Thembani. "What have you brought me today? Oh, one of those. At least they're easy to remove from there. Mainly you'll feel the injection of local anaesthetic. After a bit of scratching around it'll soon be over."

Stanley slipped on sterile gloves before extracting the bullet from the bone. There was hardly any bleeding. After removing a few clothing fragments from the damaged tissues, he placed the bullet with a slightly flattened head in a test tube.

"You are lucky this small calibre bullet couldn't pass through bone. At least you've not lost as much blood like the last time."

"Ahh. You remember Doctor. Yah, the arm is like normal. I'll trash the bullet on the way home." Thembani examined the bullet before placing the tube in his pocket.

"I expect the wound to heal well. If there are any problems, don't hesitate to return. You must take these antibiotics only if there is any fever, reddening or painful swelling in the area. Return at any time you are worried. Understood?"

"Thank you, Doctor Gershon. I always hope I never need to see you again."

STANLEY WAS DEEP IN thought after Thembani left. *I wonder what happened to Curtis and the other two friends?*

Fay, who was upgrading computer software at the practice, came in with a newspaper in her hand. "I'm sure this article will interest you. Desray showed me the latest *Cape Herald* left in the waiting room by one of the patients. She said to show you the front page."

'Hammer van Zyl cops himself!' screamed the bold-print front-page headline with a photo of the police officer alongside a black Volkswagen Beetle. In typical fashion a cigarette hung from his lips. Stanley did not read beyond the opening paragraph. Hammer van Zyl had ended his life at home with a gunshot through the head. "Lots of people will rejoice at the news. The main problem is that there are too many other van Zyls in the security police."

"Will the nightmare of our liberation struggle ever end?" Fay rubbed his shoulders from behind. Her kiss on his neck comforted him.

Troubling thoughts gnawed away at Stanley. He stared through his consulting room window. The sunset-shadowed Table Mountain seemed to look on, casting the end of the day's shroud over the somber Cape Flats. There was none of the joy he often experienced with a Cape Town sunset. He thought of Fay's words. *When will South Africa's horrors end? Will it ever?*

THEMBANI KNEW THE METAL dealers in Gugulethu would dismantle the Cortina to the last nut. He was sure Dr Gershon must have wondered where his three friends were. No doubt he would make the link when he heard the news of the station attack. From what Curtis had told him about Dr Gershon, Thembani had confidence in the GP's confidentiality. He would have liked to listen to the afternoon news, but there was no radio in the car.

Thembani had to lift his spirits. More than revenge, he had to honour his Comrades one day. The Glock pistol could come in handy. The Three Star was in his other pocket. *Maybe I can become the Gugulethu Assassin. Curtis would approve.* He managed a wry smile.

While Thembani pondered the events of the day, King Henry, Act 111, scene 3 came to mind.

We few, we happy few,

We band of brothers.

For he today that sheds his blood with me,

Shall be my brother.

Thembani put the car into gear with his cheeks awash with tears. His three pals were not just brothers, they were *Comrades*.

He had never felt so drained before. There was no consolation in knowing there were bodies at the northern end of the platform after the explosions. Driving through the side roads to Gugulethu, he struggled to regain his composure. He stopped the car on a quiet side road close to the scrap dealer. Thembani wanted to sing *Nkosi sikelel iAfrika*. His deep voice cracked when he sobbed with the first line. He could not continue. Instead, he heard Curtis sing the rest of the lines. He smiled. Curtis' Xhosa was faultless. Pat and Ebrahim joined the chorus lines.

When they finished their singing, Thembani looked towards the shadow-darkened Table Mountain. The Mother City's icon looked drab, matching his mood. How many more had to die? Would the deaths ever stop? In the shadow of Table Mountain, the Cape Flats townships had a united shroud in their Blackness, in their sorrow, in their suffering, in their deaths. With activist cells like theirs Thembani believed he had no other choice. *Apartheid must end!*

Through the open car window, he raised a tightly clenched fist to his fallen Comrades; his forceful deep voice called out, "*Amandla, ngawethu! Mayibuye, iAfrika!*"

A SPECIAL REQUEST FROM SHADLEY

IF YOU ENJOYED READING *Toti-toyi, Cape Town's War Dance,* then a short review on your Facebook or other social media sites would be much appreciated – a simple "What a read"; "Most enjoyable"; "Riveting and informative"; ... or more would suffice. An emoticon would also be good. An online review posted on Goodreads, Better Reading or equivalent sites for readers would also help.

Such is the world we live in nowadays with authors having to promote themselves with a bit of help from readers and friends! For this, ngiyabonga, I thank you all. Keep well.

GLOSSARY

A llah hu akhbar! God is the greatest!
Amandla ngawethu! Power is ours!
Afrikaner Broederbond Afrikaner Brotherhood
askaris ANC- or PAC-turned fighters working with the State
ANC African National Congress
Boere/boers White Afrikaners
boerewors traditional South African spicy sausage
bokmakierie bush shrike
braai barbeque
croes hare kinky hair
Dompas Stupid pass
dua Muslim prayer
Enkosi kakhulu Many thanks
Hotnot Racist term to describe a person classified Coloured
Ja, nee Yes, no
jy weet mos as you know
Kaffir Offensive, racist term to describe an African person
klaar finished
klapoor smack-ear
kierrie, knobkierrie bevelled or round-headed hardwood club
limonka a Russian RGD-5 hand grenade
Mayibuye iAfrika! Come back Africa!
MK uMkhonto we Sizwe, armed wing of the ANC
moffie faggot
Nkosi sikelel iAfrika God bless Africa

PAC Pan African Congress
O my God, wat het jy gedoen Oh my God, what have you done?
Perlemoen Abalone
pondok shanty, a word of Indonesian origin
rooikrantz wattle
sjamboks short rhinoceros-hide or plastic whips
skollies and *tsotsis* thugs, gangsters, street toughs
Thula, thula umntwana Hush, hush little child
UDF United Democratic Front
UWC University of the Western Cape, for Coloureds only
Veldskoene South African suede boots
Vark pig
Witdoeke White Scarves; pro-government contra forces

ADDENDUM

WHILE THE BOOK IS A sociopolitical thriller set in a historically relevant period in South Africa's history, all the characters are fictitious, likewise the details related to the thriller, except there are references to real people like Robert Sobukwe, Nelson Mandela, Steve Biko, Oliver Thambo, Phillip Kgosana, Vuyisile Mini, ex-Prime Ministers Verwoerd and Botha, ex-Minister of Tourism, John Wiley; and Reverends David Russell, Alan Boesak, Lesley Mabuza, and Jan de Waal. Shaun Magmoed, Jonathan Claasen and Michael Miranda were the three killed during the Trojan Horse massacre in Athlone.

Any similarities with other people would be coincidental.

For historical accuracy, there are many references to events in the country during the 1960-1986 period.

OTHER BOOKS BY SHADLEY FATAAR

1. *Fury and Revenge in Cape Town* – published 7.7.2023.
2. *Cape Town's Necklaces of Fire* – due out early 2024.

(These are Books 1 and 3 of the trilogy: *In the Shadow of Table Mountain, Cape Town.*)

JOIN THE AUTHOR'S UPDATING e-mails by dropping him a line at zonshad@gmail.com or for direct paperback mailing.

E-BOOKS AND PAPER BACKS can be obtained by visiting the author's new website at: ◎ https://www.shadleyfataar.com/

APPENDED FOOTNOTES ARE BELOW

[1] KTC - Kakaza Trading Company - an informal shanty housing complex in Cape Town located close to the Kakaza Trading Company store.

[2] Since its formation in 1983, the United Democratic Front became the leading national group opposing apartheid.

[3] Police resources were drained by the military whose annual budget exceeded fifteen percent of Government expenditure.

[4] The described event is based on an injury sustained by the Reverend Jan de Waal during the march.

[5] The term "NY" stands for "Native Yard". It is seen by many as a crude attempt to dehumanise black people.

[6] The State designated these rural areas as "homelands" even though many citizens had never ever lived there.

[7] Regarded as government-designated Homelands, the Transkei and Ciskei Bantustans became the enforced homes of many Cape Town deportees who had never before lived there.

[8] The worst such episode was the Langa massacre a year earlier when the police killed 35 mourners and injured 27 at a funeral in Uitenhage.

[9] The term "Comrades" was adopted by township youths as a militant identity after exiled ANC deputy leader, Thabo Mbeki's 1985 call on Radio Freedom to make the townships ungovernable.

[10] *Witdoeke* - The White Scarves were pro-government contra-mobilisation forces who wore distinguishing white scarves tied around their heads or arms during times of conflict with the anti-State Comrades in the townships.

[11] Azania was the fashionable future indigenous name used by many as the name of a new democratic South Africa.

[12] The *Afrikaner Broederbond* was an exclusive Afrikaner Calvinist, male secret society dedicated exclusively to the advancement of White Afrikaners.